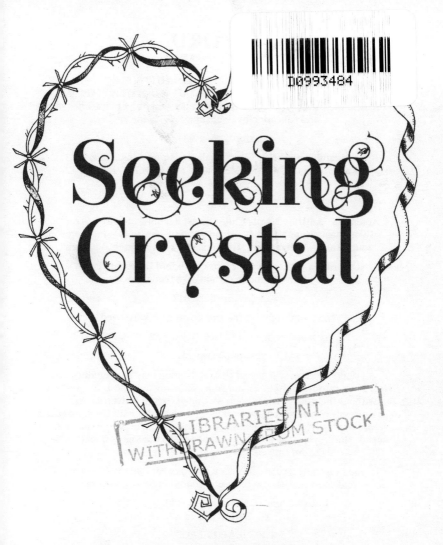

Seeking Crystal

Joss Stirling

OXFORD
UNIVERSITY PRESS

OXFORD
UNIVERSITY PRESS

Great Clarendon Street, Oxford OX2 6DP
Oxford University Press is a department of the University of Oxford.
It furthers the University's objective of excellence in research, scholarship,
and education by publishing worldwide in

Oxford   New York

Auckland   Cape Town   Dar es Salaam   Hong Kong   Karachi
Kuala Lumpur   Madrid   Melbourne   Mexico City   Nairobi
New Delhi   Shanghai   Taipei   Toronto

With offices in

Argentina   Austria   Brazil   Chile   Czech Republic   France   Greece
Guatemala   Hungary   Italy   Japan   Poland   Portugal   Singapore
South Korea   Switzerland   Thailand   Turkey   Ukraine   Vietnam

Oxford is a registered trade mark of Oxford University Press
in the UK and in certain other countries

British Library Cataloguing in Publication Data
Data available

ISBN: 978-0-19-279351-5

1 3 5 7 9 10 8 6 4 2

Printed and bound by CPI Group (UK) Ltd, Croydon, CR0 4YY

Paper used in the production of this book is a natural,
recyclable product made from wood grown in sustainable forests.
The manufacturing process conforms to the environmental
regulations of the country of origin.

For my sister Jane, who paddled across
Venice with me.

Chapter 1

Denver, Colorado

The night my life changed began with eating a truly amazing dessert: raspberry cheesecake with dark chocolate sauce. My sister and I had just arrived in America from Italy and were both battling really foul jetlag, the kind where your eyelids need to be propped up with matchsticks and your head feels so heavy it threatens to nod off your neck. Experience told us that we should try to stay awake until a reasonable hour or our body clocks would never catch up. This meant we had gone out to dine rather than fall onto our pillows as I would have preferred. And if we were going to sacrifice sleep for the cause, we at least deserved an excellent sweet reward. I had not been disappointed.

Diamond spent the last part of the meal carefully dissecting her portion, taking tiny spoonfuls, her appetite at zero. I'd already finished mine.

'Have you thought what you are going to do with yourself while I'm at the conference tomorrow?' Diamond asked. 'You could sit in at the back but I doubt "Savant Crime: Dealing with the Offenders" would make the most riveting experience of your life.'

She knew me so well. I could do without listening to a bunch of gifted people with amazing extra-sensory perception telling us all how wonderful they are at solving the world's problems. I couldn't stop my yawns thinking about it so sitting through lectures on stuff I didn't really know much about would probably induce a coma.

'Maybe I'll give it a miss.'

'I don't think they'd mind.' Diamond had picked up the yawning from me but shrouded hers with a napkin.

'Who are "they"?'

'I told you.'

Was she really going to leave half her dessert? I eyed it speculatively, twiddling my fork in my fingers. 'You did? Sorry, must've tuned that out. You know me: I just come along for the ride.'

Diamond sighed. She had given up on getting me to focus on the stuff she thought I should know, recognizing I had a stubborn streak that meant I only listened when it suited me. I'm one trial of a younger sister.

'Then I'd better tell you again as you'll no doubt meet some of the people from the conference at the social events.' Her voice was, as ever, endlessly patient with me. 'It's been organized by the influential American Savant family, the Benedicts; several of them are involved in law enforcement.'

'And this influential family just begged international peace-maker, Diamond Brook, to be their star speaker.' I grinned at her. 'They're lucky to get you.'

'Stop it, Crystal, it's not like that.' Diamond looked sweetly flustered by my cheerleading for her brilliance. 'There are no stars in the Savant Net; we work together.'

Yeah, right. Forget what she said; we all knew she was

something special. Unlike me. I was down as her bag carrier on these jaunts, roadie on the Diamond tour.

'I don't know what I'll do. Maybe I'll go shopping.' I scraped the last remnants of chocolate sauce off the plate, making artistic swirls with the prongs of my fork. 'I need new jeans and Denver looks a good place to hunt for bargains—much cheaper than home. At least I'm good at shopping.'

My frivolous plans put that look on Diamond's face, the one where her soulful brown eyes brimmed with concern. Here came the sisterly pep talk; she couldn't resist even though we were both so tired we were drooping in our seats.

'I was hoping, Crystal, that you might, you know, take the next few days to give some serious attention to your future. I picked up a stack of brochures for colleges so you can retake your exams. They're in my case back at the hotel.'

I shrugged. I really did not want to go there, not while I was enjoying the lingering taste of chocolate.

'Or if you don't want to do that, then maybe we should start thinking about an apprenticeship? You always liked fashion and design. We could ask Signora Carriera if she needs any help for the Carnival. It would be great experience learning how to run up so many different kinds of costume so quickly. I know for a fact she has lots of work right now because she's also making some for a big Hollywood movie shooting in Venice next month.'

That did sound interesting but the chirpy waiter was back, refilling our coffee cups with an actor's flair. Maybe he was one, 'resting' between jobs like me. Though, to be honest, at nineteen, I'd not even got my career off the launch pad.

'How's your meal, ladies?' he asked, his eyes on my sister, hoping for a crumb of praise. I could tell he had already fallen in love with Diamond as most possessors of the Y chromosome did.

'It was lovely, thank you.' She gave him one of her warmest smiles, her bobbed hair swaying slightly as she looked up. Diamond had the neat dark swing cut and features of a Cleopatra, Elizabeth Taylor-style. In Diamond's case, the resemblance to the queen was genuine as our mother was Egyptian. Dad had been a British diplomat who fell in love with Mama on a posting to Cairo and whisked her away as his bride. We are a truly international family—Diamond and I now living in Venice, roughly halfway between our roots in the leafy Home Counties and the dusty banks of the Nile. I didn't feel I had a strong national identity. Italy was my adopted, rather than native, country. Maybe that sense of being rootless was another part of my dissatisfaction with myself?

All politeness, the waiter finally remembered to seek my opinion. 'And how was your dessert?'

'Yeah, it was great.' I smiled but his attention had already skipped back to my sister. He retreated, satisfied, his gaze lingering on Diamond rather than me. I didn't blame him: I had inherited the striking pharaoh looks, strong nose and emphatic eyebrows but none of the prettiness, as in my case the features were topped by the lion's mane from my father's side. Savants tend to have complicated inheritances—ours no exception. Dad had had a Venetian mother with the hair characteristic of some northern Italians: a riot of curls that included every colour from dirt brown to sun-bleached blonde. You sometimes see it in the paintings of the Old Masters but mine is not a Madonna's smooth undulating wave but a choppy sea of a frizz. Beside my sister I always felt like the mangy lioness with a sleek, exquisite pussycat.

The tourist magnet of the Hard Rock Café was filling up with students and travellers, the noise levels soaring, our waiter pulled in many directions by numerous orders. I found my eyes drawn to a glass display case claiming to contain a genuine

Michael Jackson military-cut jacket, enjoying the odd optical illusion that made my reflection look as though my head was poking out of the neck. I yawned again. What had we been talking about? Oh yeah.

'You really want me to work for Signora Carriera? It would be slave labour.' I knew the costume maker who lived below our apartment in Venice quite well as I often walked her dog when she was busy. She was a pleasant enough neighbour but would be one demanding boss. It made me shudder just to think about what demands she would make on my time.

Diamond pushed her dessert aside. 'I hate to see you waste your life like this.'

'I hate waste too. Pass that over. The cheesecake is ledge.'

'What?'

'Legendary.'

My sister sighed, biting back the comment that at nearly six feet I needed to watch my weight. It wasn't that I was fat but—how did she put it?—oh yes, I was *Amazonian* compared to the rest of my sisters, blessed with average dress sizes. I didn't care. Who was I out to impress? No boys asked me on a date because I was taller than them all and they feared the mockery. 'Beanstalk' was the friendliest of the names I had endured at the boarding school in England I had attended.

'Crystal, don't think I don't understand. It was rotten losing Dad during your A level year,' Diamond continued gently.

I forked up another mouthful, defying the flash of pain her remark sparked. Rotten didn't even begin to describe the emotional gutting I had experienced. He had been my one admirer in my family, always on my side when I was disadvantageously compared to my six older brothers and sisters. He had found my height amusing, referring to me as his 'little girl' at every opportunity even though I could see the bald patch on top of his head fringed by curls when we stood side by side. No wonder I had crashed and burned spectacularly in my exams. His death had taken the best part of me with him.

Diamond touched the back of my wrist lightly, attempting to comfort me though the grief was out of reach of such gestures. 'Mama asked me to look after you. She wouldn't expect me to let you mark time like this for no purpose. She'd want to see you going after something that you really wanted to do.'

'Diamond, good try. We both know that Mama is too exhausted by raising the six of you to worry too much about me.' I had been born ten years after Diamond, who was the sixth youngest in our parents' brood of seven, a surprise to everyone, most especially my mother, who was beyond what she thought were her childbearing years. 'She's ecstatic being grandma. How many is it now?'

'Twelve between them: Topaz's six, Steel's two, Silver's one and Opal's three.'

'I'm glad you're keeping count; I'm a rubbish aunt. Twelve cute little grandkids to spoil and not have to take responsibility for—Mama is hardly going to get in a flap about me.'

Diamond, ever the peacemaker in our family as well as for the world, shook her head. She made that little circling gesture with her finger that had the waiter leaping to bring us the bill. 'Mama does care but her health is not the best these days. Not since Dad.'

'So that's why she moved in to that granny flat near Topaz without a spare bedroom, is it?' *Listen to yourself, Crystal.* I sounded so bitter. This had to stop. My predicament wasn't Diamond's fault. With Dad's passing, Mama had not just lost her husband; she had lost her soulfinder, as we Savants call our life partners. I couldn't really understand it, not having one myself, but I knew intellectually that that was a kind of death for a Savant. Her grief had held centre stage when he died and

Diamond was the only one who had stepped forward to give me a hand when I had stumbled out of school with a clutch of 'E' grades and no future. 'Sorry, I'm tired. You're right: I'll give your idea about the costumes some thought. I don't think I can face redoing my exams.'

'Good. You've got so much potential; I just want you to find a direction for it.' Diamond gave me her special smile. She was incredibly gifted at calming troubled souls and I couldn't help but feel a bit better for a touch of her soothing power. Her skills were much sought after in the Savant community and she was often brought in to negotiate between warring factions. We Savants are people who are born with that bit extra, perhaps a gift for telling the future, moving things with our minds, or talking telepathically, but it can lead to disputes as you get so many gifted people rubbing shoulders together like a bunch of divas at the Fenice Opera House all vying for the limelight. Diamond had the best power in our family. It was pretty cool to watch her reduce a slavering guard dog of a litigant to a fawning puppy. All my brothers and sisters had gifts to some degree. Except me.

I am the equivalent of what in the Harry Potter world is called a squib. A damp squib. As the seventh child, all had expected me to come loaded with the whole box of fireworks. Instead they got a girl who could tell you where you left your keys. Yes, that's right. I'm the equivalent of the whistling key fob. I see the stuff you are attached to like space junk circling the earth and, if needed, can give you the general direction where to find something you've lost. I can't do telepathy because when I connect to other Savants it's like flying right into the cloud of defunct satellites and I get knocked out of orbit, so I'm almost completely useless, my gift nothing more than a party trick and aid to the careless. Still, my family are quick to make use of it.

1

Take yesterday. Topaz rang while we were at the airport, but not to chat about me. 'Crystal, Felicity left her coat at school somewhere. Can you be a love and tell me where it is?' My sister Topaz was mother to the most forgetful girl in the world.

Within reasonable distance—this case ten miles as we were changing planes at Heathrow—my gift still works. I closed my eyes. Little bit of manoeuvring between the things whirling about in Felicity's mind and . . . 'It's fallen behind the painting table.'

'What on earth is it doing there? Never mind. Thanks, sweetie. See you soon.'

That is the kind of conversation I have with my brothers and sisters all the time. I am the Go-to Girl for life's clutter.

My gift is more a nuisance than a blessing. This is especially annoying because being a Savant already has a sting in its tail: all of us are destined to find the love that completes us only with our Savant counterpart, or soulfinder, like my parents had. They were incredibly lucky to meet each other, as our soulfinder is conceived somewhere in the world at the same time we are. Our lives are a search for that other person but the chances are low that we will find them as they could be-long to any race, any country. Just think about it—your partner might die and leave you devastated as my mama was by Dad's death, or they might be already married by the time you meet them. I'd heard stories of soulfinders who had met only when in their old age. You probably won't even speak the same lan-guage. My brothers and sisters have had mixed fortunes: Steel struck lucky, meeting his Japanese soulfinder when he was twenty-five through a dating agency that specializes in Savants. His twin, my sister Silver, had not waited to find hers and had already gone through a stormy divorce. Topaz was happy with her husband, but we all knew he was not 'the one' though he is a great guy. Opal had found hers in Johannesburg and now lived there. Our youngest brother, Peter, was like Diamond and me: still waiting.

I didn't hold out much hope for myself: if my counterpart existed, he'd either be amazingly talented to make up for my shortcomings, and that would condemn me to a life of living in his shadow; or he'd match my feeble powers and be so weak that we'd barely sense each other. I couldn't do telepathy without serious side effects; and without two minds meeting, Savants can't tell if they are a match. Sucks to be me sometimes. Well aware of my shortcomings, I preferred to avoid the company of other Savants, so perhaps a career in costume making would not be a bad direction for me to take?

Diamond settled the bill and we gathered our belongings to go. In the mile-high city of Denver, the autumn nights are cool so it took a while to button up and put on gloves and scarves. We emerged on to the street, momentarily disorientated by being in a foreign city.

'The air is so thin here.' Diamond peered up between the skyscrapers to catch a glimpse of the starry sky. 'In Venice you can always tell what you are breathing.'

'Yes, because living at sea level means it's always damp or smells of drains. If we stay there any longer, I think we'll develop gills and webbed feet.' I linked my arm through hers and began to lead her back to the hotel. It was only a few blocks away and I could find my direction by sensing where my suitcase was stowed. How strange to walk among the canyons of high-rise buildings iced with anonymous glass when we were used to streets of the ornate, quirky, and crumbling.

Diamond accepted my guidance without question, knowing I had the instincts of a homing pigeon. 'And how do you know I don't already have webs between my toes? I've lived in our grandmother's apartment for longer than you.'

I chuckled. 'I swear Nonna did. As a true bred Venetian she must have been part mermaid.'

'Well, you can't get further from the sea than Denver.' Diamond did a little twirl on the spot, semi-drunk on her exhaustion. 'It's odd but I feel so at home, like part of me has always been waiting to come here.'

'Diamond!' My warning system flared a moment too late. Three men stepped from a dark alley in a gap between shuttered shops, cutting off our retreat. I had a quick impression of dark hoodies, faces obscured by scarves pulled up over mouths, knives—shadowy, anywhere villains. One grabbed the strap of Diamond's shoulder bag and sliced it through. She foolishly tried to hang on and was swung around as he tugged viciously to get it free. I went to help but the other two tackled me; we landed in the gutter, with me on the bottom as they fumbled for my handbag. One elbowed me in the stomach as he got up; the other punched my head on the kerb.

After that, things go blurry. Pounding feet. A noise that sounded like a roar of an enraged beast.

'Police!' Click of a gun magazine being slotted into place. 'Move away from her!'

Swearing and then swift retreat of three pairs of soft-footed trainers. I lay on my back, awkwardly half-on-half-off the pavement, stars whirling.

The man who had come to our aid hurried to my sister's side. She was sitting on the ground, bag clutched to her stomach. I got to my knees, head throbbing, and pulled myself on to the kerb before I got run over by the next vehicle to pass.

'Are you all right, ma'am?' Our rescuer crouched before her.

'Yes, yes, thank you. Just a bit shaken up.' Diamond's eyes were filled with tears and she was shivering, triggering every protective instinct in a man.

He reached out to help her up. I don't think he'd even

noticed me as I was in the shadows between streetlights while she was spotlighted. When their hands touched there was a gasp of indrawn breath as they surged to their feet.

'My God, it's you! I can hear you in my mind!' Diamond gazed up at her saviour as if he was Christmas day and all her birthdays rolled into one. If I dipped into my Savant sight I could see all her swirling space junk was now centred on him, like a magnet dragging iron filings.

'Yes, it really is me.' Then, without another word being exchanged, he gathered her in his arms and kissed her.

Wow. I didn't know if to applaud or laugh. It was like watching some really clichéd romantic film—love at first sight—impromptu embrace like that famous photo of the sailor kissing the nurse on VJ Day in Times Square.

Jealous much? Of course I was.

Finally, they broke apart.

'Who are you?' At last my sister had the sense to remember they hadn't even been introduced.

'Trace Benedict. And you?'

'Diamond Brook.'

He framed her face in his hands as if he was holding the most valuable object in the world. 'I know that name. You're here for our conference. Pleased to meet you, Diamond.'

'And you, Trace Benedict.' Her gaze drifted down to his mouth.

Oh no, not again.

He bent to her again, this time giving her a sweet, tender kiss, a hello to his soulfinder. I didn't dare move. I wasn't so selfish as to spoil the greatest moment of their life by complaining that I had a slight concussion and was smeared with unmentionable stuff from the gutter. I removed a McDonald's wrapper from my leg with a flick of a fingertip. Yuck. Diamond would remember me. Eventually.

'I can't believe you walked right into my life. I've been waiting so long.' Trace rubbed his finger along her cheekbone, caressing the corner of her pretty mouth. 'I had to admit I had hoped, when I saw you on our guest list and noticed that you were my age . . . '

'We always hope, don't we, when we meet another Savant who might be the one?' Diamond smiled shyly up at him.

'I've been introduced to so many possibles with the right dates of birth; thank God that you turn out to be my one.'

I sighed and rubbed my aching temples. I feared their script was not very original but I couldn't blame them for the headache.

'Meeting my soulfinder was the last thing I expected when I accepted the invitation to come.' My sister sounded so sweet— happy and shy at the same time.

He bent to pick up her bag and handed it back to her. 'You're the peacemaker, right?'

'Yes. I have a small consultancy firm based in Venice.'

'Venice, Italy?'

'Is there another Venice?' Her eyes twinkled at him with gentle teasing.

'In America? Sure. There are probably about seven or eight. Italy, hey?' He kissed her lightly, already so familiar, unable to keep his hands off her. 'I work for the Denver police depart-ment. How are we going to work that one out, I wonder?'

Crumbs, this was fast. They had met, like, five minutes ago and already he was moving in.

'My job is easy to do from anywhere in the world; it's only Crystal I have to . . . ' Suddenly remembering my existence she pushed away from him. 'Crystal, oh my God, Crystal, are you OK?'

I waved feebly from the kerb. 'Fine. You two carry on. I don't want to spoil the hearts-and-flowers stuff.'

Diamond hurried to my side. 'You're hurt? I can't believe I left you sitting there and you're injured. Trace, please.'

I had already gathered that my brother-in-law-to-be was a capable soul. He hardly needed my sister's prompting to help me limp to a doorstep. He had a flashlight on the end of his keychain and he shone it in my face.

I blinked and shaded my eyes.

'Bump on the head but pupils responding. I think we'd better get her to ER just in case.'

An electric shock of panic ripped through me. 'I'm fine. Really. I don't want to go to hospital.' Last time I had been was my eighteenth birthday. Dad had taken me out for dinner to celebrate but had a heart attack before we'd even ordered. I ended up spending my special night in the hospital breaking the news to Mama and the rest of the family that he was gone. Even thinking about it gave me that ugly feeling like falling down a manhole into nothingness.

Fortunately, Diamond knew full well I wouldn't go willingly to a medical centre. 'She doesn't like hospitals. Perhaps we can call a doctor to check her over?'

Trace pulled out his mobile. 'I've got someone better than that. Let me call my brother. He can give her a check-up better than any machine in the ER.'

Chapter 2

We made it back to the hotel, causing a little ripple of consternation in the foyer as I limped through on the arm of the local police officer. Trace was not in uniform but he was well known to the staff as it turned out that he was the one who had booked the conference in at this venue.

'Jim, can you send my brother straight up to the ladies' suite when he arrives,' Trace asked the doorman.

'Yes, sir.' The chubby porter peered at me through his thick glasses. 'Are the ladies all right?'

'They just had a bad encounter with a few of our least favourite local characters. I'll file the report but luckily nothing was taken.'

'Actually, they took my clutch purse,' I muttered. Of course, he hadn't noticed such little details while he was saving the day. 'Not much in it but my library card and a hundred dollars.'

Trace turned all cop on me. 'Any other form of ID? Driver's licence?'

I snorted. 'We live in Venice: the streets are full of water. Good luck with the driving in those conditions.'

'Passport?'

'In the room safe.'

He nodded, satisfied. 'Then I'll refund you the money. Sorry about the library card. It's my city; I hate the fact that this was the welcome it gave you. It's such a great place in normal circumstances.'

The lift arrived and we climbed smoothly to the tenth floor. The only buildings as high as this in my city were campanile, and they tended to lean at gravity defying angles thanks to the subsidence of the centuries. The room itself was ultra modern—white furnishing, flat screens, plush bathroom with plumbing that didn't groan and drip whilst it got you clean with a blast of the power shower. The view from the window was impressive too: strings of lights spreading through the city before being eaten up by the absolute dark of the Rockies some ten or so miles away. Here the land went vertical—mountains, climbing roads, ski-resorts; where I came from, we went in for horizontals—lagoon, low-lying islands, mud flats.

I took myself off into the bathroom and washed off the gutter gunk. A thick robe was a welcome comfort after I'd stripped away my smelly clothes. I bagged them up for the hotel laundry to tackle. Feeling a little restored, I hobbled back into the bedroom. Diamond and Trace had barely noticed my absence; they were staring at each other, talking mind-to-mind, lost in the wonder of meeting their soulfinder. My heart gave a funny kind of lurch, a little bit envious but mainly so happy for them.

Diamond looked up. 'Any better, Crystal?'

'Yes, I'm fine.' I stretched out on my bed with a groan. The pounding in my head increased twenty-fold and nausea over-whelmed me. 'Maybe not so fine.'

'We'd better stop using telepathy, Trace; it makes Crystal feel sick. She picks up on the thought waves even if she can't hear what we say.' Diamond fetched a cold flannel from the bathroom. 'I don't like the look of her colour. Perhaps we should take her to hospital after all?'

I flapped my hand at her. 'Hey, I'm still here you know. No hospitals.'

Trace put his arm around Diamond, standing behind her as if he already owned the spot at her side. 'My brother's a healer. He'll let us know if we need to take her to ER.'

A loud tap at the door interrupted their deliberations.

'That's probably him now.' Trace went to let him in. 'Hey, Xav, thanks for getting here so quickly.'

'Ah, well, you know I charge double for house calls.' A tall dark-haired boy strode into the room, eyes scanning as he took note of the situation. What I noticed was about a mile of denim, wolf T-shirt and unbuttoned dark grey peacoat. Trace was about my height, but this brother had a few more inches. Where Trace was broad-shouldered and rugged featured, this brother was lean and whipcord strong, an athlete in the way he moved. His hair flipped every which way in a casual cut I'd seen on dedicated surfers, what I thought of as the 'hey-I've-just-ridden-the-wave-and-now-ready-to-party' look. He was one of those boys too handsome for their own good, doubt-less having had his ego fed with constant female adulation since kindergarten. His money must go on his clothes unless the stores begged him to model—yeah, I could well imagine that.

'This is my little brother, Xavier, or Xav,' said Trace, intro-ducing him to Diamond. 'Xav, I've got some amazing news: meet my soulfinder.'

When Xav caught sight of Diamond, he pretended to be knocked back a step. He clutched his heart dramatically. 'Awesome. Trace, you're one lucky son of a . . . very lovely mother.' He kissed Diamond's hand in a continental gesture I'd last seen practised by a real count, but with him it was part self-mocking, part just for the fun of it. 'Happily, I can announce that you're fine, Diamond. No harm done.' So he did his diagnosis by touch, did he? 'Except for that little detail of being attached to this loser, of course.' He thumped Trace on the arm, beaming with delight for his brother's good fortune. 'I've got no cure for that.'

'And I don't need one, Xavier.' Diamond smiled up at him.

He pulled a face. 'Have I done something wrong? Only our mother calls me that and then I know I'm in trouble.'

'Xav.' Diamond was already charmed. 'But it's my sister that took the knock to the head.' My sister gestured to where I lay. I gave him a finger wave, wondering if I would disgrace myself by being sick on his trendy boots.

'Oh yeah, Crystal.' He winked at his brother. 'Noticed her name on the list. My age, isn't she? How're you feeling, darlin'?'

'I'm OK.' I got up; British instilled reserve demanded that I not show weakness in front of strange boys.

Xav reeled theatrically with a second dose of surprise. 'Whoa, you're one big lady. I mean *tall* lady. I bet you never had any problem making the basketball team in school?'

How many things about that little speech did I find offensive? Let me count the ways.

'I've never played.' I tugged the robe tight. 'I'd prefer not to be examined, if you don't mind. There's nothing wrong with me that a good night's sleep won't put right. My sister is just over-reacting.' No way was I going to let this tactless wannabe doctor put his hands on me.

I felt a buzz against the walls I erected in my head against telepathic assault. I pressed my hands to my temples. 'Stop that.'

'You're one prickly lady-patient.' Xav put his hands on his hips, grinning at me. 'Won't let me help you.'

Diamond pressed me to sit back down. 'Crystal doesn't do telepathy.'

'She's not a Savant?' Xav's expression filled with disappointment.

'Not much of a one,' I muttered.

'She has a gift but it gets in the way of telepathy. Can you check her over without it?'

'I don't want him anywhere near me.' Bile rose in my throat. I was feeling desperate and not minding my manners. 'Get out of my way.' I pushed roughly past them both and ran into the bathroom, slamming the door behind me to be vilely ill.

'Well, using my special spidey sense, I'd say she just got sick,' Xav said.

The next few days went no better for me. The conference took the news that their organizer had found his soulfinder among their number with embarrassing enthusiasm. It became one long party, and I'm sure very little of the serious stuff got done. Trace's family, those not already involved in the event, rushed to Denver to meet Diamond. She was an instant success. How could she not be? Sweet, kind, talented—she was every parent's dream partner for a much-loved son. His diminutive mother, Karla, hugged her as tightly as if she was the last lifebelt on a sinking ship; his impressive Native American father, Saul, gave her a lovely fatherly embrace, his pride and joy plain for all to see. When he smiled, his dark eyes disappeared into a sunburst of wrinkles; it was one of the happiest faces I'd ever seen, a contrast to his usual composed expression.

Don't get me wrong, I was really delighted for Diamond. Aside from the annoying healer brother, Trace and his family were lovely, going out of their way to be kind to us. The soulfinders of the two youngest boys made a particular effort to make me welcome while the Benedicts concentrated on Diamond. Both girls were English in origin and as I had spent most of my life imprisoned—sorry, being educated—in a boarding school in Cheltenham, we had a fair amount in common. Sky was paired with the tallest and youngest of the brood, Zed, a scary-looking boy until he was with his little blonde girlfriend. Then he looked almost tamed. They were in their last year at High School. The other girl, Phoenix, was a more fragile character than the others, thanks to a difficult past, but she was already married to brother Number Six, the ultra-intelligent college boy, Yves. She told me she was far happier than she had ever been before. They were way too young in my mind to be hitched as they were only eighteen but that didn't seem to bother her. She only said that it was inevitable and wonderful.

Sky and Phoenix were fun to go shopping with and the Benedict boys (with one exception) charming to me. The problem was that I felt so, well, *redundant*. It was very clear that in her mind Diamond had already moved on to thinking about how to change her life with Trace in the frame; being a kind of surrogate mother to a grown sister bent that picture out of shape. She would never be so cruel as even to hint that she didn't want me around, but I was no fool. I knew things would be easier if I took responsibility for myself and got out of the way. Decisions had been hovering over me for a few months; now the flock had landed and it was time to deal with them.

So I did what I could for her. I kept a low profile, saying that I was still feeling shaky after the mugging, and changed the dates on my air ticket. She had already said she wanted to stay on in Colorado to get to know Trace's family.

'Crystal, you don't have to go back, you know.' Diamond perched on the edge of her bed, playing with the bracelet Trace had given her the night before: an expensive modern setting of the stones she was named after.

No, I really did. 'It's fine. I've got stuff to do.'

She hugged her knees. 'We've decided to get married in Venice, so all our family can come too.'

Marriage had been inevitable from the start: both Diamond and Trace were traditionally minded and we had been raised devout Catholics. I was pleased she wanted to do the dreaded deed back home where we had our roots. At least that gave me a reason for my existence over the next few months.

'OK, shall I look into arrangements? When do you want to hold the ceremony?'

She blushed prettily. 'Trace doesn't want to wait. We are thinking just before Christmas so we can take our honeymoon over the holidays.'

'That doesn't leave us more than a few weeks. I'd better get busy.'

Diamond cleared her throat, her awkwardness striking as she was rarely lost for words. 'You don't need to do anything, Crystal. Mama's going to sort it all out—she loves a wedding and it will be good for her to focus on something like that. She's already booked the church and the venue. Topaz is seeing to the catering. Silver and Manatsu are taking charge of the bridesmaids and pageboys, as we all know how good an eye Manatsu has for that kind of thing.'

'Bridesmaids and pageboys?'

'Yes, all twelve of our nieces and nephews: fifteen down to fifteen months. It is going to be a nightmare.' Diamond hugged herself with delight at the prospect.

'I see.' I realized then that I had thought that I might be asked to be one of the bridesmaids, or at least be consulted over the dresses considering how Diamond had often said I was good at design. I could see how she might not want me in the line up—the beanstalk among the pretty flowers.

'I hope you don't mind; it just seemed easier to get the parents to sort it out for the children rather than involve you. There's hardly any time. And I thought you would be busy with Signora Carriera if that plan works out.'

'Yes, of course.' I slammed the case shut and zipped it up.

I'm not good at hiding my feelings and Diamond has a gift for sensing disturbance; I wasn't going to get away with pretending I was OK with being cut out. She stopped twiddling her bracelet. 'Oh no, I've made a mistake, haven't I? I projected on to you what I would be thinking, but that's wrong. You wanted to be asked to do something. I thought you would hate the whole wedding thing and run a mile. I just wished to spare you.'

Yeah, you go on telling yourself that, Diamond. You might have thought that in the nice part of your brain, but even you have the darker side that wanted to avoid getting the disaster-area sister involved in your big day. You wouldn't be human if you didn't. 'No, no, it's OK. It's your wedding—you do what you want.'

But Diamond was now trying to repair her error. 'I've already asked Manatsu, but I'm sure she'll appreciate the help. We're getting the dresses made in London where Topaz's brood live—that seemed most convenient—but she could send you the designs. I'd love your opinion.'

Too late for that. 'Really, stop flapping, Diamond. You're right; I'm going to be busy if I do get that job. I'll be lucky if the signora gives me the day off for the wedding, knowing her.' Right now, I'd prefer not to come.

'I know what! I need someone to organize my hen party. I've already asked Karla, Sky; and Phoenix to come out early to enjoy Venice with me. Who better than you to make sure we have a great time?'

Actually, there were busloads of people better than me. 'I

don't know, Diamond, I'm not sure. What about one of your Italian friends—wouldn't they do it?'

Diamond was not to be deterred. She had decided on this sop for me and now had persuaded herself I was the answer. 'It would mean a lot to me if you did it.'

I'm about as resistant as a marshmallow. Emotional blackmail wins every time. 'Sure. OK. Just don't blame me if I make a mess of it like I do everything else.'

Diamond hugged me. 'You won't.'

But I no longer believed her. All that stuff about my talent for fashion had clearly meant nothing when it came to something that was important to her. I now understood why family weddings were such a minefield; I was feeling aggrieved when really it was nothing to do with me. She could and should do what she liked on what was her day. 'I'll see you in a month or so then?'

'Yes. You can keep living in the apartment, you know, whatever happens.'

'Thanks. I'd better get going. Didn't you book the taxi for five minutes ago?'

'Actually, Trace insisted that one of his family drive you.'

Oh no. I could guess what was coming. Just as I thought my day couldn't get any worse. 'Who exactly?'

'Xav. He's the only one at a loose end at the moment.' She nudged me. 'See, you've got a lot in common. Have you, you know, checked him out?'

I snorted. 'I don't think you mean that to sound quite the way it came out.'

Diamond laughed. 'Well, that too. Trace does come from a family of outrageously handsome brothers. And Xav is the right age.'

'C'mon, Diamond, it's me we're talking about. I'm barely a Savant and Xav is clearly a skilled healer for all his other obvious character flaws. What are the chances of two in the same family turning out to be the ones?'

She flipped my hair behind my ears, reaching up to do so. 'I know. Call me optimistic.'

'You felt it with Trace right from the start, didn't you?'

She nodded.

'With Xav, it is safe to say all I feel is a violent dislike. Chalk and cheese. Oil and water.'

'Sorry. I can't help stirring things. I want you to be as happy as I am.'

'Trust me, that wouldn't be the case if I found myself shackled to Xav Benedict by a quirk of fate.'

Diamond accompanied me down to the lobby to say goodbye. At first we couldn't see my driver, then I spotted him stretched out on a chair in reception, head back, eyes closed. Yep, Xav had really risen to the occasion: recognizing the urgency of making the check-in for an international flight, he was asleep.

Diamond shook his shoulder gently. He was fortunate she was with me; if I had been in charge of his wake-up call, I'd've grabbed an ice cube from the bar and stuffed it down his neck. I have a weird sense of humour, according to my sister.

'Wha—oh, it's you.' Xav got up and stretched, all long limbs and fluid shoulder rolls. 'Sorry, I pulled an all-nighter yesterday.'

I dumped my case near his toes, pleased when he hastily gathered them in. 'Such an exciting social life you lead.' What a witch I sounded, but I couldn't help myself; somehow all my decent impulses flew off like water shaken from a dog's coat when I came into his presence.

He grinned at me, amused by my bad temper. 'An all-nighter, at the hospital.'

Diamond elbowed me to behave. 'Xav's volunteering as he intends to study medicine.'

The one thing I had liked about Xav was that he seemed as useless as me; now that illusion was burst. 'Oh. Sorry. Good for you.'

'It's OK, darlin'. I'm glad I had you fooled. Got an image to maintain, you know? So, this all your stuff?' He eyed my modest suitcase. 'What time's the flight again?'

Diamond gave him the details as I showed signs of saying something rude.

'We'd better get going then. See you later, Diamond. I'll make sure little sister gets her plane.' He marched out towards his car, carrying my case on his shoulder like a Nepalese porter climbing Everest.

I gave my sister a hurried kiss and chased after him. For once, someone had longer legs than me and I had to jog to catch up. He chucked my case in the back of his jeep and then opened the door of the passenger's seat for me.

'Climb in, Beauty.'

I frowned at his overly cute name for me. He jokily called all women a variation on this theme—darlin', sweetness, cupcake—but I was the only one I'd heard him call 'Beauty'. I did not appreciate him making a joke at my expense but I had no idea how to retaliate in kind. If I called him 'handsome' I'd only be adding more puff to his over-inflated ego.

I got in and prepared my next remark as he climbed into the driver's seat. 'So, you want to be a doctor then?'

'Hey, are we going to have a normal conversation?' He put the car into drive. 'Yup, if I can afford it. I'm trying to earn some money to pay my way through college.' He pulled out into the traffic, following the signs for the airport.

He had better cut back on the high price fashion items then. 'But I thought your family was rich.'

'No, we're not. Only Wonder Boy Yves has the dough and none of us will touch a cent, though he does try to sneakily give us stuff. Sorry to disappoint but we're just plain working folk. Mom and Dad are ski instructors in the winter and run a white water rafting school in the summer. Dad also manages the ski lift. I'd be the first doctor in the family if I make it through.'

I had a brief vision of him wafting through a ward round with adoring nurses following on his white coat tails. 'I don't know what it's like here, but European doctors have to be very careful how they address patients. Have you not heard of political correctness?'

He smirked. 'Heard, but in my opinion that's a fancy name for being polite.'

'It might surprise you, but women like to be treated as equals. If you call your female patients "cupcake" you'll find they slap you,' I waited a beat, 'with a writ.'

He hooted. 'Don't worry: I know where to draw the line. I'll just make sure I call the men "cupcake" too so no one can accuse me of ignoring equal opportunities. But thanks for worrying about me, Beauty.'

'Please stop calling me that.' I folded my arms across my chest.

'Fine.' Drumming the steering wheel, he glanced at me briefly before turning back to the traffic. 'Hey, Beau—my respected and very equal cupcake, what've I done to annoy you? Every time I talk to you, you get all riled up like a cat. I keep expecting that any moment I'm going to get scratched to bits, you know, like Androcles.'

Andro-who? 'I just don't like people who pretend I'm something I'm so clearly not.'

'Huh?' He looked genuinely puzzled. 'You've lost me.'

'It's not difficult. When you look like me, any comment about my appearance is going to be an insult or a lie.'

He had the gall to laugh. 'What?'

'OK, I'm tall: get over it. I want to be judged for who I am, not what people see.'

'Ah, you are one of those intellectual girls who like to be admired for their brains rather than their beauty? I've heard Europe is full of those.' He hummed a little tune and moved smoothly to overtake a truck.

'I'm not intellectual,' I muttered.

'Strange, because girls here are usually happy with praise of both. I like to make people—and here I do mean girls as I'm not into sweet-talking the other kind—I like to make them feel good about themselves. Inside and out.' He gave me a wink that had the blood rushing to my cheeks.

'Just don't feel you have to try with me.'

He gave a theatrical sigh. 'You are one complicated chick.'

'Chick!'

He laughed. 'Knew you'd rise to my bait! Just knew it. You've got to realize, darlin', that "tease" is my middle name.'

'Oh, really? Did you know that "punisher-of-those-who-call-girls-chicks" is mine?'

'Nope. That really trips off the tongue, doesn't it?'

'Just bear it in mind, Mr Benedict.'

'Anything you say, Miss Brook.'

He put the radio on to cover the silence. Train's 'Hey, Soul Sister' blared out before he could adjust the volume. He was one of those who sang along as he drove, tapping the beat out on the wheel. I loved this song but now I wouldn't be able to hear it without thinking of him bopping away to the chorus. And the words—just let's not go there.

Finally the signs announced that we had arrived at the airport. Rather than drop me at the door, he took the ramp to the short stay car park. When he cut the engine the radio died.

'Before you get out, Crystal, there's something I promised

Trace I'd ask you.' He rubbed the back of his neck awkwardly, suddenly not his usual self at all, like a cloud had passed over his sunshine.

'What's that? Is it something I can do for Trace in Venice? I'm happy to help, really I am, even if I give the impression I'm a bit . . . '

He cocked an eyebrow, interested in the unexpected direction I'd taken. 'Go on: even though you're . . . ?'

'A grump?'

Xav roared with laughter at that. 'You said it. Yup, if you were one of the seven dwarfs, that's the one I'd pick for you.'

'And you're what? Dopey?'

'Got it in one. He's my role model. But no, it was nothing like that he asked me. It's just that he's got this thing that I have to check if I have a soulfinder bond with every Savant of the right date of birth even if it seems, um, unlikely.'

'Diamond's the same. But look at me, Xav, and tell me what you think is going on here. I saw your brother and my sister— bang: instant link, just like that.' I studied my nails; I'd managed to get them French polished at the hotel so could pretend to admire them. 'I don't quite see that for us, do you?'

He gave me a wry grin. 'I'm glad you said it. And no. You and I—we are, I guess, not on the same wavelength.'

'You're DVD region one and I'm two after all.'

'Yeah, exactly. But could we just do it, so I can say we tried?'

'Do what?' I squeaked, having all sorts of embarrassing images of passionate kisses in cars waltz through my mind.

Xav chuckled, a deep rich sound reminding me somehow of mellow red wine. 'Crystal Brook, be ashamed of yourself, girl! We're in a public parking lot. No, not that. I just meant could I talk to you telepathically?'

'If you want me to be sick in your car, then be my guest.'

'That bad?'

'Yes. I'm not joking. I get really, really sick when I try it with my family. It sounds stupid, but I'm not much of a Savant, and it seems that gift didn't quite take with me somehow.' I shrugged, powerless to explain what I didn't really understand.

'How about I try just the tiniest touch. You can shut me out as soon as you start feeling bad. Deal?'

I checked my watch. 'I'm not sure I have time.'

'You've printed off your boarding pass already?'

I nodded.

'Then you have time.' He wasn't going to let me get away with this.

'OK. Just a touch. And please, don't laugh at me if I am ill.'

He held up his hands. 'Would I?'

'Yes, you would.' I remembered him joking when I'd succumbed to concussion. I'd been so annoyed I'd chased him out of the hotel room and insisted on being allowed to sleep off my headache without further medical intervention.

'Character assassin.' He offered me his hand. 'I won't laugh. Pinkie promise.'

Taking a deep breath, I let the tips of my fingers rest on his palm. I closed my eyes, sensing his presence stealing up my arm like warmth from a stove on a cold day. It didn't hurt at first, but as soon as he prepared to make the mind link, my brain started to protest, my stomach churning as if I'd been strapped to a roller coaster and we were doing a series of corkscrews.

'Can't!' I whipped my hand away and clamped it over my mouth, eyes brimming with angry tears. I knew better. I couldn't do those mind tricks others found so easy. I was a complete failure as a Savant and there was no point even going on thinking of myself as one.

'Just take deep breaths. It'll pass.' Xav's tone was anything but mocking. He was no longer touching me, but his voice was soothing, helping me breathe through the crisis.

We sat in silence for a few minutes until I had pulled myself back together.

'I'm OK.' I blinked back the tears, my insides still shaking. 'Now do you believe me?'

'I never thought you were lying. I just . . . Look, Crystal, you know my gift?'

I nodded.

'It helps me see things. I sensed something was wrong in there but I can't tell more unless I look deeper.' He gestured to my head.

That got me fumbling for the door release. ''S OK, Xav. I haven't got time for that now.'

He sprang out of his side and was holding the door open for me before I'd even untangled my handbag from the seatbelt. 'I don't mean to upset you but you need to do something about it. See a doctor back home, one who knows Savants, if you don't want me to touch you.' He was a bit angry but I couldn't help the fact that I just didn't want anyone messing with me.

'Yeah, yeah, I'll do that. See doctor. Thanks.' I extended the handle of my suitcase and started trundling it across the tarmac.

'Goodbye, Crystal.'

I glanced back; he was leaning against his car watching me with the strangest look on his face. Xav, serious—no, that just did not seem right. I was really scared now.

'Bye. Thanks for the lift.'

'No problem. Take care.'

I ran for the terminal, wishing my suitcase didn't make such a racket as it bounced along behind me. I'm not sure why I felt so panicked. I think I was fleeing from the fear that he had found out that I was not even one of them. I had always believed I was some aberration, an offshoot from a true Savant. Was the truth written in my brain somehow?

As I queued to drop my bag, he sent me a text.

Hey, Lion, Let me know how it goes with the doctor. Androcles

That was the second time he'd mentioned that character. I quickly googled the name and read the legend of the Roman slave who removes the thorn from the foot of a wounded lion. I now knew what my reply should be.

Grrr.

chapter 3

Rio d'Incurabili, Dorsoduro, Venice

I let myself in to the courtyard through the canalside gate and dumped my shopping bags on the little mosaic garden table.

'Hey, gorgeous.' I knelt down to give Nonna's old cat, Barozzi, a scratch under the chin. This lazy marmalade general of the feline world had taken the plinth under the tabletop as his command post, the spot from where he hissed challenges to Signora Carriera's beagle and gazed disdainfully at the birds who had long since rumbled to the fact that he was too bone-idle to chase them. I could hear Rocco barking inside the downstairs apartment. The signora had sent me home early (by which she meant when it was still daylight) to walk him for her. I got out my keys. 'Ten second warning, Barozzi: Rocco is about to be unleashed.'

Barozzi closed his eyes. He was right not to be impressed: Rocco's idea of being a fierce dog was to let out a barrage of hysterical barking. Any hint of opposition from the cat and he fled to my skirts. Dogs are small in Venice due to lack of living space but the cats grow large as it is a paradise of many mice and no cars: the natural order reversed.

Opening the heavy locks of our neighbour's front door, I let the beagle free to do a preliminary sniff round the garden while I mounted the external staircase to our second floor flat. Venice gets newer the higher you go: Signora Carriera's apartment was late medieval, heavy timber beams and gloomy rooms. Ours had been added later and was only a few hundred years old, the ceilings high with plenty of light. As I put the groceries on the kitchen counter I could look out across the little courtyard with its strings of washing, tiny patio, and masses of potted plants to the high wall and then to the Canale della Guidecca, the broad stretch of water that separated Venice proper from its satellite islands. The sun was sinking over the cranes and roofs of the Guidecca suburb opposite, nearly horizontal shafts staining the pale walls of the kitchen apricot and reminding me that I didn't have long if I wanted to walk Rocco in the light.

Changing into a pair of black running shorts and white T, I shuffled off my smart work shoes and swapped them for trainers. Xav's warning about seeing a doctor a few weeks ago had made me more conscious about my fitness and I had taken up running. Much to my own surprise, I was even enjoying it. It had given me the excuse not to see any medical person. Without Diamond to bully me into going, I would never enter a clinic on my own. As the running proved, I felt fine, so that meant I was fine. And I was fortunate I lived on one of the few stretches of Venetian streets where it was possible to jog in a straight line. The broad pavement called the Zattere that went along the edge of the Canale made a decent track and was not too crowded with tourists.

I bunched my hair in a scrunchie and then did a few preliminary stretches, trying to ignore the emptiness of the flat.

I had never lived alone until I returned from Denver. I had always had other girls or teachers around me at school, and then I had shared with Diamond. I kept feeling as if I was only playing at being grown-up and running my own life, but then I caught myself paying the phone bill and stocking the fridge, all things that seemed the preserve of adults. I had slipped over to join their number while inside I still felt like a teenager. I couldn't even go into a decent snit when fed up with my boss, as there was no one to flinch when I slammed a door or swore a blue streak. I'd taken to talking to the animals. At least I didn't expect them to reply. I might be heading for eccentric but I wasn't insane.

'C'mon, Rocco. Let's go!' I bounded down the steps, heart lightened by seeing the beagle's uncomplicated enthusiasm, his toffee-coloured ears flapping and his white muzzle perky. We ran anticlockwise round the tip of the Dorsoduro, heading for the landmark of the bell tower in the Piazza San Marco. It rose above the roofs like a square rocket on a very fancy launch pad. Think of the centre of Venice as a bit like the Yin and Yang sign. The famous square of San Marco and the Doge's Pink Palace are in the fat bit of the black Yang side; where I live is right on the pointy end of the white in. The curve in the middle is the Grand Canal dividing the two. There are three evenly spaced bridges linking the sides, including the celebrated Rialto in the middle. If you know your way (and it is a given that strangers will get lost in our maze of streets even with a map), then you can walk between most of the famous places in about twenty minutes or jump on a vaporetto, or waterbus, and be there in ten.

It didn't take me long to reach the end of the Zattere. I sat on the steps of the church of Santa Maria della Salute and gave Rocco a cuddle. Across from me, the top of San Marco's campanile was gilded by the sunset. The tourists up there must be getting one great show as evening fell across the lagoon. I wondered if anyone had their binoculars fixed on me. I waved—just in case.

Perhaps I should rethink that whole 'I'm not going mad' thing?

Even living here, it is hard to see Venice with fresh eyes. It has been described so many times by writers, artists, and filmmakers that it is like a beautiful handcrafted yacht afloat on the Adriatic lagoon, which's become covered in a suffocating accretion of barnacles. Occasionally you need to hoist it out of the water and scrape it back to the bare planks or it will keel over with the weight. Perhaps I projected on it my own unstable grasp on the world because to me the fundamental truth of the place—my bare planks—was that Venice was experienced as a city on the brink of destruction, probably not seeing out the century when sea levels rise with global warming—a last-chance-to-see civilization. With that destiny on the not so far horizon, life here was all the sweeter: sunny squares, whistling parrots in upper storey windows, narrow winding streets, secret corners; groups of workers, artists, students who bind the city together like links in a chain; tides of tourists ebbing and flowing each day. It is an inconvenient place to live—expensive and isolated—so we all have chosen to be here for some particular reason. Mine was family ties, happy memories of Nonna, but also a wish to live in a unique place, somewhere that could feed my imagination. Diamond felt so too, not that we ever put our feelings into words for each other. We just both loved it—not an emotion I had for any other city I had lived in.

A private speedboat drew up at the Salute mooring, white wake turning pink in the sunset. I watched as a little lady dressed all in black was helped ashore by her burly pilot in a smart navy-blue uniform. I recognized her, of course; anyone who had lived in Venice a few years knew her. Contessa Nicoletta owned one of the little islands near the Lido, the long, thin barrier between Venice and the Adriatic. The lagoon was speckled with such enclaves, some former isolation hospitals, others monastic communities. The one the lady lived on was not far from here, close to Elton John's house and the exclusive hotel where all the stars stayed for the film festival in September. It was said to be a little jewel, perfectly positioned to come across to the city but giving her total privacy in her grand house. Only very ancient Italian families or rock stars owned such real estate. You could just glimpse the roof and surrounding trees from the Salute steps; it remained a delicious mystery and had become in my mind as alluring as the walled garden had been to Mary Lennox in *The Secret Garden*. The old lady knew me too—or at least she was friendly with Diamond and so may have registered my existence—because Contessa Nicoletta was also a Savant.

Leaning heavily on her pilot's arm, the old lady tottered towards the church with the others attending mass. Rocco started barking, drawing her attention my way. I got up (you did not sit when Italian nobility deigned to greet you).

First the contessa patted Rocco, and then she turned to me. 'Crystal Brook, yes? How are you, dear?' she asked me in Italian. The pilot paused to allow her to talk to me, his mirror sunglasses obscuring his expression. I imagined he had to be a patient person to put up with the contessa's frequent stops. She had so many acquaintances in this city. He had cultivated a perfectly blank face for such moments.

'I'm well, thank you. I've started work for Signora Carriera.'

'Ah, yes, I heard she had got a big order for that film company. How exciting for you both!'

So far the excitement had been very muted by the sheer amount of work involved in making the costumes. I'd not seen so much as a flicker of Hollywood stardust. 'And how are you, Contessa Nicoletta?'

'*Sempre in gamba.*' A funny phrase, which translates roughly as 'still on my pins'. Her hawklike features wrinkled in a smile, her faded blue eyes twinkling. She had features that reminded me of an old Maria Callas, the opera diva: strong nose, still dark eyebrows, bearing of a queen even if a little stooped. 'And what news of your lovely sister? I thought she would be back from America by now.'

'No, she stayed on. Did you hear what happened? She found her soulfinder.'

'Oh heavens!' The contessa clapped her hands together, swaying dangerously. I was glad the pilot still had a firm hand on her arm. 'Oh, oh, I am so delighted for her. Who is the lucky man?'

'His name is Trace Benedict—one of a family of Savants who live in Colorado. Apparently they're quite well known in law enforcement circles. Have you heard of them?'

The old lady's expression froze for a second as her faulty memory searched for the entry in her brain. Then her face cleared. 'Ah yes, I've heard of them. How . . . interesting. I'm not sure they are good enough for Diamond—I'm not sure anyone is.'

'I know what you mean, but I think he's an excellent match for her.'

The bells started ringing for mass. The contessa squeezed the pilot's arm to signal she was ready to enter the church. 'Do send her my best, Crystal. I'll see you, I expect, when I call for my costumes for the Carnival.' Her parties for the pre-Lent celebration were famous and attracted high society figures from all over the world. 'That is if Signora Carriera can fit me in this year.'

I smiled and reassured her. No one would be so stupid as to snub her custom, even when a film crew was in the city. Directors came and went; Contessa Nicoletta was for ever.

Rocco and I jogged back to our courtyard. By the time I let us in, Signora Carriera had returned. My heart fell when I saw the piles of fabric she had brought with her. Taking work home was an evil habit and with me upstairs she had started to assume I was a willing pair of hands. Rocco had no such fears: he bounded to his owner with puppyish enthusiasm, leaping around her and licking her fingers. A willowy lady with blonde highlighted hair, the signora was doing an excellent job of disguising the fact that she was in her early sixties. She wore her glasses on a diamanté chain around her neck. They were bumping against her chest now as she shook out a wonderful piece of emerald green velvet.

'How was your walk?' she asked. I assumed she was addressing me though she was paying more attention to Rocco.

'Good, thanks. We saw Contessa Nicoletta going to church. She says she'll call by soon about her costume order.'

Signora Carriera ran a distracted hand through her hair. 'Ay-yay-yay, how will we cope?' Her lips curved in a little smile as she thought of the profits. 'But cope we will. Would you like to have supper with me? I'm expecting special guests so I've cheated, naturally, and brought in a lasagne from the restaurant across the street.'

I rather fancied the idea of having someone other than the cat to talk to. 'Yes please. Who's coming?'

'The director from the film company and his head of costume. They phoned just after you left.' She snipped off a loose thread on a gold tissue petticoat.

I thought of the last few masks I was still to complete, the dresses with seams only tacked and not properly sewn. 'But we're not ready!'

She shrugged in a 'what can one do?' gesture. 'I know, but they want to see what we've done so far. They realize we cannot deliver the final pieces until Saturday. Filming starts on

Sunday so there is not much time for changes if they don't like my approach.'

I was already regretting agreeing to attend. If there were multiple alterations, guess who would be asked to do them while my boss dealt with her usual customers?

'That's all I have time to do now.' Signora Carriera put her little scissors away. 'Why don't you go and change into one of your dresses—the purple wrap, I think.' The signora assessed me with her professional look. 'Yes, that brings out the best in your colouring. Dramatic, like your features.'

I choked on a laugh. 'I have a best to bring out?'

'Oh stop that, Crystal!' she said smartly. 'I don't know where you got this idea that you are ugly.'

From the mirror? I thought.

'It is most ridiculous! I have heard enough of it. You are one of those girls whose faces are arresting, not merely pretty. Hundreds of women can do pretty; few can do stunning.'

My jaw dropped. Then again, a cattle prod could do stunning.

Having begun on this theme, Signora Carriera was on a roll. 'Look at the top model agencies, they do not go for what the world calls beautiful; they choose faces that you remember and who can wear the clothes rather than let the clothes wear them. That, *bella*, is you.'

Well, wow. Just wow. After a couple of rotten weeks, I suddenly felt a hundred feet tall—in a good way. 'Thanks. I'll go get changed then.'

And with the encouraging smell of baking lasagne to spur me on, I took time to dress for dinner. After all, I was going to meet two guests used to rubbing shoulders with the most sophisticated people in the world. I did not want to let Venice or myself down. I peered at my face in the mirror as I applied mascara, trying to see what Signora Carriera had described.

Drama? Hmm. I still looked like me, dark brows, funny-coloured eyes, rioting hair, but if I pretended I was beautiful like she said, maybe I'd begin to be the person she saw rather than the one I did? Worth a try. I added a necklace I had made from Murano glass beads—bold colours threaded on silver wire—and a pair of my nonna's heirloom earrings. There: I was done. I still couldn't see any beauty when I looked at my reflection, but I could see memorable.

The director, James Murphy, turned out to be a friendly Irishman, if somewhat highly strung at the moment as he had a multimillion dollar movie riding on his shoulders. No giant, I noticed I had a few inches on him when I shook his hand, but he made up for height with width. He wore a grey polar neck under his jacket and jeans—California's version of the head guy's suit. The costume designer, Lily George, was surprisingly young for her job, in her late twenties I would guess. She was a funny combination of ethereal looks—flyaway blonde hair, pale skin, size zero—with a raucous voice and earthy laugh. I liked her immediately.

Mr Murphy twirled his *vino santo* aperitif, lounging on Signora Carriera's ancient sofa. It was impossible to get comfortable on that instrument of torture but I doubted the signora ever had time to sit on it to find that out. 'If there is a moment before we eat, signora, can we see your costumes? You know the look I am trying to create: the moody night of the Carnival, a time for lovers and assassins to be abroad.' He sketched his ideas in the air, threatening to douse us all in his drink. 'I want our hero, who will be dressed in his signature black suit, to be framed by the outlandish jewel-toned costumes of the participants in the revels. They must be everything he is not: out of control, colourful, loud.'

The film was the third in a successful spy thriller series, a modern bitter twist on the Bond character with a leading man who walked more often on the dark side than that of the good. It had made the career of the actor, Steve Hughes, whose fair-haired good looks could both chill and tempt with one smouldering glance at the camera, sending his female admirers into a swoon of longing.

Oh, did I not mention? I'm a big fan.

Signora Carriera nodded and got up. 'Yes, we have time to show you a few pieces. Crystal will model the costumes for us.'

I put down my Coke. 'I will?'

Lily George got up from her perch on the window seat. 'Great. I loved the ones you've already delivered. Sorry to ask for a few more so late but James got carried away when he saw what you'd done—made the scene much bigger.' She gave the director a fondly exasperated look.

'What, *moi*? Carried away? Surely not.' James grinned.

'Show me how to fit them and I'll then be able to brief my team for dressing the extras on Sunday.'

We processed into the signora's spare room where she had laid out the costumes. The basic idea behind the fancy dress was an eighteenth century lady's gown or man's breeches and jacket, topped by a robe called a domino, mask and hat. It was the mask that really made the costume and these were where the signora's skill really came into play as she was brilliant at thinking up modern versions of the traditional patterns, using urban themes such as graffiti or technology to twist the old-fashioned into the shockingly new. But first I had to be laced into the gown, which involved a fearful amount of corsetry and petticoat fluffing to get the right silhouette. The dress—a red and white satin embroidered with gold—fitted me perfectly.

Lily made me stand at the far end of the room. 'Yes, yes, excellent. James wants the extras to cast long shadows across the set—this will work well. They are supposed to tower over Steve, larger than life.' I was disappointed to learn from Lily that my favourite actor was only five ten. Apparently many leading men were, as the camera preferred them that way. 'Put the hood up. Even better. Which mask?'

Signora Carriera chose a blood-red one made up of a fili-gree of overlapped words—Death, Sin, Danger, Passion. They formed a lacy network covering two thirds of my face.

Lily caressed it with a fingertip. 'Oh, I want one. I could wear it on a bad day at the office. That'd put the fear of God into my girls in the workroom. Come, let's show James.'

I spent the next half an hour being turned and prodded as they worked through the potential of each costume. I was even asked to wear the male domino and mask just to see the general effect. Everything was approved and the three of them were buoyed along on creative enthusiasm for what could be done with the outfits. Not daring to speak up, I was also caught up in the mood, remembering how much I loved my textile course at school, which had allowed me to conjure shapes and silhouettes with fabric, but nothing on this scale or budget.

Over a fantastic dinner of local scallops followed by the lasagne and green salad, James toasted his host. 'You've ex-ceeded my expectations, signora. You've produced everything you sketched for us but added magic. It will make fantastic cinema.'

'*Grazie tante.* I could not have done it without my assis-tant.' She gestured generously to me.

Lily tapped the back of my wrist. 'Crystal, you must come along on Sunday—be one of the extras. You don't need to do anything more than you've done tonight but you looked fabu-lous. I'm itching to get my hands on dressing you properly. Don't you agree, James?'

The director's BlackBerry buzzed. He glanced down and checked his message. 'She looked great. Yes, come along, Crystal. You might find it fun. There will be a lot of standing around but that's the movies. I've got to cut this short, I'm afraid. Steve's just landed his helicopter at his hotel and wants to talk to me—some problem with the press in the rumour department. Thank you so much for the meal, signora: it means a lot to meet real people when you go on location. The film world bubble can get in the way of a genuine response to a place.'

Signora Carriera left the room to show him out. Lily made no move to leave with the director, taking a sip of her wine and sitting back with a fond smile of contentment rather like Barozzi the cat after a good supper.

'He's nice,' I said, topping up my water.

'Yes, James is a really lovely man,' Lily twiddled a lock of her short hair in thought, '—nervous at the moment because so much money is riding on the project but he never takes it out on his team. I really enjoy working for him.' Her gaze shifted from contemplation to concentrate on the present moment, taking on a wicked glint. 'Your signora is quite something too.'

I smiled. 'A hard worker, that's for sure.'

'And an artist when it comes to clothes. I could learn a lot from her.'

'Is that why you're still here—to pick her brains?'

Lily laughed. 'Of course. When we needlewomen get together, we can't pass up the chance to talk the language of dressmaking with someone who really understands. But I'm also interested in you, Crystal. You're not what I expected to find in Venice.'

I shrugged. 'I'm only part Italian—a quarter. I went to school in England, which is where my mum and one sister still live. The rest of us are scattered all over.'

'I wasn't talking about your nationality. I meant someone with your looks. Have you ever been approached by anyone? You obviously have the height and there is just something about your face that screams to be photographed.' Thumbs and index fingers together, Lily mimed capturing me in a frame.

'Oh, um, well, no. You're only the second person to say that and the other was the signora earlier today. Must be my day for being talent-spotted.' I chuckled at the irony. 'Funny because I always thought I looked, well, *odd* compared to other girls.'

'You do.'

Caught mid-sip, I almost spat out my mouthful of water. I swallowed and managed a wry 'Thanks.'

'No, I mean it. You have an unusual face, but the eyes now— what colour would you call them?'

'Light brown?'

'Uh-uh.' She shook her head. 'They're really striking—gold flecks, a hint of hazel and green. You've got the colouring of a chameleon; you'll photograph differently depending on the shade you are wearing.'

Our hostess returned and sailed on through to the kitchen. 'Does anyone have room for ice cream?'

'Yes, please,' replied Lily. 'I was just telling Crystal that she should think about modelling as a career.'

From the kitchen came the sound of the freezer compartment being tugged open. The signora came back bearing a tub of locally made ice cream. 'I tell the girl she has the looks but does she believe me?'

I helped get out the dessert dishes, lovely antique ones with gold leaf edging. 'You're beginning to persuade me, but I always thought my features were too large.'

'Ah, but that is why they work,' said Lily. 'Think of Julia Roberts and Anne Hathaway—mouths the size of aircraft carriers but it didn't do their careers any harm.' Lily accepted a large serving of strawberry ice cream while I sketched the outline of my lips self-consciously with a fingertip. Aircraft carrier? 'I know people in the industry. If you're interested, get some studio portraits taken and I'll send them around. In fact, I insist. I'll get one of the photographers on set to do it free. I have this hunch about you and I want to crow that I discovered you when you are rich and famous.'

The signora gave a huff. '*I* discovered her, Lily.'

Now they were fighting over the right to claim responsibility for my non-existent fame.

'OK, Maria, *we* discovered her.'

The two women smiled at me expectantly.

What could I say? 'Um, thank you.'

'James said there was a lot of standing around on set; now we know what to do with the spare time, don't we?' Lily dug in her spoon. 'Excellent ice cream, Maria.'

By the time I had helped clear up and let myself into my own flat, it was nearly midnight. I felt ridiculously happy and took Barozzi for a little waltz round the kitchen, much to his disgust. He scrambled out of my arms and disappeared through the window. Ever since Xav had raised the idea that there was something wrong with me, I'd felt as if I'd had no future, not as a Savant at least. Now Lily and Signora Carriera had helped me see that my path did not have to follow the rest of my family's; the vast majority of the population lived happy fulfilled lives in the normal, ungifted world. I could make a name for myself there that would mean my lack of Savant proficiency was entirely overshadowed. All I needed to do was push on the doors they were pointing me towards. Maybe modelling wouldn't be the thing for me in the end, but it was a place to start.

I was just about to switch off my bedside light when my phone flashed that it had a message waiting from Diamond. I quickly tapped on the screen.

Arriving back tomorrow. If you get time, please make up spare beds for two. Love ◊.

Two? Trace plus one. My guess would be that Androcles might well be coming to find out why the lion had not sent him a paw report. Damn. And it had been such a good day.

In no hurry to make my explanations to Xav Benedict, I left Diamond a note on the kitchen counter saying I would have to stay late at work. When Signora Carriera hinted in the afternoon that Rocco might benefit from a jog, I did not leap at the chance as I normally would, but busied myself pasting sequins on the last of the masks we were making for the film. She let the subject drop, occupied as she was showing her costume ideas for the next Carnival to Contessa Nicoletta. The old lady had come to the shop as she had promised; her ever-present pilot left on the street outside like a bouncer manning our door. The two Venetians were cackling together like witches over a cauldron, thoroughly enjoying themselves. Each threw in snippets of themes, touches of colour, to the palette of designs Signora Carriera was going to make for the old lady's guests.

My phone rang. 'Hey, Crystal, I'm home.' Diamond's voice sounded crackly on the line.

'Diamond! Good flight?' I flicked a sequin off my nail but it kept getting stuck to another finger. I moved to the window overlooking the little bridge and canal in the back street. Light rippled across the ceiling like a veil of billowing watered silk.

'Very good. No delays, thank the gods of air travel. I've brought Trace with me. He's decided to hold his stag party here as I've roped his brothers' soulfinders in to mine. They're all going to fly over next week. His employers have been great; they've given him a whole month off—can you believe it?'

I imagined that the Denver police department were clever enough to realize the benefit of having one of their top cops married to a first class peacemaker. 'That's really nice for you both.'

'Only two weeks to go till the big day! So we thought parties next Friday. Will that be OK?'

'Sure. What do you want to do for yours?'

There was a brief pause. 'I thought you were organizing it for me.' Diamond sounded a little aggrieved that I hadn't made any preparations. Should I have done? I'd imagined we would book a table nearer the time.

'Of course I will; it's just that we've been really busy. I've had some ideas though.' Or I was going to make sure that I had by the time I got home.

'Humph.' I could hear Diamond thinking that it was just as well that she hadn't asked me to do anything more serious towards the wedding. I hadn't meant to disappoint, but again I had been proved a waste of space in our family of high achievers. My beautiful dreams of success and new hope took on a little tarnish. Who was I fooling? I couldn't even manage to arrange a party for my lovely sister without making a muck of the whole thing.

'Well, if you need any help, just ask Xav.' Diamond couldn't hide the tone of reprimand. 'He's here to organize Trace's night out and is full of really amazing ideas. He was telling me on the flight—a champagne cruise, the casino, water skiing down the Grand Canal.'

'Oh really? Xav's arranging water skiing for his brothers?' Crumbs, I had been thinking more on the lines of a meal out and all of us going to a club wearing those daft hen night outfits. I'd have to up my game.

'He should be with you any moment. I sent him over with Rocco—that dog needs to get out more—you should've heard the racket he was making when we got in. Anyway, I gave him a map and the dog-lead so hopefully he and Rocco should be with you in about half an hour if they only get lost once or twice.'

Xav hot footing it to see me the moment he arrived? 'Why's he coming all the way over here?'

'Oh, he said he wanted to see where you worked. Trace and I will cook supper. See you soon. Love you.'

'Love you too.'

I put my phone in my pocket and noticed that the two signoras were watching me with interest. 'Diamond's back,' I explained.

'So we heard. You are arranging her chicken night, yes?' asked Contessa Nicoletta.

'Hen night,' corrected Signora Carriera.

I nodded glumly.

The old lady clucked at my expression. 'Do not worry, Crystal, I will help. We will make sure she has a night to remember. Better than the water skiing arranged by this Xav Benedict, I promise.'

She had heard that, had she? 'Better than that?'

'Oh yes. These Americans can do action but only we Venetians know how to do true sophistication.' She tapped the side of her nose. 'Your sister will adore it.'

'Thank you. You might just be a lifesaver—at least as far as Diamond not killing me for messing up.'

My boss looked surprised to hear that we were on such close terms with Contessa Nicoletta. 'I didn't know you knew Diamond so well, Contessa.'

'Oh, we have ties.' The old lady waved her hand vaguely in the air. She meant through the Savant network but it allowed

Signora Carriera to infer that we were some kind of distant cousins.

The old lady picked up her heavy black handbag, vintage Chanel if I knew anything about accessories. 'I will be in touch early next week with my suggestions. It is too long since I have held a party at my house.'

Her house! Wow and double-wow! Take that, Xav Benedict: you might bid water sports; I'm going to raise the stakes with an invitation to the most exclusive estate in Venice!

I beamed at her. '*Grazie mille*, that is so kind of you. I know that Diamond will be over the moon.'

Contessa Nicoletta gathered up her scarf and handbag. 'Ladies only, naturally. Maria, I hope you will be there.'

Signora Carriera glanced at me. 'Oh, I'm not sure. These young girls won't want an old bird like me.'

'Nonsense. Who else will supply the costumes?'

Costumes too? Diamond was just going to die when she heard all this. I hurried to secure the deal. 'Of course you must come—my sister wouldn't dream of having a party without you. Besides, her fiancé's mother will be there. I'm sure Karla will love to meet you.'

My boss smiled, genuinely pleased to receive the invitation. 'Then I'd be delighted.'

Contessa Nicoletta reached the door. I hastened to open it for her. She paused to admire the display of masks we had in the window, her face taking on a keen expression. 'Such skill,' she sighed in appreciation. 'I do love those who use their gifts as God intended. Goodbye, Crystal.' She tottered off on the arm of her manservant and over one of the little hump-backed bridges that spanned the canal outside.

'Hey, Cupcake of Complete Equality. We found you.'

I turned round. 'Hello, Xav.'

Chapter 4

'Missed me?' Xav let Rocco pull him over the threshold into the shop.

'Yeah, like I miss having toothache.'

He grinned, let the dog off the lead and began rummaging through the masks on display. Everywhere you looked in this shop you were met with the blank-eyed gaze of carnival masks—feathered, plumed, and sequinned. They had not lost their sinister air even though I'd worked here a few weeks. I preferred not to be the last person to lock up. Xav picked up one with a big curved beak—the plague doctor theme. 'What do you think?' His brown eyes twinkled through the holes.

'Huge improvement.'

He passed me a lacy affair with diamanté and pearl fringe. 'Go on.'

'I can't—I work here, remember.'

'Aw, you've no sense of fun.'

I slapped the mask over my eyes. 'Satisfied?'

He pulled my hand away then put it back, head to one side like an expert judging a painting. 'Nope, I like the original better.'

Was that a compliment? I began to soften a little towards him.

'With a mask on, you seem all fairylike, none of the lion Crystal swatting me away with a few cutting words. Rr-rarr.' He aped slashing the air with curved claws.

I dropped the mask back in the basket he had taken it from. 'Well, thanks, kind sir.'

He bumped my forehead with his beak. 'Don't mention it.'

Rocco had unearthed Signora Carriera from her workroom and she emerged to find out who had brought him.

'Ah, so this must be one of Diamond's new family!' she exclaimed in Italian. She held out her hand and switched into English. 'Please to meet you.'

Xav whipped off the mask and bent to kiss her wrist. 'I'm Xavier Benedict—or Xav if you prefer. You must be Signora Carriera; I have heard so much about you from Diamond.'

My boss positively melted under the warmth of his smile. Was I the only one who felt like spitting when Xav turned on his charm? 'How sweet of her! And thank you for bringing Rocco over for his walk. I hope he behaved?'

'Not at all: he was extremely ungentlemanly, chasing all the lady dogs with no discrimination in the slightest.' He leaned closer. 'I fear he is a rogue and a heartbreaker.'

Rocco cocked his head, gazing up at Xav with eyes of pure innocence. Even the dog was besotted.

The signora gave a lovely liquid laugh, one I rarely heard from her, and patted her beagle on the head. 'You little terror, you!'

The bell over the entrance rang. Lily George whirled in, wearing an eye-catching patchwork coat. 'I hope you are ready for me, Maria!' she called. 'I need those last masks to show make-up.' She stopped when she saw we had a customer. I took the plague doctor mask out of Xav's hand and placed it carefully back on the rack.

'Yes, I've everything boxed up for you.' Signora Carriera reached beneath the counter to find the order. Xav gave me a wink and wandered to the other side of the shop to look at the cloaks on the rack of costumes. 'I have some last minute ones in the workroom. Give me a moment, Lily.'

Taking a good look at our visitor, Lily sidled over to me. 'Crystal, why did you not tell me you meet such gorgeous Italian men working in this shop? I'd like to take that one home with me, wrapped in a bow.'

I blushed and cleared my throat. 'Erm . . . Lily . . . '

Xav turned round and arched a brow at us.

Lily gripped my arm. 'Don't tell me: he understands English. Just kill me.'

Xav laughed. 'Now that would be a shame.'

'Oh my gosh, and he's American! I am totally, totally mortified. Crystal, find a cloak and throw it over my head. I need to hide.'

I shook her back to her senses. 'Don't worry, it's only Xav. My sister is marrying his brother in a couple of weeks. Xav, this is Lily George; she's doing the costumes for the new Steve Hughes movie that they're filming in Venice this week.'

'Nice to meet you.' Xav offered Lily his hand. She gave it a quick shake before clapping her hands to her blushing cheeks.

'And you too. Ignore me: I have this terrible thing where I go like a beetroot even when I shouldn't be embarrassed. I thought age would cure me of it.' She flapped at her face.

Signora Carriera returned from her search for the various boxes she had packed for Lily and placed them on the counter. 'That is everything, I think, Lily. Do you want to check them?'

'I'll take a quick peek.' Lily went through the boxes, humming her approval. Xav loitered at her shoulder to get a preview. She held one up to his face. 'Fabulous.'

Did she mean the mask or Xav? I wondered.

Lily put the mask back in its box. 'You know, Xav, you could come along with Crystal on Sunday if you like. Casting are having difficulty finding enough extras who are tall enough for what the director wants. They'd love to have you, I'm sure. You might find it interesting.'

Selfishly, I had thought of the film as my special experience; I rather hoped Xav would turn down the chance, but no.

He rubbed his hands. 'Hey, I've only been in this country a few hours and I'm already starring in the movies—I love this place.' He addressed the last remark to Signora Carriera, cementing his reputation as her favourite.

'I take that as a "yes"?' Lily put the boxes in one of the shop's large bags decorated with Carnival masks. 'Crystal knows where we'll be. Early start, I'm afraid. Make-up call at six.'

Xav beat me to the door and opened it for her. 'We'll be there.'

'Thank you for these, Maria. See you two on Sunday then.' Lily swept out, the bag swinging jauntily in her grip.

Rocco scampered out of the workroom, fighting a long piece of gold braid. Signora Carriera gave a cluck and untangled him with difficulty.

'It is high time this dog had his supper,' she said in Italian. 'Will you take him home and feed him for me, Crystal? I'd better see what mess he has made in there before shutting up the shop.'

'Of course, signora. C'mon, Xav. Home time.' I fetched my coat and clipped the lead back on Rocco's collar.

'Goodnight, signora!' Xav called as we left the shop.

'*Arrivederci*, Xav!' The door locked behind us and the shutters snapped closed.

'That's an amazing place to work.' Xav turned to go in

completely the wrong direction. Rocco and I headed towards home, the beagle looking mournfully over his shoulder until Xav realized we weren't with him.

'I'm sure we came that way,' he said, catching up with me and pointing to the other side of the bridge.

'Maybe you did, but that isn't the quickest way back. Follow me.'

My gift had proved useful in Venice in the first few months here, as the network of streets was bewildering. Still, it didn't help with the sudden blind alleys or streets ending at a canal, which thwarted you from carrying on in a straight line; only local knowledge could solve that problem. Many streets here are so narrow you have to proceed single file, but on the maps they are drawn as main routes. Tourists can be forgiven for hesitating before marching along a path that in any other city would only lead into someone's backyard or wheelie bins. I was rather pleased to be able to display my expertise to Xav, threading our way without making a single mistake, until we reached the Accademia Bridge, the southern-most of the three over the Grand Canal.

We paused at the top of the arch to admire the view. Even after more than a year in Venice I always stopped to remind myself of the incredible city that had become my home.

'This place is extreme.' Xav leant on the parapet, watching the gondoliers pass under with a cargo of Japanese tourists. I stood beside him. I love this view of the church of Santa Maria della Salute, the very one that I ran to daily. It sat at the end of the Grand Canal like a very fat question mark. While Venice is mainly about horizontals, long, low islands and winding river channels, here the view emphasized the verticals: tall palaces rising directly out of the jade green water, candy-striped mooring poles, wooden piles driven into lagoon mud. I've often thought it would make the good basis for an abstract fabric print—just the hint of Venetian colours and lines. I should sketch it sometime and show the signora.

'So, how did the visit to the doctor go?' Xav tapped the parapet restlessly.

'It didn't. I didn't go.' I tugged Rocco away from a fallen ice cream cone and started down the opposite slope of the bridge. 'I've been feeling fine.'

'You, Beauty, are enough to drive a boy to drastic measures.'

I let the pet name pass on this occasion; Lily and Signora Carriera had helped change my mind about that. 'What can you do? It's my body.'

'I could tell your sister.'

'And what happened to doctor-patient confidentiality? You may have the spidey sense, as you called it, but that comes with responsibility—I've seen the movie.'

'Rocco, bite her. Someone needs to make her see reason.'

The beagle looked up at Xav, puzzled to hear his name.

'Don't bring him into it. That's not fair.'

'I seem to remember someone promising to see a doctor when they left Denver.'

'Well, I changed my mind. Let it go.'

'Will you let me take a closer look then?' He made a step towards me but I dodged his touch.

'So do you think Steve Hughes is the greatest actor of his generation or not? Personally I'm a big fan. I'm hoping we'll get to meet him.'

'Good try but changing the subject won't work with me. You saw Rocco with that gold stuff in the store—that's me with the little matter of someone's health.' He grinned, expecting me to appreciate the self-mockery.

I was not in the mood for his brand of charm. 'I'm not a child; it's my life: I can make my own decisions.'

'Like that's turning out so well for you.'

I felt he had just cut me off at the knees. Xav had teased me frequently but he'd never been cruel before. I looked away before he saw that he had upset me. 'I repeat: it's my life; if I want to make a mess of it then that's my decision.'

He sighed, reaching out to me then dropping his arm when he saw me move away. 'Sorry, I shouldn't have said that, but you drive me crazy.'

'So it's my fault you were rude? Oh yeah, I get it. My little life here isn't enough for the amazing Benedict family—or my own family for that matter. Basically you all despise me for not being a high achiever like you lot.'

'No!'

'Yes!' I echoed back, using exactly the same tone. 'You might wish you'd not said it but at least I know what you really think under all that charming gloss of words you spray over everyone you meet. You're the equivalent of a verbal water cannon.'

'Crystal, I only meant that you weren't taking care of yourself as you should.'

I accelerated, leaving him lagging until he matched my pace.

'I'm sorry, really sorry.'

'Just shut up, Xav. I don't want to talk to you.'

'Cupcake . . .'

'I'm not your cupcake, your beauty, your anything! I'm not even a proper Savant so just butt out of my life!'

He held up his hands. 'OK, OK. Message received. Sorry for caring.'

I shoved open the courtyard door. 'Come on, Rocco, let's find your supper.'

Even Diamond, absorbed as she was by her soulfinder, sensed that all was not well between Xav and me. She and Trace carried the burden of the conversation at dinner until it became awkward for everyone. I had been pleased to see her but the way she looked to Trace over the dining room table, speaking with glances, underlined how she no longer belonged with me, if she ever had.

'So how's your new job, Crystal?' Trace asked kindly after he had entertained us with an account of his investigation into a recent financial fraud. His gift enabled him to track where things had been and it had led them right to the door of the guilty party who had taken to the old fashioned crime of printing his own money.

'It's fine, thanks.' I twiddled spaghetti on my fork. The poor man didn't have much to go on with that answer. Manners made me elaborate. 'We've been busy doing the costumes for a film company.'

'That must be really interesting.'

'Yes, it has been.'

Silence fell again. I could sense Xav seething on the other side of the table. 'Crystal's hiding something.'

I looked up sharply: he wasn't going to betray me, was he?

'What she hasn't said is that they've asked her to be an extra—me as well.'

'Oh, Crystal, that's wonderful!' Diamond latched on to the good news with embarrassing enthusiasm.

'It'll just be a very short scene—a few seconds if that—bit of Venice atmosphere.' I shrugged. 'Probably end up on the cutting room floor.'

'Still, but the experience will be fascinating. It hardly matters what they do with the footage.'

'I s'pose.' I wondered if I should mention the modelling thing. 'There's this costume designer who's taken an interest in me.'

Xav helped himself to more Parmesan. 'I thought it was me she has a crush on.'

'Cute.' I grimaced at him. He returned the gesture—we were acting as if we were in the primary school playground in our treatment of each other.

'Xav,' Trace said quietly. Why did I get the impression his whole family spent half their life reining him in?

I didn't need telepathy to hear him think 'well, she started it'.

'Anyway, as I was saying before I was interrupted,' Xav gave me a mocking bow, 'Lily—that's the designer—thinks I might photograph well. She's going to get a friend to take some shots on set so I can send them to modelling agencies.'

Diamond looked at Trace, her brow furrowed. What had I said?

'I'm not joking: she said I had a face that would, you know, be memorable. She thinks I could go the whole way—become famous and everything.'

'Oh dear.' Diamond pushed her plate away.

'What? You don't think I could do it?'

'No, no, nothing like that. I think you could—that's the problem.'

'You're worried I'm going to succeed? That doesn't make sense. You've been pushing me to do something—well, here it is.'

Xav stepped in. 'That's not the issue, cupcake—sorry, *Crystal*. It's the kind of success you'd be aiming for.'

'What do you mean?' I examined their faces—they all knew something I didn't but I had no idea what.

'We Savants can't become famous—not in ordinary circles,' Trace explained. 'We have too many enemies and people would use us if they knew we had certain gifts.'

'But I'm not trying to be famous for being a Savant.'

'We understand but the same still holds true. If you are well known, people will start digging for dirt and asking questions.

There is no one more examined than a celebrity. If they find out about you, you'll become a target. At the moment you're safe because you are unknown.'

'Sorry, Crystal, better not take off that mask on Sunday.' Xav pulled the bowl of spaghetti towards him to help himself to seconds.

Diamond, sensing the explosion about to come, held up a hand to silence him, but it was too late.

'I can't believe this!' I shoved my chair back and leaned both fists on the table. 'I finally find something I could do—somebody who thinks I've got a future—and you're telling me to forget it! Oh, it's all right for you with your shiny gifts and your reputations in the Savant world, but what do I have? Nothing!' My head started to pound, eyesight blurring. 'You all know I'm worse than useless in the Savant world so why the hell should I let that hold me back?'

'You're not the only one who has to make sacrifices, Crystal.' Trace managed to make me sound like a child in a tantrum. 'Xav here has had to turn his back on a promising skiing career.'

'Yes, but he has something worthwhile in its place—his healing. I want this—I want this new life. If it means cutting myself off from the Savant way of doing things, then fine, I'll do that.'

'But your family belongs to that world. You haven't thought this through.'

I folded my arms, gulping against the lump in my throat. 'I'm not the one saying I have to choose.'

'Crystal, please.' Diamond rested her forehead on the back of her hand. 'I'm sorry, but I can't deal with this now—what with the wedding and everything else on my mind. Can't it wait? We'll talk it over when that's out of the way.'

'You know, you might not get anywhere in any case. No

point driving a truck through the family harmony for something that might not happen. It's a competitive industry.' That was Xav's brand of peacemaking; he should leave it to Diamond.

'Thanks for the support, guys. Really, I'm overwhelmed.' I took my plate to the counter, scraping the uneaten food into the bin. 'I think I'll go for a walk. I expect you'll want an early night as you've been travelling. I have to get up at dawn for work so, well, see you sometime.'

I made sure the door banged loudly when I went out. One benefit of sharing the flat with others again was that my temper had an audience so the gestures were worth making.

I didn't go far. I sat by the vaporetto stop near our apartment on the edge of the raised boardwalk that we used during high tides. In late autumn and winter we often had to slosh through puddles as the lagoon swamped the edges of the city twice a day. There was a siren system for dangerously high water or *acqua alta*, as we called it, but just at the moment the tide was low and no one was walking on the raised platform. A street seller with an eye for the late trade of tourists visiting the restaurants shot little glow-sticks into the air; they hovered for a moment before falling back to the pavement—a tiny firework. A breeze came in off the Adriatic, bringing the scent of diesel and saltwater. Boats came and went from the mooring platform. I pictured them in my mind like needles tacking together the edges of the city in a constant circle. Venice is a good place to sit alone; something is always happening and no one questions why you should want to stop and people-watch for a while. It is a place used to being on display.

I replayed the dinner table conversation. I still felt hurt and my brain was coming up with all sorts of over-dramatic responses, ranging from refusing to attend the wedding and never speaking to my family again. But the saner part of me knew this was like one of those angry emails fired off in the heat of a temper and regretted afterwards. No one was trying to harm me; they just saw things differently, thought they knew what was best. My impulse to slam doors and shout that no one understood, that it wasn't fair, was that of a teenager. Technically I was still one, but I no longer had the luxury of being able to indulge my own mood swings. People were expecting more from me—I was expecting more from myself.

But that didn't mean they were right. I was correct when I said my future wasn't the same as theirs. I had few attractive options in the Savant world so would need to forge my own path. If it conflicted with the usual Savant practice, well then, I'd cross that bridge when I came to it, work out how to reconcile the two. Opportunities like this didn't come along every day and certainly wouldn't wait for a wedding to come and go.

I got up, more at peace now I'd made my decision. Diamond, Trace, and Xav would not approve, but I was going to have those pictures taken and then go from there.

Chapter 5

Realizing things had not gone well between us, Xav tried to be nice to me for the next two days but I didn't make it easy for him. My response to the situation was to become the master of disappearing either to work or for a run. But I was touched, though, when he left a little bunch of silk violets in my bedroom, which some street seller no doubt conned him into buying for far too much money. Still, it was the thought that mattered to me, even if he was doing it just so I didn't spoil his brother's wedding by fighting with him all the way to the big day.

The first time we spent any time together was at the crack of dawn on Sunday morning when I went into his bedroom to wake him at five. I discovered he was not a morning person, which pleased me no end, as I was the one that got to drop a cold flannel on him.

'Hrr-murph!' He flung the flannel into a corner and buried his head under the pillow. I would have normally tried to ignore the display of tanned arms and glimpse of toned midriff this flailing about revealed, but, hey, I have hormones like the next girl. Some things in life are worth seeing.

'Rise and shine, cupcake. Hollywood awaits.'

His answer was a grunt.

'Oh well, that's fine. I'll go on my own then. Shame, I made coffee—I'll just have to drink that too.'

'There's coffee?' A face appeared from under the pillow.

I put the mug down on the bedside table—my version of a peace offering as I recognized it had taken two of us to fall out. 'Just don't think I'm making a habit of it.'

I went back to my own bedroom to get ready. Lily had already warned me not to do any make-up or hair myself, as the make-up artists wanted a clean palette to work on. I left my hair loose which of course meant it was spiralling all over the place as if I'd just stuck my finger in the power socket. My dream of modelling had never seemed more ludicrous.

Xav had shambled into his clothes by the time I returned to the kitchen. Why do boys just look gloriously rumpled when we look as if we've been dragged through a hedge backwards? 'Thanks for the coffee. I can't get going without a shot of caffeine.'

'Me neither.'

He clapped a hand to his chest. 'Stop press: we have something in common!'

'Yeah, yeah, hold the front page. Now, have you got a coat?'

He grabbed his jacket. 'Yes, mother.'

'Wellington boots?'

'What? Ah no, I haven't. That would be because I was packing for sunny Italy, not rainy England.'

'Hmm, Diamond really should've said. You will need them.' I stuck my own feet into my favourite pair of polka dot ones.

He thought I was joking. 'Must you?' He gestured to the boots.

'I really must.'

'C'mon then, fashion disaster—let's go.'

I was the one to be laughing once we were outside. The early morning tide was high and the pavement outside our courtyard was awash. His trendy boots were going to be toast. 'Piggyback?'

He looked grimly at the toes of his leather Timberlands. 'Like you could carry me, Beauty.'

'I'll give it a go—just to the bridge. Then there should be walkways all the way.'

'Don't tell my brothers.' He stood on a garden chair and I took his weight. He was pretty heavy, I must admit, and I staggered a few paces before getting my balance. We managed to cross the short distance without falling into the canal. I dumped him on the dry ground by the bridge.

He gave me a jaunty salute in thanks. 'How much do you charge?'

'What, for rescues? You couldn't afford me. That's your one freebie. After this the Timberlands will have to be sacrificed.'

We made our way through the streets back to the Accademia Bridge over the Grand Canal.

'Where are we going?' Xav had only now really woken up.

'Filming is taking place at the Piazza San Marco. I don't think they're going to actually do any proper stuff until it gets dark this afternoon. We've got to be there so they can set up the shot.'

'You mean I could've stayed in bed?'

'If you are Steve Hughes, you probably are still in bed. We extras are done first so the stars don't have to wait around. Lily warned me it might be a bit boring.' I rather hoped Xav might turn back. 'You could bow out if you want—no one would mind.'

'No way. If you can put up with standing around, so can I. It'll give us a chance to talk.'

'Hmm.' I didn't want to mention in our little ceasefire that I had arranged to spend my spare time with Lily's photographer friend.

The film crew had taken over one corner of the piazza for their costume and make-up marquees. We checked in with an assistant director and then joined a queue. Xav and I took one look at our fellow extras and burst into laugher. It was odd being with so many other tall people, as if the world had suddenly divided into us normal folk and the munchkins who dressed us. There were lots of good-humoured quips between the two sides. I wasn't even the tallest girl; there was one who must have been well over six feet.

Xav was led away to the men's side of the marquee, his lack of Italian meaning that the locally hired make-up ladies pulled and prodded him like a child where they wanted him to go. They were enjoying the opportunity to have such a good-looking boy at their mercy and he looked a little bewildered by their attentions.

'Be gentle!' I heard him plead as he was pushed into a chair in front of a mirror.

From the giggles that comment provoked I guessed they understood more English than they let on.

When my turn came, the make-up artist explained that the cosmetics would be applied quite lightly as most of our faces would be hidden by masks. Emphasis was on blood-red lips and glitter on the eyelids.

'But Lily asked me to do you a special treatment as you are having some photos taken, yes?' Marina, my artist, dusted my cheeks with a faint blush. 'Nothing too heavy, just a little emphasis to bring out your features.' She stood back, pleased with the final effect. 'Hmm, Lily was right: there is something about you. After costume, go to Paolo in wigs and hair: he knows what you need.'

I rejoined Xav in the next bay, which was devoted to the costumes I had helped make. As we arrived together we got a matching set: his consisted of a dark gold jacket and breeches with crimson waistcoat and cape, mine the reverse, crimson gown with gold accents and cloak. I was handed the mask I'd already seen: the one made up of a lace of red words; Xav's was a simple gold demi-mask that made him look like a very high class cat burglar.

Last was the hair department. As we both had long hair we were spared the need to wear a wig. Xav's was tied back in a ribbon, which completed the eighteenth century gentleman look nicely. Mine took much longer as the artist wanted to pile it up on my head in an intricate arrangement.

'You have amazing hair, Crystal,' Paolo exclaimed, running his fingers through my curls. 'Such body, such structure. You won't even need any padding for what I have in mind.'

He twisted my hair so that it tumbled from the tiara he had kept for my costume like some kind of wacky waterfall. He softened the effect around the face by letting a few wisps escape and one long lock to stray down my neck and onto my décolletage. He finished the whole arrangement with a sprinkle of gold dust so that hair and skin glowed subtly. With the mask in place I did look like an exotic creature.

I stepped out from behind the curtain to find Xav waiting for me at the coffee point. Seeing him standing nonchalantly with the other guys, cape flung loosely over one shoulder, did make my heart pick up its pace. Modern clothes were so boring by comparison. He was unfairly handsome in his outfit—a Mr-Darcy-cum-wicked-highwayman dream—but I would prefer to have my toenails pulled out than admit that to him.

'What do you think?' I did a spin, enjoying the unfamiliar sensation of masses of petticoats swirling around my legs.

The Italian extras lived up to my expectations and piled on the compliments, offering outrageous praise and undying devotion, all with the twinkle in their eye of professional flirts. Italian men are raised from birth to flatter females. Xav frowned at them, not understanding what they were saying but getting the gist.

'Xav? What's the verdict?' I tapped the mask. 'I helped make this one myself.'

'Yeah, it's great.' He looked over my head.

'And what about me?'

He forced himself to look back at me. 'Cupcake, you look good enough to eat as I'm sure you know. Be careful: I don't want to have to rush to your rescue when you get overwhelmed with admirers. I don't trust these guys.'

'Hey, Xav, we are good boys!' protested a rogue by the name of Giovanni. 'We make-a no move on your lady.' He gave me a wink and lapsed back into Italian. 'At least, not while he is watching, agreed?'

I laughed. 'I'm not his lady, Giovanni. He's . . . ' What was Xav exactly? 'He's family.'

Giovanni wiggled his eyebrows. 'Ah, even worse. We have to be very, very careful. He may call us out if we impugn your honour.'

Xav hadn't understood the exchange. 'What did he say?'

'He's taking this whole eighteenth century costume thing too far—expecting a duel if he flirts with me.' I grinned at Giovanni. 'Pistols or swords?'

Lily came up behind me and tapped my shoulder. She must have heard part of the exchange because she was smiling. 'Sorry, guys, no duels: health and safety won't allow it. You all look fabulous. Boys, if you wouldn't mind going over to the lighting director, he wants to test his colour scheme on your costumes.' Xav, Giovanni and the others obediently headed for the set, which had been rigged in part of the colonnade that ran around the edge of the piazza. 'Crystal, come with me. Joe's got his camera set up and has half an hour free.'

I thoroughly enjoyed my brief photo call with Joe. As the production's official photographer, his role was to record the proceedings for the website and DVD extras but as Steve Hughes had not yet arrived on set, Joe was free to snap what he liked. A weather-beaten Scot, the photographer had a wrinkled face that would have suited a highland shepherd used to squinting into a northerly wind; his concentration was totally absorbed as he lined up the shots he wanted. I sensed that I became almost abstract to him—lines, shadows, and highlights interacting with my background of gondolas and palaces. I did the same when I thought of fabric designs, blurring out the foreground details and seeing the image as a whole.

Finally, Joe checked his watch. 'Sorry, Crystal, that's all I've time to do today. Steve Hughes is due to arrive at eleven. You've been wonderfully patient with me—a natural. I'm sure I've got some great shots.'

'Thanks, Joe, for sparing the time.'

'It was a pleasure—really it was. I'd enjoy working with you again if there's time. Perhaps we could try it with your normal clothes—a good contrast to this dramatic look you have here.'

'If you think you can manage it, I'd love that.'

He shook my hand. 'It's a deal then. I'll give you a call when I know I've a spare moment. There should be time at the end of this location shoot.' He changed the lens on his camera, glancing towards the canal in case Steve Hughes's boat was already approaching.

'Where are you off to next?' I decided to hang around, hoping to get a glimpse of my hero.

'The Alps. The next location is a big action sequence involving helicopters and all sorts of stunts.'

'Wow.'

'Yes, it should be exciting to watch but these things are tedious to set up as you have to get every detail just right.' Joe smiled at my expression. 'As you are probably already aware, movie making is ninety-nine per cent boredom and one percent action. We are at the mercy of the camera and lighting people, not to mention the director.' The rumble of an engine alerted him. 'Ah, here's Steve now. Things will move more quickly once he's on set.'

I stayed at Joe's shoulder to watch the white motor launch slip into the moorings. I couldn't see Steve at first but then I realized he had driven himself. A very famous crop of blond hair emerged as he handed the skipper's hat back to the pilot. How cool was that! He jumped up on to the landing stage and waved to the little gaggle of fans who had gathered at the edge of the roped off area the city authorities had allowed the film company to commandeer. He strode towards us, heading for the costume marquee behind.

'Hey, Joe, how's it going?' Steve asked the photographer as he swept by.

'Fine, Steve, fine.' Joe didn't stop taking photos as he replied.

'Whoa, that's one amazing costume.' Steve had spotted me—not hard as I was a very obvious confection of red and gold standing among people in ordinary clothes. 'Are all the extras dressed like that?'

My mouth went dry as I realized he was addressing me. 'Er . . .'

'Steve, this is Crystal.' Joe dipped between us, snapping the moment of my meeting my idol. 'She helped make the costumes.'

'That's great. And you look great, sweetheart.' Steve's attention was already moving on. 'Where's James?'

One of the director's assistants took him by the arm and led him away, briefing him on the sequence they were planning to shoot.

Joe grinned at my stunned expression. 'Remember to breathe, Crystal. Costume department would get me sacked if I had to cut your corset strings.'

I patted my chest. 'He's . . . amazing.'

Joe put his camera back in its case. 'Yeah, he's nice enough for an actor. Always remembers names, which says a lot about him.'

I wandered back in a daze to the extras' green room—another marquee where a refreshment table was laid out for us to keep ourselves fed and watered until we were called. Xav pounced as I entered.

'Where've you been?' he asked. 'I was beginning to worry you'd changed your mind about this whole thing.'

'No, no, nothing like that: I just met Steve Hughes.'

Another female extra heard my comment. 'Oh, you lucky thing! What's he like?'

I mock-swooned. 'He's gorgeous.'

Xav's expression soured. 'I've heard he's short.'

'He's average height, but that doesn't matter; he's perfect.' I sat down on a bench, careful of my costume. 'Don't mind me: I'm just going to savour the moment.' I waved Xav away. He stomped off to the other end of the tent where some others were engaged in playing cards. He couldn't be jealous, could he? Well, if he were, it would be good for his soul as usually he would be the one the girls swooned over.

Filming began properly in the late afternoon as darkness fell. The director called the extras together for a briefing.

'OK, ladies and gentlemen.' He spoke through a translator going from English to Italian. 'This is the Carnival. You have to imagine you have been up all night enjoying yourselves and have reached the hours just before dawn, the darkest and most sinister period when emotions are at their height. You are not so much individuals but symbols of what the Carnival means to Venice. I'm going to split you into groups. Green and black—that couple there—you are Anger. I want you to stand over by that column and pretend to be having one enormous row about something. I want lots of arm waving and threatening gestures—you're Italian so I don't have to teach you how to do extravagant body language.'

The Italian extras laughed at that.

'The men in the black cloaks and plague doctor masks, I want you to be walking through on the prowl, restless, the kind of gang looking for trouble and finding it. That's what you are: Trouble with a capital T. Girls in silver and blue, you take the chairs and benches over there: you are looking to attract the guys to join you. You are Seduction. Lady in white—you are Loneliness. I want you drifting, looking tragic as if you're just about to throw yourself off a bridge. Red and gold—you are the Lovers. I want you standing on the steps doing romance—you got that?'

What! I glanced up at Xav. He looked as horrified as I did. Neither of us replied.

'Red and gold—oh, it's you, Crystal.' James's tone became warmer, less businesslike. 'You can handle that, can't you?'

From the murmurs behind me, I could tell that the other extras were impressed that I was on first name terms with the director. There was only one possible response now we'd come this far.

'Yes, no problem.'

'Great.' James swept us all with a keen gaze. 'Be careful what you say to each other. I know you are wearing masks and it gives the illusion you can get away with anything but there are lip readers out there who will be writing to me like a shot if you don't keep in character. No wisecracks; no discussion of what's for supper. Decide what your character's story is and remain in it until I say, "cut".'

I bumped shoulders with Xav. 'You OK with this? It's a bit more than I expected. Lily said we just had to stand round looking impressive.'

Xav had recovered some of his usual confidence after the shock of finding some acting was required. 'Sure. Like you said: no problem. I have a good imagination.'

We took our positions for the run through. The star wasn't even on set yet and we all knew we'd be doing this several times so it would be perfect for him. Xav and I took our place on the flight of steps, adjusting our stance as James directed from behind the bank of cameras. I couldn't help thinking how much more enjoyable this would be with anyone but Xav as my partner. It would not have mattered with Giovanni or one of those guys; we could have laughed about it and put on a show. I couldn't find the same light-heartedness with Xav's arms around me.

He bent his head to mine. 'You know the theory of infinite universes?'

A blast of dry ice bubbled through the set to make a pre-dawn mist.

'No, what's that?' Had we ever been so close before?

'It's one of the explanations of how our universe is like it is as all others exist somewhere else.'

I wrinkled my brow. 'What's this got to do with acting?'

He shifted so that his arm angled across my back and he bent towards me. 'I was just thinking that that means somewhere there's a universe where you and I are lovers and this would be real, not make-believe.' His mouth hovered above mine.

I licked my lips, feeling the warmth from his skin on my cheeks even though he wasn't touching my face.

'And cut! How did that look?' James was checking the lighting for the rehearsal with his chief technician.

I broke away from Xav, unsure how to make a landing after that free-fall of an embrace. 'If that theory is correct, then there's also a universe where you have purple spots and I've green skin.'

'True.' He squinted at me, pretending to line me up for the camera. 'Yeah, green would suit you.'

Steve came on set with his entourage of assistants, his entry drawing all eyes among the extras. The girls all perked up, voices louder, gestures more feminine; the guys looked at each other and shrugged, doubtless wondering what he had that they didn't. I could have told them: charisma. There was only one other on set that had it and he was standing next to me.

'How's it going, James?' Steve asked in a carrying voice, slapping the director on the back.

'We're almost ready for you. I want you to enter from that arch over there and walk through the Carnival crowds. You'll be carrying this.' James passed him an open bottle of champagne from the props table. 'Remember, your character has hit rock bottom, doubting his motivation, doubting his soul— these extras are an externalization of your inner demons.'

I gripped Xav's arm and whispered:

'And that's what makes these films so great—a bit of magical realism threaded through a gritty plot! Isn't it amazing to see it being created before our eyes?'

Xav shrugged. 'I just like them because they blow stuff up.'

I slapped him lightly in the stomach. 'Huh, boys!'

He tapped my nose, not daring to disturb my elaborate styling with a hair ruffle as he might otherwise have done. 'Huh, girls!'

'OK, ladies and gents, this time we're going for a take. Steve, are you ready?'

The star gave James a thumbs-up from his position at the far end of the colonnade.

'Cue mist . . . and action!'

Xav held me to his chest and smiled down at my upturned face, finger stroking along the edge of the mask. There was something in his expression I'd never seen before, something incredibly tender. I found that I was falling into his dark eyes, totally unaware that Steve Hughes had just swept by.

Steve who?

'Cut.' James huddled over the monitor with his star, heads together as they muttered over the effect of the staging. 'Right, ladies and gentlemen, men in black I want you to enter a few seconds earlier—you were in Steve's path and I want you clear by the time he reaches the second archway. Woman in white— excellent—keep on doing that. Lovers—that was sweet but I want passion. Kiss the girl, for heaven's sake, man. Think: you've got a babe in your arms, looking a million dollars and I've given you the excuse you need to lay one on her lips. What are you waiting for?' The extras laughed as Xav gave a sheep- ish wave to say he understood. 'We're going again. Positions!'

My heart was pounding; I could hear it and I feared Xav could too. I wished I'd remembered to suck a mint since my last cup of coffee. I felt all awkward limbs and aircraft carrier mouth; I was sure I'd get the romance wrong, bump noses or giggle at the wrong moment.

Xav must have picked up on my tension. 'Shh. It'll be fine.' He rubbed my back in a little circle. 'It's just make-believe. He's right. You do look incredible. A princess. I've been dying to kiss you for days now.'

I told myself he was just doing this for the lip readers, but the cameras weren't rolling yet.

'And action!' shouted the director.

This time I promised myself I'd resist Xav's spell and notice

Steve Hughes going past but then Xav's lips touched mine and all other thoughts fled. His kiss was incredibly soft and tender. Tingles ran from my mouth and down my spine, radiating to every inch of my body. My bones seemed to melt and I could do nothing but hold on to him with that perfect point of contact joining us. Cold dry ice whirled around my ankles. Warm arms enfolded me, keeping me upright. A hand cradled my head in just the right position to deepen the kiss, lips exploring, touching the curve of my jaw, the column of my neck. I was so enthralled that I had not even heard James shout 'cut'. Xav lifted his head; I stepped back only to find us in the centre of some very amused technicians.

James cleared his throat. 'OK, guys. I'm so pleased some of you really take my direction to heart. Well done, Lovers, that was very . . . convincing. Let's go again from the top.'

I put my hand on Xav's arm. He was trembling and I was feeling pretty shaken myself. I was relieved I hadn't been the only one affected; it would have been horribly embarrassing to find him shrugging the moment away as of no account.

'That was . . . ' I broke off, lost for words.

'That was the most amazing kiss I've ever had.' He touched my collarbone with the tip of one finger and toyed with the stray strand of hair. 'Thank you.'

I looked down to where my hand rested on his linen shirt. 'That was my first ever kiss. A proper one, I mean.' I was beginning to feel sad that this was all just acting.

Xav sighed. 'With kisses like that, I wish this was the universe where you were my soulfinder.' He leant his forehead against mine, steeling himself for the onset of yet more incredible emotions as we kissed again for the cameras.

'I do too,' I breathed, letting his lips meet mine.

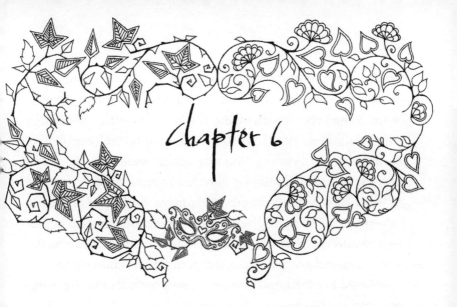

Chapter 6

How do you recover a normal way of treating someone while still reeling from the most wonderful kisses of your life? The shot had required ten takes and none of the embraces had felt routine. By the end, I was a wreck and I don't think Xav was much better. Of course we knew that we both had soulfinders somewhere; I'd only expected to experience this kind of intensity of feeling with mine. It was profoundly disturbing to discover I felt all that for Xav too. It wasn't just physical attraction; I'd begun to like the person under the charming exterior. Though we more often than not annoyed each other, he had been so incredibly sweet about the whole situation. He could have teased me but when he realized we were both feeling the attraction, he did not mock or pretend it was nothing, which would have been taking the easy way out of an awkward situation; he treated me with respect and the experience with wonder.

It hit me as we made our way home in the early hours of the morning that I'd fallen a little in love with him.

The streets, so rarely quiet in Venice, were hushed. A few fishing boats were making their way down the Guidecca

Canal, returning from their night's work in the lagoon; their engines purring against the lap of the waves. Soon they would be unloading their catch at the fish market on the Rialto; the cooks would emerge to buy the fresh seafood and haggle over the fruit and vegetables; the city would shake off sleep and go back to business; but for now it belonged to us and to the cats that prowled the alleyways. At night the streets could not help appearing sinister, haunts for assassins and ghosts; present melted into the past; canals whispered broken promises in old voices; ancient grievances lurked in the shadows.

Xav took my hand. He swung our arms between us, humming softly. His playful mood kept the bad spirits away as if we were walking in our own bubble of happiness.

'You know, Crystal, we might have to revisit the question of whether there is a bond between us or not. We never did really test it properly, did we?'

Mellowed by the moonlight and the peace, I did not respond with my usual counter attack. 'I tried to explain to you in Denver. I can't do telepathy.'

'But you have a gift?'

'A small one. I find stuff for people—things that belong to them.'

'Like Trace does?'

I shook my head. 'Nothing as fancy as that. He can track anything that someone has touched. With me it's got to be something you own, like your keys or favourite teddy bear.'

He squeezed my hand. 'I don't know why you call that a small gift; there are millions of little children everywhere that would love that. Their parents would go down on their knees and thank you for finding their kid's comfort blanket.'

I smiled at that picture. 'Yes, I know. My brothers and sisters find it useful sometimes. Not that they've ever gone down on their knees.'

'They've taken you for granted, I guess. So why are you scared of telepathy?'

'You think I'm scared?'

'Aren't you?'

Perhaps I was. 'It's just always been so bad for me. Like a bird strike on a plane's engines—my brain being the engine and all that stuff that surrounds people the flock of seagulls. I can just about manage when I chart my own course through people's minds, but when they reach out to me I get over-whelmed and crash.' We paused on the top of the Accademia Bridge. Who would not stop when the moon is silvering the inky waters of the Grand Canal? 'I think I'm really scared of finding out that I'm not a proper Savant like the rest of you.' There: my secret was out.

'Then what are you?' He turned to face me.

I was grateful he was not making fun of my fears. 'I don't know. A kind of offshoot maybe? Have you ever met another Savant who can't communicate telepathically?'

'No, but that doesn't mean they don't exist. I wish you'd let me take a look at you with my gift. I might be able to tell you why you find telepathy so hard.'

Last time he had proposed this I had immediately panicked and run. Fear had driven that reaction. Now, feeling a lot calm-er and a lot closer to Xav, I no longer felt so afraid of him; it was only the prospect of finally knowing what was wrong that scared me.

He put his arms around my waist and I moved to lean against his chest. After hours of doing so for the cameras, it no longer felt strange. It was almost as if I now had a re-served parking spot right there against his heart. I smiled at the thought.

'I don't know what we are to each other, Crystal, but I do know that I want at the very least to be a friend. You can trust me to take good care of you. If there's something wrong, isn't it better to know from me than from a stranger?'

I nodded. 'Yes, you're right.'

He shook with silent laughter. 'Can I have that in writing? You think I'm right about something.'

'No, you can't because you'd never let me forget.' He smelt so good: a hint of aftershave, the lotion they had used to take off our make-up and something that was just Xav. I had to stop myself nuzzling at the skin on display through the open top buttons of his shirt. 'I'll let you take a look but not now.'

'Not now,' he agreed. 'It must be four in the morning. Definitely not now.'

I forced myself to move away. 'Maybe we should wait until after the wedding? If it's bad news about my Savant gift, I don't want to know yet, and if it's good, it won't matter if I hear it later.'

To my surprise, he agreed. 'Yeah, I'd prefer to do it with my family around. With Zed's help we can pool our skills and give you a thorough examination. My older brother Victor is very gifted with mind control so can find out if someone's tampered with your head at any point.'

I hadn't agreed to let his entire family in on my flaws. 'But Xav, I don't know them. I wouldn't be happy to have them all involved.'

'I wasn't thinking all of them—just Zed and Victor. Zed as the seventh son has a touch of most of our skills and can hold us together when we do a joint investigation. He's a pain in the neck but a useful one.' I could tell from his tone that he meant nothing of the sort; Xav was much closer to his brothers than I was to my family. 'Both Sky and Phoenix in different ways had bad stuff planted in their heads when they met my brothers. It was tough for a while until they got sorted. It isn't unusual in the Savant world for some of us to fall victim to such abuse;

there are as many of us out there doing bad stuff and mind control is an obvious way to go.'

'But I'm sure no one's ever done anything to me. I've always been like this. From what Sky and Phoenix told me, they fell into the hands of some evil people; I've had a sheltered life—school, family. Nothing's happened to me.'

'Then we won't find anything like that. But I just want to be sure.'

'OK. But I'm not promising. Let me meet Zed and Victor again. Don't tell them what you've planned. I want to decide for myself if I can let them in.'

'Please, Crystal.'

I held up a hand. 'Stop right there, Xavier Benedict. I've given enough ground tonight.'

'*Xavier Benedict!* Now I know I really have overstepped my bounds when you use my full name.' He swung me into a waltz twirl around the Campo di Santa Agnese, a little square near our apartment with some of the few trees growing on the Dorsoduro. 'Are you going to box my ears too?'

'Don't tempt me.'

He lifted me onto a bench to promenade me to the end, and then bowed as I stepped off. 'Will madam ever forgive the presumption of her humble servitor?'

'I see the eighteenth century dress has rubbed off on your manners.' I rubbed my knuckles against his skull. 'Dimwit.'

'That's Sir Dimwit to you, my lady.'

When we reached the bridge near our gate, we both realized at the same moment that the tide was high once more.

I raised my foot and displayed my boot to him. 'Another piggyback?'

'No, my pride can't take it.' He sat down on the hump of the bridge and pulled off his Timberlands. He thrust them in my arms. 'Here, hold these. Don't, whatever you do, drop them.' Then before I could think what he intended, he swept me into his arms and strode into the calf-deep water.

'Xav! I've boots on—there's no need.'

He hugged me closer. 'There's every need, my lady. Have you not read the Gentleman's Guide to Gallantry?'

I shook my head, giggling as he hissed when his toes registered the cold water.

'On page twenty-eight, it definitely says something about being drummed out of the ranks if a gentleman accepts a second piggyback from a lady. He must sacrifice his toes to keep her dry.'

'But not his Timberlands?' I held the boots by the laces over the water.

'Not his Timberlands.' Grinning, he put me down by our gate. 'I think I'll take those back before they come to harm.'

The thaw in our relationship carried over to the week that followed. Though I was still busy at work, I no longer avoided our houseguests and Xav even came running with me a couple of times. He was much fitter than me and thought my little jog along the Zattere a very tame event as he had been brought up in the mountains with endless forest tracks at his disposal, but his remarks were teasing rather than sneering so Rocco and I gave him a pass. The dog's short legs provided me with the excuse I needed when I took a break and Xav was kind enough to go along with the ruse.

Where we were competitive was over our rival hen and stag night parties. After my shaky start, I had got the bit between my teeth and had begun organizing in earnest. Neither of us would divulge the full details of our separate plans but were not above throwing a tantalizing hint to the other to make them worry that theirs would be overshadowed.

'Diamond, don't forget, you have to get a really special dress for Friday—top designer, top dollar. I don't care if we eat off paper plates at the wedding as a result, but you can't let the side down with anything less,' I announced to my sister on Monday evening over supper, making sure the Benedict brothers heard every word.

Xav raised an eyebrow. 'You haven't stolen my idea of going to the casino, have you? I should never've let so many details out at the beginning.'

I waved my hand dismissively. 'Casino? No way: that's far too predictable and, dare I say, ordinary. Any old tourist can wander in there.'

Xav spluttered into his glass of wine.

Trace took Diamond's hand and rubbed the back of it with his thumb. 'So, honey, where are you going that needs a bank raid to fund your clothes? Remember, I am a police officer so I should warn you that anything that you say may be used against you when this comes to trial.'

She laughed. 'Don't worry, darling, I'm not going to do anything illegal . . . '

He grinned.

'No, I'll just get your mother, Sky, and Phoenix to do it for me.'

Trace groaned. 'Don't even suggest it, Diamond. The three of them would make an unstoppable team: Mom sees the future, Sky is pretty amazing at moving stuff with her mind now, and Phoenix can freeze time. Between them they could break into Fort Knox and no one would be any the wiser.'

I really had to ask the girls more about their powers next time we met up; that all sounded intriguing. 'It's OK, Trace, you should know by now that Diamond has quite a healthy little business going so she won't need to do a smash and grab to pay for her wardrobe. I, however, as your impoverished sister-in-law-to-be working for a pittance, should be the one who would need to take desperate measures.'

I could tell by his expression that Trace did not know if I was joking. The guy spent far too much time with criminals. 'I remember that it's tough when you just start out on your own. If you need anything, Crystal, you must let us know.' He glanced at Diamond but she was smiling fondly at him.

'At ease, officer, Crystal is far more resourceful than you can imagine.' Diamond patted his cheek.

Aw, they were so sweet together. 'Yep: I work in a costume shop; I'll be making my own outfit, not lobbing a brick through the window of the Versace boutique.'

Xav grabbed the salad bowl from his brother. 'While the girls are fooling around with dresses, Trace, I need to know your measurements for your suit and the other equipment you'll need.' Xav sprinkled olive oil on his lettuce. 'Lola was very particular that it all had to fit properly.'

'Lola?' squeaked Diamond. I wanted to warn her not to rise to the bait Xav was dangling in front of her but it was too late.

Xav added some Parmesan and pepper. 'Suspicious, Diamond? You should be. This is a bachelor party I'm organizing, not a school outing, and it is going to tick all Trace's boxes. Lola is either a very efficient water sports instructor or an exotic dancing girl; I'll leave it to your imagination.'

I rolled my eyes at Diamond. 'Maybe she's both. I mean, the guys would really go for that, I guess. Don't worry, Di, Luigi and his crew will not disappoint us girls.' Luigi was in fact Contessa Nicoletta's little bespectacled chef with whom I had been consulting about the menu for Friday, but the Benedicts weren't to know that. 'He has promised to provide something suitably spicy for our tastes.'

'Um . . . Crystal.' Diamond now looked anxious, making me wonder if anyone in the room really knew me. 'You haven't taken things too far have you? I mean I went to Marie's hen night and the male strippers were a huge step beyond the bounds of good taste.'

I mustered an innocent expression. 'Oh, of course not. Luigi and co are going to be the very epitome of tastefulness.'

Diamond's eyebrows winged up until she saw my wink. She sat back in her chair. 'Excellent. Roll on Friday.'

Trace and Xav exchanged a long look. Both knew Diamond would never hire a team of Italian Chippendales but neither quite trusted me. Oh, I was enjoying myself!

I leaned forward, sharing confidences with my sister. 'I've told Luigi, nothing too raw, you know? I stressed that we were all ladies of refined palates. He should make the display hot, but not too hot.'

'Oh my!' Diamond flapped at her cheeks with her napkin.

Xav was now studying me with suspicion. I may have pushed the cooking metaphor a touch too far. He nudged my foot under the table.

'What?' I mouthed as Trace and Diamond went into one of their little romantic whisper routines. In consideration of me, they didn't use telepathy when I was around.

'Hot but not too hot? Cupcake, that doesn't suit you.'

'I'm thinking of my sister,' I said primly.

'Good, because I've kissed you and I can say that you are the female equivalent of red chilli.'

I blushed. 'Sssh!'

'Why? It's all there on film for the world to see.' His gaze dropped to my mouth.

'Stop it!' I was worried that Diamond might notice. Fooling about with her brother-in-law was not the most sensible thing I could do for the future harmony of family relations.

He shrugged. 'Can't seem to help myself. Maybe I should give Lola a ring to adjust our plans for Friday. Looks like I'll be needing a distraction if I'm not to succumb to temptation.'

Succumb! My rebellious mind shouted, even though it knew it would drop me in so much trouble. I concentrated on feeling aggrieved that he could even consider exotic water ski instructors a distraction.

'Fine, phone Lola.' I gave him a smile that was all teeth and no humour. 'But just bear in mind, cupcake: your party may be mildly diverting; mine is going to be unforgettable.'

On Wednesday, Diamond was called to Rome on an emergency reconciliation job with two feuding members of the same Savant family. Writs had been exchanged and tempers running dangerously high. Trace and Xav went with her for the ride. That was just as well because Lily turned up in the shop with a proposition I knew none of them would approve.

'Crystal, will you do me an enormous favour?' Lily asked as she breezed into the shop. Dressed in a vibrant red jumper and skirt, accessorized with lightning bolt silver earrings, she seemed to run a thousand volts through my quiet afternoon of sewing.

'I'm not sure—depends what it is.' I threw my work to one side. 'I always read the small print before I sign up to stuff.'

'Wise girl.' Lily leaned on the counter. 'But you are going to love this. In fact, I'm the one doing you the favour really.' She picked up my discarded dress—blue, hand-embroidered silk—which I had been hemming. 'Nice.'

'For my sister's hen party on Friday.'

'Hmm. It'll look fabulous. But first things first: what are you doing tonight?'

I wasn't expecting the others back until late. 'No plans. Signora Carriera will keep me busy I imagine.'

'Then I will ask her to release you early. I have a mission for you.'

'That sounds promising.'

'Steve Hughes—remember him: jaw-droppingly good-looking actor with a bank balance the size of Monaco?'

I grinned. 'I might just have noticed him.'

'Well, he's coming out with James and me to the opening of an art exhibition this evening. His agent thinks it looks good on his profile to be pictured doing high culture. He needs a story to counter some bad press about a broken re-lationship.'

'James and you?'

She waved that away. 'We're friends—just friends. Or don't you know about his boyfriend back in LA?'

'Oh, sorry.'

'Back to Steve. Girlfriend *du jour* was given the old heave-ho last week over some kiss-and-tell story she sold to the tab-loids.'

'Love rat.'

'Exactly. Now Steve needs some pretty young thing on his arm tonight to show that he's so over her and has moved on—someone he can trust.'

Was this leading where I thought it was leading? 'I don't do pretty.'

'Bad choice of words: I meant stunning and unusual. And what better start to your modelling career than to have your name linked to Steve, however briefly? Your face will be in all the gossip columns from here to Seattle.'

'Steve wants me to go with him?' I felt a strange mixture of emotions—part exhilaration part terror.

'Er . . . he doesn't actually know it is you I am lining up for him.' Lily tapped my nose. 'Don't go getting all romantic about this—it is one date, a photo opportunity really. He's not going to fall in love with you and whisk you away to his Hollywood palace so dial back those expectations.'

Actually, I didn't want him to take me anywhere; there was only one guy that made me think of happily ever afters and his name did not start with S. 'I know all that, Lily, but it is a bit lowering to find I'm just a name on a list you are running through.'

Lily laughed. 'If it is any consolation, you were at the top. Will you do it?'

Spend the night straining my eyesight sewing on sequins or rubbing shoulders with film stars? 'I'll just check with my social secretary, put off Taylor Lautner till Tuesday, move Robert Pattinson to next week, but it looks as though I'm free.'

'Thank you. I'll just sort things out with the signora and we'll go get you dressed.'

I looked down at my jeans and jumper combo. 'You mean I can't go like this?'

'Just you wait, Crystal Brook, I've got something special in mind for you.'

Chapter 7

'I can't be seen like this!' I hissed to Lily as we waited for Steve and James outside the Fenice Theatre. The white-pillared entrance loomed above us like an entrance to Olympus; it was guarded by a phoenix, which hung, carved and freshly gold tinted, over the flight of stairs. The organizers had staged this evening's art exhibition in the sumptuous foyer of the opera house and I could already see the brightly-coloured evening dresses of the ladies mingling with the black tie suits of the men. White jacketed waiters wound between the groups of art lovers offering delicate nibbles and flutes of champagne. They were the gods of the international social scene; I was one very unimportant human interloper and we all knew what happened when mortals messed with deities. I tugged the hem of my outfit lower—it was mid thigh and I was not used to displaying so much leg. 'I'm not dressed for that crowd.'

Lily glanced at the guests and sniffed. 'Not a scintilla of fashion taste among them. Those dresses have been in their wardrobes for years. Classic, classic, classic, yawn, yawn, yawn. You, girlfriend, are wearing a signature piece from Julien

Macdonald's latest collection, London Fashion Week's star turn.'

'I am not wearing a signature anything because I am wearing not very much!' The hem finished at the top of my leg before it barely got started. The V front and back meant not very much material had been used in the bodice either. The only place there was any coverage was in the floaty train that billowed from the back which was what made it qualify as evening wear.

'You look lovely in cream and gold. You know, the embroidery on that alone costs more than the average family car.'

'Oh God. Lily: I order you to keep me away from the red wine.'

'Just be careful. Julien was more than happy to lend it to me as he knew that he'd get some nice shots in tomorrow's press but I did promise to get it back to him in the same condition in which I received it.'

'This is such a bad idea.' If Lily hadn't been holding on to my arm, I would have picked up the train of my skirt and run for it—high-heeled gold boots notwithstanding—a Cinderella who bottled out before the ball.

My little panic attack amused Lily but she did not make the mistake of letting go. 'You can't change your mind now. Just think of the negative press for Steve if he gets stood up.'

'How on earth would they know?'

Lily rolled her eyes at my naivety. 'Because they have been tipped off that they can get a shot of him leaving the party at around ten with his date. These things are not spontaneous, you know.'

Two men stepped out of the street running down the side of the church opposite the opera house. One short and fat, the other medium height and slim: our dates had just arrived. Steve's burly minder closely followed them.

'Quickly now: Steve won't want to hang around outside in case any press have come early. Candid shots never look good.' Lily tugged my arm and we fell in behind the director and his star, through the glass doors and into the foyer. Cloakroom attendants were on hand to take our wraps and coats. Only then did Steve relax and greet us.

'Hey, Lily, you're looking amazing!' He kissed the wardrobe mistress on the cheek twice.

I had to bite down on a scream: I was in the same room as my hero. I was HIS DATE!!!!!

James gave us both a hug. 'Hi, Crystal. Feeling up to this?'

I gave him a weak smile.

Lily brushed a loose thread off the film star's lapel. 'Like the jacket, Steve. Tom Ford?'

'Yes. It's one of my favourites.' Steve turned to me.

Deep breaths, Crystal. Don't disgrace yourself.

'Hi, you must be Crystal. Thanks so much for agreeing to this madness tonight.' He leant forward and gave me two kisses as he had Lily. 'Love the dress.'

'Thanks,' I squeaked.

He gave me an understanding look. I imagine any normal girl must act really strangely around him so this was not the first time he had reduced someone to a blithering idiot.

'Here's the deal, Crystal: this whole gig is in honour of a friend of mine, so we sip champagne, say "hi" to a few folks, support the cause, then we split.' He rubbed his hands in a workmanlike fashion. 'I've got a heavy poker night lined up with the guys from the crew back at the hotel, so I want to leave in about an hour. Is that OK with you, Crystal?'

Not very flattering but I was hardly going to demand his undivided attention all evening.

'No problem.'

'Great. Let's go mingle.' He offered me his arm, which I

took. I hoped he couldn't tell that I was shaking in my four-inch heel boots. Fortunately he seemed unfazed by the fact that I towered over him. 'So, tell me about yourself. Lily said you were an extra for the movie?' He checked his reflection in the wall mirror as we passed.

'Yes.'

'So, do you want to be an actress?'

That was so far from being my ambition, I couldn't help but laugh. 'No way!'

He gave me a quick grin, almost making me swallow my tongue as I got a blast of his cobalt eyes. His onscreen charisma was even more obvious in real life. 'I'm getting to like you more and more. Wannabe actresses are a pain in the butt and I meet far too many of them. What do you do?'

'I make carnival costumes—you know, like the masks and robes we were wearing at the weekend. It's a Venice tradition.'

'Hey, now that's really interesting.' He patted my hand in what I couldn't help but think a patronizing gesture—well done, the little people. 'I don't think I've ever been on a date with someone who makes things. People who make scenes, sure; but not useful things like costumes. Dating a talented craftswoman shows I've got hidden depths, doesn't it?' He winked to undercut the egocentric nature of the comment but I guessed he probably meant it. He guided me into the crowd smoothly, people turning to look as he joined them: sunflowers following the sun. Not betraying that he had noticed how they reacted, Steve took me straight to the artist whose work we were supposed to be appreciating. I had not had a moment to see what pieces were being exhibited. I brushed past a tortured clown sculpture as we cut our way through the gathering and glimpsed a ravaged ballerina on one paint-splattered canvas so I hazarded a guess that the exhibition had a theatrical theme.

Steve thrust his hand out to a diminutive man dressed in peacock blue. 'Hey, Sebastian, great show you've got here.' Not that he'd seen it.

'Oh, Steve, you made it!' The artist fluttered in a nervous little circle, his flute of champagne slopping over his fingers as he switched hands to shake Steve's palm. I retreated a step, mindful of my dress. 'How perfectly darling of you!'

'I wouldn't miss it. Allow me to introduce you to my friend here—Crystal . . . um . . . Crystal.' A blush stole over my cheeks. Steve didn't know—or had forgotten—my surname. 'She's a Venetian fashion designer.'

I was a *what*?

Sebastian Perry (as I now worked out he was called thanks to the brochure another guest was clutching) kissed me as if we were old friends. 'Crystal, lovely to meet you. Which label do you work for?'

I couldn't carry off pretending to be something I wasn't even if this was the usual modus operandi for Steve. 'I think you've misunderstood, Mr Perry. I work for a Venetian cos-tume maker—carnival costumes.'

'*Mr* Perry!' The artist tittered. 'Your manners are impec-cable, darling, but do call me Sebastian or I'll feel about a hundred years old.' Some of his show-nerves dissipated and he winked at Steve flirtatiously. 'I can see why you chose this one: she's a poppet.' That was the very first (and possibly last) time anyone a foot shorter than me had called me a poppet; I warmed to him immediately. 'But, Crystal, I am intrigued to hear more about what you do. Traditional theatrical skills such as mask making are very close to my heart.' He flicked his fin-gers towards another canvas of what looked at a distance like a heap of massacred carnival participants.

But Steve was already pulling me away. 'Later, Sebastian. I must go and drum up some buyers for you.'

'Do that, sweetie, and I'll be ever in your debt!'

Steve was already on the move. I glanced back and saw the artist jokily patting his heart for the benefit of his little circle. I know how he felt: Steve was all action man, enough to make anyone's pulse race.

'How do you know Sebastian?' I asked, accepting the glass of sparkling water Steve snagged from a tray.

Steve's eyes were roving the room, working the angles for his press profile. 'Oh, how do I know anyone? Bumped into him at a gig like this—bought a couple of his canvases as my financial adviser said they'd increase in value.'

From what was on display, I decided that I liked the artist more than I liked his work. 'Where have you hung them?' I was struggling to imagine my little apartment with one of these nightmarish pictures on the wall. I'd only just taken down my Twilight poster and had moved on to Monet.

'Oh, they're in a vault somewhere. I don't have a home right now—just a rented house and a few staff to keep things ticking over. I spend most of my time working. My personal assistant has got very, very good at packing suitcases for me. Hey, Mary, long time!' And he was off on his second encounter for the evening: this lady turned out to be a reporter for the *New York Times*. I hung on at the edge of the Steve show, finding the position very familiar. Had it not been a bit like that for me with Diamond in Savant circles? The idea of making a name for myself had never seemed more attractive. I'd far prefer to be the one people queued up to talk to, rather than the afterthought tacked on to the evening to buff up his image. Steve wasn't an unpleasant companion—far from it—but once I'd got over my breathless hero-worship I realized that he just wasn't that interested in me or anything beyond his career. Why should he be? This whole evening fell under the 'you scratch my back, I'll scratch yours' category.

I began to have wild thoughts. I was a hanger-on now but I wasn't powerless; if I felt really bitchy, I could scupper his little publicity voyage if I so wished. I imagined turning to the next journalist and saying 'Hi, I'm Crystal. Do you know Steve likes to kick puppies and flushed his sister's gerbil down the loo when he was ten?' It wouldn't be true but he'd have to spend the next week living the rumour down.

And I'd be sued.

Yeah, well, I wasn't actually going to say anything so stupid; I was just enjoying the sensation of flirting with the edge of the abyss. Xav would get the joke. I'd never look at another edition of a gossip magazine with a 'girlfriend' clutching the arm of a celebrity without wondering if she was contemplating kamikaze tactics just to get real.

Pausing in his conversation with the local mayor, Steve glanced at his watch—one of those fancy kinds that retail for thousands. My gold(ish) bracelet one sells for twenty euros; I wonder if this crowd would recognize the difference? Probably had nannies that trained them in that sort of thing before they learned their alphabet. Steve gave a sigh and looped his arm around my shoulder. 'Sorry, Mr Buccari, Crystal here has another party to go to and I promised I'd get her there on time.'

The mayor said something flattering and very Italian about beautiful girls being in demand.

'I know—I have a hard time fending off all the other guys.' Steve kissed the back of my hand, making it sound as though he and I were an item.

The mayor slanted a glance at me. 'But you are Steve Hughes—you won't have a problem keeping your girl. And if you do, there is no hope for the rest of us!' The little group around the mayor laughed in appreciation of the quip.

I did my bit, hanging on Steve's arm and looking suitably adoring. And I did still adore him a little, but only when I imagined him as the onscreen presence rather than the man beside me. What did that say about me? Shallow, anyone?

We returned to the cloakroom. Steve's expression became very serious as he looked me up and down.

'No coat and you'd better freshen up your lip-gloss.'

'What?'

'For the press pack, honey. This is what you came for, isn't it?'

I suppose it had been but my feet were more than cold, they were ice cubes. Had I really thought this through? No. I'd let Lily bounce me into this as I chased a dream I wasn't sure I wanted.

'No coat? I'll freeze.'

'It'll only be for a minute. My assistant will bring it along.' He gestured to a young man waiting on a chair by the entrance who doubled as bodyguard. 'John, bring Miss Crystal's coat will you?'

'My name is Brook, Crystal Brook.'

Steve was too busy checking the lie of his hair to listen, but his bodyguard had.

'I'll look after your coat for you, Miss Brook,' he said giving me a kind smile.

'Thanks, John.' I leant closer, sensing an ally. 'Does he do this kind of thing often?'

'All the time, Miss. You'll get used to it.'

I laughed and shook my head. 'You won't catch me freezing my butt off for publicity again. I'm just doing this for Lily.'

The bodyguard smiled again but I could tell he didn't believe me. I suppose in the publicity hungry world of Los

Angeles what I had just said was the equivalent of a habitual drunk promising to go teetotal.

'Ready?' Steve asked as I slipped my lip-gloss back in my little clutch bag.

'As I'll ever be.'

'The press will want to know your name. I assume Lily has given it to my PA?'

Had she? I had no idea how this kind of thing worked. 'I guess.'

Steve put his arm around me. 'I'll hustle you through. Smile and try to look as though we are good friends, OK?'

One more act in his life of acting—it was sad really.

'Understood.'

We emerged from the privacy of the cloakroom and headed straight into the lightning storm of camera flashes.

'Hey, Steve, how's the movie going?'

'Great, thanks, guys,' Steve replied.

'Crystal, Crystal, look this way, love!'

Caught off guard, I turned my head towards the shout. They already knew who I was. I imagine I looked like a startled rabbit.

Smile, you twit, I told myself.

The press mobbed us. My name ricocheted from all directions like pinballs. Now Steve's arm was genuinely reassuring.

'Give the girl room to breathe!' he joked.

'Steve, what did Jillian say when she heard about your new relationship?' called another reporter.

Steve shrugged. 'Why don't you ask her? Look, guys, Crystal and I have places to go, people to see.'

'Crystal, what's this rumour about your career as a page three model?'

What!

'Are you really fifteen?'

Oh God.

'Ignore them,' whispered Steve, his grip on my arm tightening in his anger. 'They're fishing for a story. John, take note of who asked those asinine questions and cut them from our list.'

Then, jostled by the scrum, someone trod on my floaty train and I felt a rip—and it wasn't stopping.

'John! Coat!' I begged, clapping my left hand to my rear.

Steve did not pause. 'Keep going—almost through.'

I'd had enough of this master/servant relationship. Anger made my hero-worship go pop. 'Steve Hughes, unless you want my underwear on display on the news-stands tomorrow morning, we are stopping!' I ducked out from under his arm and grabbed the coat John was hurrying to wrap me in—he at least had had an eyeful of the problem. I whipped it around my shoulders, making sure it flicked a few of the most persistent reporters in the face. 'There. Now we can go.'

I stomped away, head held high. It took a split second for Steve to realize I was on the move. He hurried to catch me up, caught my arm and swung me round.

'You were magnificent, darling,' he said loudly, then planted a kiss on my lips. He nuzzled my ear. 'Now they'll have to choose between putting that or your superior rear on the front page.'

I relaxed in his hold. He wasn't making an ill-timed move on me but trying to help.

'Thanks,' I whispered.

'Don't mention it.' He patted the back of my coat over the offending rip. 'You needn't worry—either will be very flattering.'

* * *

Back in the safety of my bedroom by ten thirty, I heard Xav, Diamond, and Trace return half an hour later. I'd already confessed my wardrobe mishap to Lily who said it wouldn't matter as long as the photos mentioned the dress that had almost been ripped off me. She thought the whole Steve/dress ripping thing might be thought very sexy and help shift a few couture items for the designer.

It had felt far from sexy to me—more like feeding time at the zoo with me as the hunk of meat. If I could magically blank out all the digital shots including me, I would have cast my spell. I knew though that it was far too late and already the images would be syndicating around the world. I'd done a search on the Internet—so far nothing—but it wouldn't be long. I'd consoled myself with looking up other wardrobe failures of the rich and famous—and there are a few far more embarrassing ones out there.

Diamond stuck her head round my door. I was tucked up in bed wearing my PJs. 'Hi, Crystal.'

I slammed the laptop closed. 'How was your day?'

'Oh, it went well thanks. Peace and harmony restored.'

Trace appeared beside her. 'She was amazing—I loved seeing her at work.'

'Yes, Di is a marvel.' I gave them a bright smile that shouted 'fake, fake!' if they had but known.

'Hey, cupcake.' Xav poked his head round the door. What was this: a pyjama party?

'Hi. Did you enjoy Rome?'

'Fantastic—could have spent a week there. How was your day?'

'Um.' I went on a date with a hot movie star and may have got my picture taken with my knickers showing at the back of a hardly-there dress. God, I hope not. 'It was fine.'

'Great. See you in the morning.'

Not if I could make a run for it before they woke up. Maybe if I fused the electricity so the router was down and then bought up all the newspapers in a half-mile radius of our apartment, I'd be OK? 'Yeah. Sleep well.'

The door closed. Oh my God, what had I done?

Chapter 8

The wisdom of the new morning did not offer any comfort. I crept out of the apartment, bypassing breakfast and my run, and hid in the workroom of the shop.

'How was your date last night?' Signora Carriera asked as she checked her invoices against her bank statement.

'Hmm,' I replied, keeping a mouthful of pins.

'That good?' She smiled. 'I have always hated those art openings—much better to go and admire the work when there is space to appreciate them properly. And how was your escort? Surely he made it special?'

I put the pins down. 'He was lovely, but I didn't make much of a blip on his radar, if you know what I mean.'

The signora chuckled with understanding. 'Still, I hope you got some nice photos taken. That was the point, wasn't it?'

Was it? I was no longer sure. Now I examined my motives it appeared to me that I was more like a person treading water, flailing about to reach a rope to pull her out of her predicament. I'd really not asked myself properly if I wanted to model, do all that posing and preening, let alone pay the price of fame. When it came down to it, did I not get more satisfaction from making something with my own hands rather than being the object another artist was moulding? Steve had been right about that. It had got mixed up with my feelings of inadequacy and wanting to prove I was more than Diamond's ugly sister, but that wasn't enough on which to base my life.

Conclusion: I'd messed up big time. It had been nice to feel beautiful rather than a freak for the first time in my life but that wasn't enough to sustain a career. I suppose many people were unsure what they should do at my age but it looked as if I had just done my experimenting in an unfortunately public fashion. Well, I should chalk it up to experience, keep the lovely set of shots Joe had done for me for the grandchildren, and hope the newspapers would be lining compost bins before my presence was noticed by my nearest and dearest. Then I should get serious about taking my ambitions to do fabric design further. Retakes and college: that was what I should be thinking about now.

But if I became world famous I could do a Kate Moss and then go into design.

What was I? A seesaw? I couldn't stick with a decision: modelling up, modelling down. Why couldn't I just know what I wanted?

The front door to the shop banged open.

'Crystal!'

Damn, damn, damn—it was Xav. I ducked my head. Signora Carriera, who had got up when the bell rang to serve the customer, raised a brow.

'That's your young man, isn't it?'

Not exactly my young man. 'Is it?' I croaked.

'Crystal, I know you're here,' Xav bellowed.

The signora checked her watch. 'Why don't you take your lunch break? It sounds like he has something he wants to get off his chest.'

'Aren't we busy?' Please let us be busy.

'Crystal.' The signora looked disappointed in me. 'If he wants to make a fuss, I'd prefer it to happen off the premises. I do have a business to run.'

With a sigh, I got up. I couldn't refuse her. By the end of the day, Signora Carriera might be my only friend in Venice.

I breezed into the showroom. 'Hi, Xav.'

He slapped a newspaper down on the counter, folded back to the gossip column. 'What the hell is this?' He stabbed the photo of Steve kissing me. The coat had fallen open and it was a nice shot of the Julien Macdonald creation. You couldn't tell it was ripped. Phew: they'd gone for the clinch rather than the dress failure. Perhaps the coat had covered me in time?

'Oh that. Do you like the dress? Costs a packet according to Lily.'

'Shove the dress. Look what it says.'

His finger was close to drilling a hole in the offending article. I'd never seen him this incandescent with temper; he always cracked a joke or diffused tension, never ramped it up. With a feeling of dread, I read the words to which he was objecting:

Steve Hughes and his new girlfriend, model Crystal Brook (19), can't keep their hands off each other. Has the iceman of the screen finally met his true love? Sources close to the actor said he met Crystal while filming his latest movie in Venice.

'Ha-ha!' My laugh was pathetic. 'Just goes to show you can't believe anything you read in the press.'

'Is that you?' Xav folded his arms, spearing me with his lethal brown-eyed gaze.

'Um, yes?'

'Are you Steve Hughes's girlfriend?'

'I was his date—for an hour. Lily set it up so he had some-one to go with.'

'Of all the brain-dead things you could have chosen to do . . . !'

Signora Carriera had decided we had done enough damage to her business. 'Ah, Xav, lovely to see you.' He managed a nod. 'I was just suggesting to Crystal that you take her to lunch.' She opened the door for us. 'Off you go.'

I walked ahead, Xav on my heels like a prison guard making sure I didn't make a run for it. Tempting: I could lose him in these streets, no problem. His silence spoke volumes. I was getting a bit angry myself: what right did he have to come marching in and tell me off for a damn photograph? It was a free country last time I looked. I hadn't done anything illegal or hurt anyone. Reaching for my own mad, I felt more equipped to face him over our sandwich lunch.

After buying a couple of ham and cheese specials, we sat down at a little table tucked in the corner of a local sandwich bar, the only other customers a couple of off-duty gondoliers in their striped tops. I took a swig of my lemonade.

'I can't believe you'd be so stupid!' he hissed.

I clunked my glass down. 'I went to an art show with Steve, that's all. End. Of. Story. And who appointed you my judge in any case?'

'It is not the end. These pictures are all over the world, Crystal—I only showed you this one.'

I gulped. I really, really hoped that the coat had hidden the damage.

'You don't have any idea why I'm upset, do you?' He ripped his sandwich in half and took a bite.

I had taken a guess that it might be some weird kind of jealousy. We had spent most of the shoot kissing and now my photo turned up in the press locked in the arms of another man; he might feel a bit confused by that. But that didn't explain his outrage.

'Not really. I'm not going on another date if that's what you're worried about. I was just doing Lily a favour.'

'Do you have any idea how many enemies your sister and my family have?'

This was a new tack. 'No. I'd have thought none for my sister. Everyone likes Diamond.'

'Believe me, they don't. She has her own notoriety in Savant circles, as do my family, for being on the side of the good guys. There are plenty of Savants out there who would prefer to be without us as we stand in the way of using their powers to make mountains of cash for themselves.'

'What has this to do with me?'

'We tried to explain to you the other night. We survive by keeping as low a profile as possible and protecting ourselves. We do not put our face and personal details in the international press for any guy with a grudge against us to track us down.'

I shrugged. 'Still, I'm just not that important. Who cares what I do?'

'You just don't get it, do you?'

'Cut the patronizing tone. No, I don't understand what terrible sin I've committed by going out for one night.' I pushed my sandwich aside. No way was I going to get to eat it. Shoving it down his throat seemed the most attractive of my limited options. Why were Xav and I like this: oil and water was a tame description; butane gas and match was more accurate.

'In the summer, thanks to Phoenix and Yves, we took down a large criminal gang of Savants—a worldwide one. It was a very big deal—happened in London when they gathered to plot their carve-up of the international crime networks. They're now in jail in their home countries waiting prosecution.'

'Well done you.' I wish my tone had been less sarky; I actually did admire them for this but it was hard to get that across when I was rubbed raw by his attitude.

'Can you imagine how delighted their people would be if they could get us back?'

'From the prophet of doom tone you are using, "very" I guess is the right answer.'

'It's a matter of public record that Trace is marrying your sister thanks to the fact that to be legal they have to register it. You bet that the first thing any Savant with a grudge will do is find out all they could about her and what weaknesses she might have. And then, glory hallelujah, they hit the jackpot because they see her idiot sister splashed all over the front pages telling them exactly where to find her. You might as well have painted a target on your sister's forehead. The more you expose yourself with this modelling thing, the worse it will get.'

I got up. This interview was pointless. He was determined to hold me responsible for the actions of others. He hadn't even asked if I was thinking of continuing on the modelling route, just assumed I was. Some advice, some sympathy would really help when I was so confused.

'Thanks, Xav, for listening. You know, it's really great how you take my feelings on everything into account. I mean, it wasn't as if I didn't have a pretty scary time last night fighting off the press pack. So kind of you not to expect me to live my life just so you and your family won't be inconvenienced.' I threw a few euros on the table. 'I've got to get back.'

Xav got to his feet. 'Crystal, this isn't over.'

I took a last long look at him, cursing the little flip of attraction I could not stop when I was in his company. I was in a 'no win' situation getting tangled up emotionally with him. 'Actually, I think it is.'

I felt a complete outsider in my home for the next few days, like a child sent to the naughty step for daring to break with the Savant unwritten code. It did not help that my own family were less than impressed by my press debut. My sisters, including the bride-to-be, called me irresponsible, risking the wedding and their safety. My mother picked up the phone for the first time in a while so she could tear a strip off me. Her complaints centred on the damage I'd done to the family reputation; apparently the Brook family had always been noted for being discreet in Savant circles. At least my brothers, Steel and Peter, when they called, were worried that I was being taken for a ride by an older man; I didn't mind their scolding as they were basically on my side and less worried by the publicity I had attracted. Sure, I had had to dodge speculative reporters a couple of times who had hung around the shop in case they could catch another glimpse of me with my supposed boyfriend; but they knew how these things worked too and when he was a no-show decided that the 'stormy break-up' was the next angle on the story and were content with a few shots of me hiding my face behind sunglasses or shopping bags when I passed them.

It was not the best atmosphere in which to continue organizing the hen party. Contessa Nicoletta had been incredibly generous: she had hired a first rate band so we could have dancing after dinner and her chef was clearly a genius. I'd tried the samples he brought to the shop: they melted in the mouth and made the taste buds do a rumba. The Venetian hair ornaments and delicate half-masks that Signora Carriera and I had designed were also ready. The idea had been to go exclusive on the usual hen night fancy dress: rather than the stubby wedding veils, pink tiaras, and fairy wings you often see groups of girls staggering about in on their party night, we had created fantasy versions in diamanté angel masks, costume jewellery, and a special crown for Diamond with a cascade of white lace. With the evening dresses, we should look gorgeous and very much up to our surroundings on the lagoon's most elite island.

The overseas guests who could make the hen and stag parties arrived the night before. We had booked out the waterfront Hotel Calcina near our apartment, as we could not host everyone in our limited space. I was relieved when Xav and Trace shifted to join their brothers, leaving the guest room for Sky. Trace's mother Karla and Phoenix stayed with their husbands at the hotel, naturally, but spent most of the day with us as the boys were plotting their night's entertainment. Our older sisters and mother hadn't been able to make the party due to school and grandmotherly commitments but would arrive a few days before the wedding. That left the party guests, in addition to the American contingent, to be made up of Diamond's Italian friends—and there were plenty of them. She had always been very popular.

'OK.' I put my file of arrangements on the table in front of Sky and Phoenix. Karla and Diamond had gone off to do some last minute shopping together, a trip from which the two younger girls had mysteriously begged off, muttering something about not wanting to risk it when they had perfectly nice dresses in their suitcases. 'Will you help me marshal everyone into position this evening?'

'Of course.' Sky yawned and rubbed her eyes. She was still in her PJs and her curly blonde hair was going every which way. Sweet and seventeen: she was exquisite and I could tell when I saw them together that Zed knew exactly how lucky he was. 'But aren't you going to fill us in on the gossip while the others are out?'

I leafed through my plan for the evening. 'Gossip?'

Phoenix laughed: a strangely throaty sound from a girl who looked like a pretty elf; sharp-cut brown hair that spiked around her face before falling to her shoulders. I could see her as a rock chick Tinkerbell. She was married to the intellectual genius of the Benedict boys, the one she had described as her Clark Kent. I knew what she meant: to any girl with taste, Clark was way more attractive than the underpants-wearing Superman that he turned into; Yves made science geek look sexy. 'Don't try to dodge the question, Crystal. We are talking about *the* story—you and Steve Hughes.'

'If you want to have a go at me for that, get in line.'

Phoenix snorted. 'Have a go? You've got to be kidding.'

'I'll have a go,' butted in Sky, 'but only in the sense of "way to go, girl!". I can't believe someone I know went out with the hottest movie star on the planet.'

It was so wonderful not to feel judged and scolded by people I cared about that I felt a bit like crying.

'He's not that hot really,' I mumbled, fishing for a tissue.

'Aw, your colours are all sad ones,' Sky said, reaching over to give me a hug. 'Don't get upset, Crystal. What did Steve do to you?'

I tried a laugh but it caught in my throat like a fishbone. 'Not Steve. He was OK really, just a bit self-obsessed. Who can blame him? I mean he's like stratospherically famous and I'm, well, I'm me.'

Phoenix topped up my coffee cup. 'So it was one of us who gave you a hard time?'

'Not one—everybody.'

Phoenix's eyes misted for a moment. She was using her gift to sift my thoughts, a shortcut to finding out the events of the past few days. If she took it further, she could freeze my thought patterns so that it would seem like time stopped but that wasn't her intention just now. 'Xavier Benedict: you are an idiot!'

Sky narrowed her blue eyes. 'What did that joker do now?'

I cleared my throat. 'I don't think he was joking at the time. He told me off for endangering the family.'

'But I don't get it: I can see how your family might feel they have something to say on the issue, but Xav? His link to you is distant—a brother of your not-yet brother-in-law.'

I crumbled up my croissant. 'Well, he and I . . . it's complicated.'

Sky's face lit up with a mischievous grin. 'Complicated? Phoenix and I like complicated.'

'We spent last Sunday kissing . . . '

'What!' squeaked Sky.

'No, no, not like that; for the camera—as extras on the Steve Hughes movie.'

'Uh-huh. Not such a distant link then.' Phoenix smiled at me.

Confession time. 'It was special, but weird. We sort of became friends and then he took offence about the date thing with Steve Hughes.'

'Now we're getting the picture.' Sky folded her arms and exchanged a look with Phoenix. 'Xav would not like to see his girl in a clinch with a guy who outshone him.'

'Oh, Steve doesn't outshine Xav; he doesn't have Xav's sense of humour for one.'

'Really?' Phoenix was struggling not to laugh. 'Xav is better than an A list actor? Does he know you think that? It might make him calm down a bit and stop acting like an idiot over a few photos.'

'You . . . you think he's jealous?'

'Hell, yeah, cupcake.' She affected a Xav-like drawl, which made me smile.

'But we're not . . . you know . . . soulfinders or anything. I can't do telepathy so that won't happen for me.'

'Oh, Crystal, that's terrible.' Sky looked really upset on my behalf. 'We knew you were uncomfortable with it—that's why we don't use it with you around—but I had no idea it was so bad.'

'Yeah, 'fraid so. I'm a dud Savant.'

Phoenix's eyes snapped with anger. 'You are not a dud, Crystal Brook! Don't you call yourself one again!'

'OK, OK,' I laughed, holding up my hands to ward her off. 'I get the message. But I'm still not firing on all cylinders. Xav thinks there's something wrong. If he's still talking to me after the wedding, he might have a go at sorting it out.'

Sky cheered up at that news. 'I can tell you now that even if he is still spitting insults he'll want to cure you. He has "healer" running through his bones like words in a stick of rock.'

'Wow, isn't that something to look forward to.'

Phoenix tugged the list of arrangements from my fingers. 'Let's get down to business. What do you want us to do?'

Chapter 9

'Crystal, I apologize for having any doubts about your talent for organizing a fantastic hen night.' Diamond leant on the balcony overlooking Contessa Nicoletta's walled garden. Tall cypress trees stood to attention either side of the path, an honour guard from the private mooring where the last of the guests were arriving, their laughter reaching us as we waited to greet them. My sister looked truly lovely dressed in a silver evening gown topped by our bridal coronet. I had made myself a sky blue silk strapless dress so I felt pretty special too—if a bit cold.

Note to self: design something with sleeves next time you do a winter party.

'It was easy once the contessa was involved. What is her Savant gift by the way? I know very little about her.'

Diamond played with her bracelet, the stones catching fire in the torches that flared from brackets either side of the main doors. The naked flame added an old world touch that perfectly suited our venue of crumbling stone mansion. All buildings in Venice are disintegrating—it goes with the maritime climate. Owners like our hostess have always had to fight a race against time to see what would win: repairs or collapse.

'I know she's a powerful telepath but I get the impression she doesn't use her gifts very often now. She has a son, I think, also a Savant, and grandchildren. She claims she's too old for dabbling in all that stuff and leaves it to the younger generations. She once told me she enjoys holding her position in Venetian society and doesn't need her gifts to do that, just wise investments, which, with the way the world economy is going, is a full time occupation.'

I quite liked the sound of Contessa Nicoletta's approach to life. Later I'd ask the contessa what I could do if I didn't 'dabble' in Savant powers either. Her experience that you don't have to use Savant gifts even if you have them could be really helpful to my singular circumstance.

'Hey, Diamond, this is just . . . just incredible!' called Anna, one of Diamond's closest friends. She hastened up the flight of steps and hugged my sister tight. 'Congratulations!'

'Thanks but it's all Crystal's hard work,' Diamond said generously.

Anna kissed me on the cheeks. 'Wish I had a little sister like you. Mine is still in the bugging stage.'

I handed Anna her mask and hairpiece. 'Here: this is for you.'

'Oh that's amazing! This is going to be just the best party ever.' She hurried away to the foyer to fix her costume jewellery in place.

All the guests were equally thrilled by the unusual party favours. Signora Carriera stood back to let me take the praise but I could see her casting a pleased and professional eye over our handiwork. My boss was resplendent in a sweeping emerald green gown with matching jacket. She had already struck up a friendship with the groom's mother, Karla, who looked wonderful, if a touch over-flounced, in a red flamenco dress recalling her Latin heritage. Sky wore a darker shade of blue than my dress and Phoenix burned in a sizzling orange that she carried off really well against her creamy complexion and dark hair.

I gave myself a pat on the back: after a difficult week, this at least looked as if it was going to be a success.

A gong rang in the foyer.

'Dinner is served,' intoned the butler.

Diamond sighed. 'Oh, I just love him. Wish I had one of those to announce meals. He makes them sound so important.'

'Ah, but this is going to be important. You haven't met Chef Luigi.'

'You mean Luigi of the not-too-raw-but-a-bit-spicy display?'

'That's the one.' I smiled at the memory of the silly conversation of a few days ago. I wished I could recapture that easy relationship with Xav but it had all gone so wrong. 'I wonder how the boys are getting on with exotic Lola?'

Diamond took my arm to go indoors. 'Good luck to them. They won't beat this.'

The evening passed off just as I hoped. The meal was superb. Whatever Contessa Nicoletta paid the man to run her kitchen, he was worth every penny. The band was also surprisingly good. I had imagined the contessa would hire a group that would play a rather staid semi-classical repertoire but she understood Diamond well and had engaged musicians who played arrangements of recent pop music and jazz. Hen parties are about celebrating the years of singlehood so the band judged it just right with their noughties hits which we could all sing along to and do girl-dancing, unfettered by having no boys around to watch our fooling about. I was enjoying myself so much; I had forgotten since moving to Venice and leaving old friends behind how much fun it was to do a girls' night out.

It seemed no time at all before the motor launch was back at midnight to start ferrying guests over to Venice. We went in reverse of our arrival: Italian friends first, family last.

Signora Carriera gave me an affectionate embrace as she got on board the second transport. 'You did very, very well, Crystal. You should be proud of yourself.'

'Thank you.'

'I will see you on Monday, if not before.' She couldn't resist reminding me of work, but just then I really didn't mind. I had come to look forward to the creative excitement of her shop. Seeing the things we had made looking so fabulous on the girls was immensely rewarding.

Contessa Nicoletta invited the remaining family guests to her private sitting room while we waited for the return of the launch. Her butler served us drinks and we relaxed—but not too much—on her antique furniture. Worried I was going to do a Goldilocks on one of her flimsy chairs, I wandered to the grand piano to look at her collection of family photos. As Diamond had said, the contessa had a son. There were lots of pictures of him doing all sorts of different activities: yachting, skiing, in dinner jacket outside the opera. Quite the sportsman even though he must be in his fifties.

The contessa joined me at the piano, her veined hand gripping the top of an ebony walking stick.

'Do you recognize him?' she asked.

'No, but I'm guessing he's your son.'

'Yes, Alfonso. He is the present count of Monte Baldo, of course.'

'Does he live in Venice?'

She sniffed. 'He used to.'

'Oh? Where is he now?' I wondered if she felt upset that her only child had left her alone in her old age.

'He is in prison.'

O-K. 'I'm sorry.'

'It is not your fault, Crystal.' Her hawk-bright eyes went to the others in the room as if looking for the guilty party among them. 'He was unlucky.'

I was intrigued that she didn't say he was innocent, but it would be the height of bad manners to return her generous hospitality with intrusive questions. There was always Google to check up on him later. A count of Monte Baldo arrested for criminal activities was hardly going to go unnoticed no matter where the incident took place. I thought it tactful, however, to change the subject.

'Contessa Nicoletta, I have been meaning to ask you: how have you managed without using your gift?'

'What do you mean?' The old lady straightened the photo frame I had moved.

'Well, my gift is really pathetic and I can't do telepathy.'

'Can you not?' She studied my face for a moment. 'That will be a problem.'

'Yes, it already is. I get sick when I try. Diamond says you manage really well, retired as you are from using your Savant powers. I was wondering if you have any advice for me because it looks as though I'm going to be in the same boat, so to speak, but not by choice?'

I regretted immediately asking her. The contessa's lips thinned and her eyes glinted with what looked very like contempt. I was suddenly thrown back a couple of hundred years and knew exactly what a peasant would have felt when having incurred the wrath of a countess.

'We share no boat, Crystal. Diamond is wrong. I use my gifts all the time—as you are about to find out. It is just that people do not remember that I have—that is the difference.'

I was finding her attitude a bit creepy. I decided to retreat to my sister's side. 'I'm sorry if I offended you, contessa. I see that that would explain it.'

Her claw-like hand gripped my forearm. 'Don't go. The best part of this charade is about to happen. You wouldn't want to miss this party for the world.'

'What's going on?' I looked up and noticed that the footmen and butler had appeared by the doors.

'My son was arrested in London thanks to the Benedicts. A count of Monte Baldo in an Italian jail—it is not to be borne! Diamond has presented me with the perfect revenge.'

I did not hang around to hear any more.

'Diamond!' I shouted, pulling free from the old lady. 'Get out of here!'

'It is too late for that.' The contessa signalled to a footman to restrain me.

'Crystal, what's the matter?' Diamond started towards me but the butler got in her path and pushed her back into her chair, the casual violence of the movement a shock after the sophisticated evening.

The contessa pointed at Diamond, Sky, Phoenix, and Karla with her cane. 'I know my price. Their soulfinders for my son's freedom. We have four of them in the room. The Benedicts will do anything to get them back.'

'The woman is mad!' spluttered Karla. 'Phoenix, Sky, do something!' She closed her eyes to send out the distress call telepathically to her husband.

'Too late!' declared Contessa Nicoletta. 'Far, far too late.' She pressed her hands to her temples and I felt the pulse of power ripple from her, sweeping through the room. I went to my knees: it was a form of telepathic assault, pressing on our minds like a tidal wave. I retched. The contessa grabbed the knot of hair piled on top of my head and pulled me to face her. 'When I was younger, child, I renamed myself the eraser. You won't remember why.'

Darkness.

Chapter 10

I woke up when a wave slapped my face. Taking an unwise gulp, I rolled to my knees, spitting out seawater, grit, and shell fragments.

Jeez, I was cold.

I rubbed my bare arms, hugging myself to stimulate blood flow.

Where was I? More to the point, how did I get here?

Opening stinging eyes, I saw a muddy beach stretching ahead and behind, low dunes of rusty sea grass, an empty iron-grey sea. My only companions were seabirds. A large gull pecked at an empty crab shell a few feet away, uninterested in the arrival of a blue evening-gowned stranger on his patch.

Racked with shivers, I staggered out of the shallow water and up the beach to the relative shelter of the dunes. I smelt really strange—fishy and, I promise you, that was not the perfume I'd put on last night.

Diamond's party. Bits and pieces were coming back to me. Come on, brain, get in gear! I'd heard that hen and stag parties can get wild, with far too much being drunk, and the groom left tied naked to a pillar in Piazza San Marco or on a one-way trip to Rome, but this made no sense. I could not remember drinking—I'd been too busy checking the arrangements. Diamond was hardly the type of sister to trick me by spiking my drinks and then abandoning me on a beach.

I searched my surroundings for clues. I knew I had started the night in Venice and this did look like the Adriatic in front of me. Perhaps I hadn't gone too far? Maybe I was on one of the barrier islands, washed up on a deserted stretch of the Lido for example?

But lots of people lived on the Lido. It even had roads, cars, and a bus service. I couldn't see any buildings, let alone a bus stop.

OK, now I was scared. This did not feel like a hen party jest gone wrong. This felt like being shipwrecked. Had the launch sunk on the way back from the contessa's island? Was I the only survivor?

When I was younger, child, I renamed myself the eraser. You won't remember why.

Oh my God, I did remember! The contessa had turned into some psycho bitch out for revenge over her boy. The tiny woman packed the largest telepathic punch I had ever met. We'd all gone down for the count—an unfortunate pun as it was all about her criminal son, the Count of Monte Baldo.

But she had not erased my memory—only stunned it— probably because I had always maintained out of habit superstrong shields against telepathy. I knew exactly who I was, why I was here, but not how I had got on the beach or where it was. Two out of four—not too bad. At least now I knew what I had to do: get home; raise the alarm; not freeze to death.

I decided moving was good—it was either that or turn into an iceberg. I clambered up the dune, my silk dress catching at the hem where it caught on a scrap of twisted iron jetsam. It was hard not to be distracted by just how perishingly cold I felt.

From the vantage point on top of the dune, I saw that my island was tiny—a little haven for wild fowl and not much else. The long low mudflats of the lagoon stretched on the other side facing towards the mainland. On the side I was on, there was nothing but sea and the distant shape of a tanker chugging to the oil refinery west of my position. I could just make out the smudge of Venice lying low at the other end of the lagoon. For some reason, I'd been dumped well to the north-east in the wilderness of salt marshes, a place to which only huntsmen and fishermen ever came. They would be along eventually, but I couldn't wait for a day-tripper to come and rescue me. Time for the others might already be running out.

Why had I been dumped at all? It made no sense. The first thing I would do is make my way back and raise the alarm.

It struck me then that that must be what the countess was counting on me doing. This was a hostage situation. I was like the ransom letter. I'd been left far enough from home so that it would take me hours to get back, giving her time to spirit her captives away from the area. I was of no importance as a hostage as I was not one of the soulfinders; I had been expend-able. She probably wasn't too bothered if I got back before hypothermia set in. And I had even told her that I couldn't do telepathy and raise the alarm; she'd exploited my confidence ruthlessly.

Fury filled me, the rush of blood bringing a welcome warmth to my fingers and toes. I was not going to fall passively into step with her plans. She had wanted time and I was not giving it to her. I was going to alert the Benedicts even if it meant spewing my guts out on the beach.

I dipped into my mind. I didn't really know how to do telepathy, let alone over distance, having always avoided it. I did know how to get a fix on a direction though, which should help.

Find home, I told my brain.

But my brain was different from the last time I had tried this. All my junk—thoughts, belongings, random stuff—was no longer whirling about in a cloud but streaming like an arrow in one narrow direction. Somehow the attack had burst through the barriers in my mind and completely reorganized it. Experiencing no sickness, I found following the arrows easy, like skiing down a well-marked run. I just didn't know what was at the end of it.

Hello?

What the—? Whoa, is that you, cupcake?

Xav! Oh my God, Xav!

What are you doing talking to me telepathically: you'll make yourself sick! He then let out a string of swear words that were not edited by the link. *You're my soulfinder, aren't you? No question. Yes, I know you are.* I could feel the burst of jubilation, dancing on the spot happiness, at the other end of the conversation. *Well then, cupcake: get yourself back here, 'cause you and I have some serious kissin', huggin', 'n' plannin' to do.*

I couldn't share his joy right then—I had to shelve that bundle of feelings for the moment and examine them later. Xav—my soulfinder. Brain just did not compute. Too cold—too shocked.

Please shut up, Xav. Just listen. I'm trying to tell you something.

He laughed. A telepathic laugh is lovely: like a gentle tingle down the line. I'd not known. *Oh, Beauty, this is going to be so much fun. Only you would meet this realization by telling me to shut my mouth.*

No, I'm serious. This is an emergency.

I felt his change in mood abruptly. Gone was the teasing boy; on the line was someone I could rely on one hundred per cent. *What's happened? Is everyone OK? Do you need me? The guys and I did wonder why you weren't back.*

Oh, it's so much to explain, but the short version is Contessa Nicoletta is the mother of someone you arrested in London.

Mr Rome? I don't know the names of all the guys we caught in our net, but there was an Italian.

At the end of the evening, she turned into this mad harpy bent on revenge. She's taken the others—Diamond, your mum, Sky, Phoenix—and is holding them hostage.

What!?

She wants to bargain for his freedom.

But you're not with them so where are you? Are you safe?

I'm OK but I'm not sure exactly where I am. Best guess is I'm on an island near Torcello—the wild part of the lagoon.

A little motor launch appeared, heading my way. Its wake cut a white bracket in the muddy waters. *Hang on: I can see a fishing boat nearing the shore. I'll see if I can attract their attention.*

If you can't, I'll get a speedboat to you but if you can get them to take you that'll be fastest. I'll tell the others. Victor and Trace will know what to do. Get yourself back here ASAP.

Yes, sir.

Crystal, you and me: this is good news, really good news.

Even though we fight all the time?

<u>Especially</u> *because we fight all the time.*

The fisherman was as surprised as I had been to find me stranded on the island. He gallantly stripped off his waterproof jacket and bundled me up in it.

'How did you get here?' he asked. A banker from Milan, he had not bargained for this little side trip on his fishing holiday. He pulled his knitted cap down over my cold ears.

'I was a guest at a party that went bad.'

He tutted and shook his head. 'I have a teenage daughter like you.' He set the motor in reverse to pull away from the beach. He spoke with his hands like a conductor in front of an orchestra. 'I warn her all the time to watch who she socializes with. Young people can be very foolish.'

I would have liked to point out that my 'bad friend' was in her eighties but it would be too long an explanation. I just wanted the fisherman to get me home as quickly as possible.

'I'm sorry that I'm asking you to go so far out of your way.'

'No problem. It is not every day I get to fish a mermaid out of the lagoon.'

My kind rescuer dropped me at the little jetty near our apartment.

'Someone seems to have missed you,' he commented, pointing to Xav who was waiting by the ramp to shore, blanket in hand. 'Hey, young man, make sure you look after her better: she could've died out there!'

'It's not his fault,' I muttered, embarrassed that the fisherman had assumed Xav was to blame. Fortunately the reproof had been in Italian. 'Hen party.'

'Humph: what are girls coming to these days? Weren't like that when I was young.' He threw a line to Xav who tied up the boat by the pier. 'Mind the step, mermaid.'

Xav reached down and pulled me into his arms. He hugged me so tightly against him I could barely get out a muffled 'thank you' to my Good Samaritan.

'Thank you, sir, for bringing Crystal back.' Xav reached down and shook hands with the fisherman. 'We'd like to pay for your trouble—the extra gas at least.'

The fisherman understood English but refused the offer. 'No need for that. Here's my card in case you have any questions where I found her. Someone should be punished for that—absolutely criminal leaving her there without even a coat.'

Xav tucked the business card in his pocket. 'You're right about that. I'll make sure they don't get away with it.'

The fisherman cast off and chugged away to his now much truncated day of sport.

'Oh God, Xav, how did it all go so wrong?' I asked. 'It's my fault isn't it? I organized the party. I had no idea about her.'

'You are not responsible for every bad Savant, darlin'. From what you said, she would have been plotting this from the moment she heard Diamond was going to get hitched to my brother. Through you, or from Diamond herself, she would have heard sooner or later. It's not something we could hide.' Xav wrapped the blanket tighter about me then bundled me into his arms as he had once before.

'You're beginning to make a habit of this.' And one I wouldn't mind encouraging.

He carried me towards our garden gate. 'What was the going rate for rescues? I seem to think you considered charging me for the same service.'

'I'll pay anything, just tell me that you've found the others.'

''Fraid not, but getting you back is one massive step forward. My dad, Trace, and Victor are on the case with the authorities but we need an Italian speaker.'

'I'll get on to it right away.'

'No, you will get warm right away, have something hot to eat and drink. Yves is in the kitchen making your breakfast.'

'He needn't have bothered.'

'You're doing him a favour keeping him busy. We had to give him something to do, as he is worried sick about Phoenix. Zed's climbing the walls with anxiety for Sky. If you can put their minds at rest that they aren't in physical danger from that old witch, it would help.'

'I don't think they are. They're hostages so I think she wants them alive and well.'

Xav kicked open the gate and climbed the stairs. The Benedict men were waiting for me in the living room, trying not to pounce on me with their questions. Xav had obviously laid down the law as far as letting me have a chance to warm up. They were an impressive group: all sharing the dark looks of their parents and their father's height. Yet they were by no means copies of each other as their characters varied widely from the quiet, still waters of Uriel, the second eldest and the academic among them, to the easy going Will, to the combustible Zed who was spoiling right now for a fight. Xav held his own though, despite the enormous pressure he was under to get answers, and I was given time to change. Ten minutes later I was sitting wrapped in a duvet on the sofa, drinking hot chocolate, and telling Victor, the one who worked for the FBI, what had happened at the party.

'The Italian police will be here in a moment, Crystal.' Victor flipped over a page in his notebook. 'It's difficult making them believe us as the contessa is so well respected. I think they believe we've misunderstood the situation and that the women are all on some surprise side trip.'

'I can understand that.'

'They've already spoken to Signora Carriera downstairs and all she could tell them was that you had a lovely party and all went your separate ways at the end.'

'Yes, that's what she saw. The contessa made sure she had plenty of witnesses to a normal evening. I wouldn't believe it of her either unless I'd been there.'

Yves got out his laptop. 'There must be something I can do. Can we track her boat? Give me time and I'd probably be able to work out a program how to do that. Maybe I could tap into the military surveillance satellites that were overhead last night?'

Will, the middle son who was built like a rugby player but with a calm, no-nonsense manner, pushed the lid firmly closed. 'And get caught by the Pentagon? Way to go, little brother.

Phoenix won't want to spend the best years of her life visiting you in jail.'

'I wouldn't get caught.' Yves tugged the lid open again.

'My gift tells me that trying it would be dangerous for you right now. Admit it, Yves: you can't think straight when she's in danger so it's hardly time to try something that requires you to be at the top of your game.'

'What if she needs me, Will?' Yves's expression gave away the torment he was experiencing.

'Of course she needs you, you idiot.' Will cuffed his brother lightly. 'She needs you to keep your head.'

Zed crumpled up a newspaper in his fist. 'I can't stand this. Why don't we go over to the countess's house and take it to her doorstep?'

His father put a hand on his youngest son's shoulder. 'I know what you mean, Zed, but kicking the door down won't help if Sky's not there. She isn't there, is she, Victor?'

Victor, the most severe of the seven brothers, shoulder-length hair tied back, grey eyes and a mind like a dagger: sharp and incisive. He could manipulate your thoughts but fortunately had chosen to be one of the good guys. 'No. The police said there was no one in residence but the caretaker. That's the most suspicious thing: so soon after a big party, the contessa has cleared out, taking her entire staff with her—and, we may safely assume, our girls.'

Xav wriggled into the space behind me on the sofa so I was leaning against him. 'I think we're missing something obvious here. We've got a weapon the contessa underestimated.'

'What weapon?' Zed asked.

'My soulfinder.' His announcement raised a brief smile from the others even though they were out of their minds with worry for their own. 'Crystal has always talked down her gift, but she finds stuff you are connected to.'

'Things, Xav, not people,' I corrected.

'Are you sure about that? I felt that telepathic link you forged right to my brain: it was the strongest I'd ever met, built of our bond. You don't do telepathy like other people, cupcake.'

'I don't?' I couldn't know that, as it had been my first attempt.

'No, you do your own brand. I'm not surprised you find it so hard to do our sort because you build yours of the stuff that binds us together—friendship, fun, and, um, love.'

My cheeks flushed. He'd sensed that, had he? Not the moment I would've chosen to make the admission that I was way more in love with him than I had let on.

Uriel took the chair next to me. He had the lightest colouring of the boys: hazel eyes and gold-shot brown hair like the mane of a lion, similar to mine but without the maddening frizz. 'That's fascinating, Crystal. I'd not considered there were more ways than one of doing telepathy, but why not? It sounds like you do something similar to me: I can track things back through time by their relationship to people and places—see glimpses of where they've been at key moments in their existence. The resonance of the emotion sticks to them. What you do seems to focus on the here and now and sounds much more useful.'

I wasn't sure about that but he was very sweet to say so.

'If I've got this right, does it mean you can find Diamond as you have an emotional link to her?' Uriel glanced over to Trace who was pacing by the doorway to the kitchen.

I bit my lip. Could I? I'd never put it to the test. 'I could if I had a sense of where to start looking, I think. I still get this problem of being knocked out of orbit by the hundreds of links we all have. I can do simple things like find keys as that is straightforward and people usually have an idea where they left them. It's going to be tough to do it when there are so many options as to where she is.'

Xav squeezed my shoulders. 'I think you'll need something a bit stronger than your sister-to-sister bond. What I was thinking is you should follow the soulfinder link from Trace to your sister, or my dad to our mom. You had no problem following ours, did you?'

'No, it was channelled right at you.'

'Too right it was.' He kissed the top of my head.

Yves dumped the laptop and crouched beside me. 'So you can also track my link to Phoenix?'

Zed leant over the back of the sofa. 'What about Sky and me?'

With an alarming groan, Mr Benedict sat down heavily in an armchair. 'Oh lord.' He had tears in his eyes, so unexpected with his usually stoic face.

Trace hurried to his father's side. Moving me, Xav half got up, ready to administer any healing that was required. We all shared the worry that the older man had succumbed to the stress of losing his wife. Mr Benedict held up a hand.

'Please, don't get up. I'm fine, boys, more than fine.' He pinched the bridge of his nose to stop the tears in their tracks. 'You just don't know how fine.' He sat back, hands dangling on his knees. 'Crystal, my darling girl, you are a soulseeker.'

Xav settled back behind me.

'A what?' I asked.

'It's your gift. It's so rare I've only met one other and that was the man who found my Karla for me. There are only one or two born in a century. Why did no one realize this sooner?'

I shrugged, not doing a good job of hiding my shock behind nonchalance. 'I didn't show the right signs, I guess, until forced to by last night.'

'But you're from a family of Savants: they should've identified your gift so you could help those of us without our soulfinders. Their neglect of your talent is verging on criminal.'

Victor's jaw dropped—the first time I'd seen the coolest of the Benedict brothers completely astounded. 'You mean she can find my soulfinder—Will's and Uriel's too?'

'She can. But right now, she can find the girls for us, which is something the contessa is not expecting.'

I was still reeling. To discover my soulfinder and hear I had an awesome gift all in the same morning was a lot to take in. Still, I had the rest of my life to sort this out; right now we had to focus on saving the others.

'Let's give it a go. How do I do this?' I looked up at Xav. 'Tell me more about what it felt like to be linked with me and how that is different to normal telepathy.'

Xav caressed my cheek. 'It was incredible. I could feel you zooming right in to my consciousness so smoothly it was a joy to watch. In telepathy, it is normally more like a gentle touch on the shoulder to gain your attention—a kind of mind-to-mind phone call. With you, you arrived like a plane coming in to land. I could see you a few seconds before you touched down—I suppose I could've blocked you then but why would I want to? I didn't have to hold the bridge between us—you did all that.'

I shook my head. 'I didn't do anything. I just followed what was already between us.'

'Even better. So it didn't hurt?'

'No, bizarrely it was the most natural thing I've ever done.'

'OK. So you need to see if you can transfer the skill to other minds. Dad, any suggestions?'

'Mr Benedict, how did the seeker help you?' I asked.

'Please, call me Saul. We're family now in so many ways.' Saul reached out and took my hand, his rough thumb rubbing across the back. 'The seeker was a very old man, a revered elder among my people, who had been doing this for years so he had had time to perfect his method. As I was just a callow youth when he helped me, he did not share his secrets. What I sensed was that he was able to get into my mind somehow and then shape and follow my link. You have to remember I hadn't met Karla then so he took the step of turning me in the right direction, channelling my connection towards her.'

'OK. Hmm, that sounds advanced stuff. But you all have your links readymade so perhaps I just have to be able to get into your mind somehow and do my zooming in to land thing from there.'

'I have an idea.' Zed squeezed himself on to the end of the sofa. Any more Benedicts around me and I'd be well and truly sandwiched. 'I hold my brothers' gifts together when we want to work on something important. You are already linked to Xav, right?'

'Sure she is,' Xav confirmed.

'Then, we try adding Crystal to the Benedict family bond. With Vick's understanding of the mind, Uriel's experience of tracking through time, Trace's of tracking through space, Yves's general genius understanding of everything, Dad and Will being very hot on sensing when we hit dangerous territory, we should be able to help Crystal find her way. A kind of crash course on being a soulseeker.'

'Without the crash part,' added Xav.

'We hope,' continued Zed, looking happier for the first time since I'd broken the news of the kidnap. 'Anyway, Xav here is good at tending the odd bump or two so we've got that covered.'

I was going to do it, of course I was, but that didn't stop me being a bit worried. 'What will they see if I let everyone share my bond with you?' I asked Xav.

'We're very polite—we won't look,' Zed promised, hand on

heart though with a less than reassuring glint in his eye.

'Don't worry, darlin', I'll stomp on anyone who trespasses on our stuff, OK?' Xav kicked his brother off the end of the sofa.

'I wouldn't,' vowed Yves, 'and Zed will behave.'

'Of course, he will.' Saul made this a pronouncement that I could not doubt. 'There's too much at stake to fool around and Zed knows that.'

'How have I become the one everyone grumbles at? That used to be Xav.'

Xav smirked. 'Yeah, but I'm now partner to a soulseeker—major respect time, guys.'

For all their teasing talk, the Benedicts were already getting down to business. Trace had moved the chairs into a circle so that we could all touch hands. Uriel had drawn the curtains to dim the lights. Will had eased the cat outside so no interruptions of the feline-seeking-attention kind would disturb us.

'Ready, darlin'?' Xav linked one hand with Zed and the other with his dad. The fact that I was sitting cradled in his lap was considered connection enough with me.

I gulped. I so didn't want to let them down. 'Let's give this a whirl.'

Allowing so many people to have access to my mind reminded me of walking out in public in a bikini for the first time. I was scared everyone would be looking at all the bits I wanted to keep hidden, but then I realized it wasn't a big deal for anyone else and I should get on with the job at hand. The sensation was so eerie: I could feel the Benedict boys' different natures surrounding me, but most clearly I felt Xav's presence. He was totally focused on supporting me; it was like being carried in his arms again, but this time in thought. How had I not appreciated that side of him till it was almost too late? I had known he was caring from the start but I'd spent more time arguing with him than letting him show his best side.

Because arguing is fun, he whispered in my mind. *Think of all the kiss and make up we get to do afterwards.*

Xav, chided his father, *focus.*

Give the guy a break. He's only just found her, said Will. I could feel his humour ripple through the shared mind-conversation.

You're only saying that so she can find your girl first, countered Uriel. *I'm going to argue privilege of the eldest.*

Boys. That was Saul again.

Just settling her in, said Xav. *She doesn't do this telepathy stuff like us. I'm working out how to protect her from the things whirling about in your heads.*

I then realized I was only prevented from feeling my usual nausea by the fact that I was within Xav's mental space, hearing the conversation through his filters. I didn't have those in my mind, which was doubtless why I had spent most of my life being knocked about by telepathy.

Yeah, darlin', that's me: your force field. He projected an image of the Starship Enterprise with its shields on maximum, ploughing through an asteroid belt.

I just hope the engines can take it when we get going on tracking one of the soulfinders. Who shall we try? I knew all of them were eager to volunteer. *I know Diamond best, obviously, but she is the newest. Should we go with your dad and mum?*

The link is strong between soulfinders no matter how new, said Saul graciously. *As you know your way round your sister's mind a little, I think it should be her.*

Trace? Xav reached out to his eldest brother.

Ready. And I could feel he was: locked and loaded like he would be before any dawn raid in his job.

I was feeling embarrassed about what I was about to do and they must have all sensed it.

Don't be shy, Crystal. There's nothing between Diamond and me that she wouldn't want shared with you for this purpose, Trace reassured me.

OK. I'm going to follow your feelings for her—that's the clearest thing for me to sense. I touched his mind with Xav's help. And there it was: the stream of thoughts and emotions all focused on his soulfinder. I didn't want to examine it too closely, a general sense of direction was all I needed, but I couldn't help glimpsing little bits of their courting, jokes, private moments, concerns shared and carried together. I featured in that last bundle; Diamond has been talking about me to Trace a lot. Ooops. Don't look too close: eavesdroppers always come to grief.

Crystal, you need to focus. You're sliding off track. That was Zed who was keeping a watch on my progress as he held all the gifts together.

Sorry. Uriel, Trace, any advice how I do this?

Don't think of the trail getting fainter as it gets further from you, said Uriel. *That's just your mind projecting an imagined weakness. For mental paths, distance is meaningless. The trail is there.*

I find points of certainty, like supports of a bridge to make sure the trail doesn't collapse on me, added Trace. *Feel rather than try to see.*

Good advice. I tried to follow it but it wasn't as clear as it had been with Xav. I felt that the end of the thread was flapping about in the wind, like a loose kite. *It doesn't feel right.*

Where are you, do you think?

I pulled back a little. Mountains. Cold. West-north-west. The effort was making my head spin; the trail was fading.

That's enough, guys, announced Xav. *She needs to rest.*

Zed gently let the telepathic connection lapse. Last to leave my mind was Xav and I came to still wrapped in his arms.

'I'm sorry. I'm not very good at this yet.' I felt terrible that I hadn't come up with a full answer, only fragments.

Trace had his head in his hands. 'It's not your fault, Crystal. I felt what you saw. There's something seriously wrong with Diamond. She's, well, she's just not there.'

'Oh my God, you don't mean she's dead, do you?' I began to panic. I'd assumed this was a hostage situation, but what if the contessa was really insane and had killed them all?

Trace shook his head. 'I think, no, I would know if that was so.' He clenched his fists and flexed them, struggling to keep control of his feelings. 'What I meant was that she was a blank. Switched off somehow.'

'That's not possible,' stated Zed. 'Nothing can override a soulfinder bond.'

'Are you sure?' Trace's eyes were filled with pain.

An ugly idea came to me. 'The contessa called herself the eraser. I thought she meant that she could wipe our memories, but what if she meant something more?'

Saul was trembling. He looked older than I'd ever seen him. 'If she has done something to our soulfinders then we will find them even if they don't know us. Once we get them back, I vow that I will find a way to reverse the damage. She is not stealing my soul from me.'

'We'll find a way, Dad,' promised Will. 'Mom won't let an evil old bird like her wreck thirty plus years of marriage.'

Yves stood up and opened the curtains. 'Thanks to Crystal, we've got a chance. Her directions were close enough to start a search. I'll just call up a map of the area she located.' He fired up his laptop and called up a satellite image of the area overlaid with names. 'Crystal, here's what I got from your mind. Can you narrow it down any?'

I knelt beside him and scanned the image of the Dolomites, the alpine range in the north of Italy. 'I think I can.' I tapped the area near Lake Garda. 'And I don't need mind power to work it out.'

Xav ruffled my hair. 'Clever. Monte Baldo. Of course, she's gone back to the area of her family's ancestral lands. How else can she hide what she's done unless she has some stronghold staffed by those loyal to her? We should've thought of that.'

'You would've done eventually,' I said. 'It's just all been too much of a shock.'

Victor was on his computer already, tapping into the international law enforcement databases. 'The guy we arrested in London, the investigators listed a villa in the mountains among his assets.' He pulled up an image. 'Damn, it looks impregnable.' It was not so much a villa as a castle built for defence high on a mountain crag, ramparts shaped with bladelike crenulations; picture postcard pretty if it hadn't really been turned into a prison. 'Suggestions?'

'There's only one real option for us,' said Saul. 'We drive up to the main gate and ask for them back. It may look medieval, but this is modern Italy. She can't get away with keeping them from us if they are there.'

'I'm pretty sure that's the place I felt.' I could feel shivers running down my spine—the castle looked beautifully cruel, like an eagle perched on a rock.

'Then what are we waiting for?' asked Zed, halfway to the door. 'Let's go rescue our girls.'

Of course it wasn't as easy as that. Trace and Victor immediately set about hiring a couple of four-wheel drives to take us to the mountains. Not knowing what condition the girls would be in once we found them, we decided we would need our own base rather than hope that they would be up to the long drive back to Venice. Searching online, Zed and Yves found one near to the contessa's villa. Fortunately, out of season and before the skiing got into full swing, they were able to track down the owner of a large house in a town on the eastern shore of the lake not far from Monte Baldo. The plan was to fetch the girls and take them there for the night so they could recover.

Victor and Uriel offered to drive. Everyone saw the sense in this as, not having their soulfinders in immediate danger, they were expected to be the calmest in this situation. Will was nominated the navigator with me as his GPS signal to home in on the destination. We had assumed we were right about the contessa's villa but it was always possible I had leapt to a conclusion and missed the girls' true position. My job was to sit in the back of the lead car, with Xav to help, keeping a fix on Trace's connection as far as it went. Uriel followed with Yves, Zed, and their father as his passengers.

Once we had picked up the cars and crossed to the mainland on the long link of the road bridge, Xav and I were left pretty much on our own. Trace was occupied with phone calls to his police contacts. I could hear him pulling in every favour, tugging on every string he had in international law enforcement. I had offered to deal with the Italians but he said that could wait until we got to Lake Garda. Will and Victor had the roads to negotiate.

I leant my head back on Xav's shoulder, his arm around me, savouring this little moment of calm. 'You OK? You must be worried for your mum.'

He played with a curl that had come loose from the quick ponytail I had made of my hair. 'I feel pretty mixed up. I'm worried for Mom and the others, especially now you say something's wrong with them, but I'm also doing a little Happy Feet dance inside to have found you. It makes me feel really conflicted—I don't know what to feel first.'

I smiled at the image of hundreds of penguins jiving through his brain. Yes, that was how it felt. 'You make a good team, you and your brothers, and your dad too. I don't think the contessa will know what's hit her once you arrive on her doorstep.'

He kissed my hand then rubbed it against his cheek. 'Thanks. It helps that you believe in us. And don't forget who is our secret weapon.'

I turned in towards him so I could see his face. 'Do you think your dad is right—about me, I mean?'

'Do you?'

'I suppose . . . well, maybe. I'm just worried I'll be a dud one of these soulseeker things like I am at everything else.'

'Cupcake, I'm warning you.' He wriggled his fingers in the air.

'What?' I squeaked, trying to get away from the threatened tickle.

'I'll take drastic action if you run yourself down again in my hearing. You've just been told that you are the once-in-a-generation gift to Savant-kind and now you're saying you think you won't be good enough.'

'But . . .'

'No buts. When are you going to wake up to the fact you are not the Ugly Duckling but the swan?'

'Aw.'

Before I could get soppy over his lovely compliment, he went for my midriff with his fingers.

'No!' I yelped, curling up and batting his hands away.

Trace frowned and tried to shield his call from my shrieks.

'Admit it: say,"I am a swan".'

'You are a swan!' I gasped, falling into giggles again.

'Urg! Confess!'

'OK, OK, I am a swan. We both are. Everyone is. There: we are a whole flock of swans.'

'You make enough noise to be one, that's for sure,' grumbled Trace, though I could tell he was not too upset. He probably welcomed the distraction, which, I guess, was exactly why Xav had done it.

It was late afternoon by the time we reached the mountain road to the castle. For what was a route leading only to a national park, the track up Monte Baldo showed signs of many vehicles having passed recently: the verge churned up, mud mixed with the snow lying at these high altitudes.

'You think she's preparing for a siege?' asked Xav, only half-joking.

I spotted a sign tacked to one of the trees at a junction, one spur leading to the villa the other up to the snowfields. 'Actually, I don't think it has anything to do with her. I reckon Hollywood has come to town. Remember what they said on set, this week they were shooting in the Italian Alps? Well, that's where we are. They've got here before us.'

'From the looks of it, they didn't head our way.' Victor signalled to turn down the narrow road that snaked around the crag; the tyre marks of the heavy vehicles had carried on up the mountain.

'No, they must be further up. If I remember right, it was some shot to do with skiing and helicopters.' But I was comforted to know we had possible allies not so far from here who might be counted on to take our part if we had to go head-to-head with the Italian authorities to get access. Lily could vouch that I wasn't a nutcase when we approached the local police with this kidnapping story.

Darkness had fallen by the time we reached the gates. As our vehicles got within range, security lights went on. There was no visible guard, just an intercom.

Victor drummed his fingers on the wheel. 'So, we just go up and knock?' He would have preferred a person on whom he could use his mind powers.

'I guess so.' Trace got out. 'Stay in the car, guys.' He held up his hand to the passengers of the other vehicle. 'I'll do this. Let's not give them too many targets, hey?'

'Does he really expect someone to take a pot shot at him?' I whispered to Xav.

Xav shrugged, tension running through his body like a low voltage current.

'Is it OK, Will?' I asked.

'Not OK—but the threat is general. Not aimed at Trace.'

We watched in silence as Trace pressed the intercom.

'*Si?*' crackled a voice at the other end.

'My name is Trace Benedict. Do you speak English?'

'*No.*'

Trace swore under his breath. 'OK. Moment. Crystal?'

I was already on my way out of the car, Xav shadowing me. I pressed the 'speak' button.

'Hello,' I began in Italian, 'I'd like to speak to the contessa, please.'

'She is not receiving visitors. Please go away: this is a private residence.'

'I'm afraid I can't do that; you see, you have my sister there and . . . and I need to speak to her urgently—a family emergency.' Well, it was, wasn't it?

There was a pause. The camera on top of a nearby pole swivelled to take a good look at us. 'I will send a snowmobile to fetch you. You may come in.'

'Tell them you're not going in alone!' hissed Xav.

'My friends won't let me come without someone else.'

'You and one other. The older man—not the young ones.' The channel switched off.

'I'm not liking this one bit,' Trace said as his father jumped out of the other car. 'We can't send her two more hostages.'

'She already had her chance to take me. I doubt it's hostages she is after but messengers.'

Saul put his hand on my shoulder. 'Are you all right with this, Crystal?'

'Of course, she's not all right with it.' Xav was working himself up to an eruption of temper. He hadn't anticipated this twist and couldn't accept that I'd head into danger without him. 'You expect me to let her walk right into the lion's den?'

'Xav!' I warned in a low voice.

'What?' He turned his anger-filled eyes on me.

'I'm not of interest because I'm *not* a soulfinder, remember?'

Even when furious, he put my safety first. Moving away from me, he tried to look as if he wasn't about to strangle us all. 'Yeah, cupcake, it's not as if you are our crown jewels or anything, is it? Jeez, I want to kick something.'

The buzz of snowmobile engines was heard before we saw the vehicles gliding down the driveway towards us.

Saul began firing orders to his sons. 'Stay with the cars. I'll keep in touch if I can but I wouldn't be surprised if she has some kind of telepathic dampener around her.'

'My kind of telepathy might get through that if it is unique as Xav claims.' I gazed worriedly at his back. He was currently stomping on a rut of snow.

He wheeled round. 'Not if it gives you away.'

'Of course not. I'll be careful.'

'I don't call heading in there being careful!'

'Xav!' Saul was losing his temper now, something that rarely happened in this family.

'What?' he snapped.

'Look at me, Xav.' My soulfinder raised his eyes to meet his father's steady gaze. 'You can trust me to look after her. I swear on my life I will make sure no harm comes to her—or your mother, or Diamond, Phoenix, and Sky for that matter.'

'You can't promise that,' Xav said quietly, his anger stamped off into the snow.

'What I can say is that if things go badly wrong, you have my permission, Yves, to blow the gates to kingdom come and all of you can charge in to the rescue. Just for now, let's try talking our soulfinders out of there. It is the safest way.'

Zed swore while Yves gave a guarded nod. Trace hugged me tightly.

'Take care, little sister,' he murmured. 'Diamond would not like me letting you do this if she knew.'

Two snowmobiles swept into view, turning so as to face back towards the house. The drivers did not get off, or even say anything to us, their faces obscured by their helmets. They could've been aliens under there for all I could see. With a little hum, the one half of the gate opened just wide enough for people to slip through in single file. The contessa wasn't taking any chances, which was hardly surprising if she knew which gifts she was dealing with when it came to the Benedict family. Victor in particular was not going to be welcome at this particular party.

'OK, guys, see you in a minute,' I said with false cheerfulness. Following Saul, I squeezed through the gate. As soon as I was clear, it hummed closed. Xav was trying not to look at me but he did shoot me an agonized glance.

Saul was assessing the two men on the snowmobiles. 'You go with that one, Crystal.' He motioned me towards the bigger of the two drivers.

I was surprised. I would have guessed that he would steer me towards the other.

'Brains not brawn is usually the threat,' he whispered, helping me take my seat behind the silent man. 'Your driver is reading as mostly harmless.'

Gingerly, I took hold of the driver's waist. He didn't wait for Saul to be seated, but set off at high speed back to the castle.

There was too much noise to ask questions so I did my best to note the way back in case I had to find it on my own. The drive was clearly marked by posts to show the track in the deep snow. On either side stretched fir plantations. Round the turn and we came upon the gardens, mysterious in their winter covering but I could just make out some terraces, hedges, and statues. Above loomed the castle, now a dark silhouette against the sky, crenellations clawing at the stars as if envious of their freedom from an earth-bound existence. I had tumbled out of everyday life into a fairy tale; it was very easy to believe that a rational discussion about releasing the girls would seem foolishness here, like trying to reason a werewolf out of savaging you.

The motor died. I swung off, not able to bring myself to thank my escort. Again, without a word, he drove off, taking the vehicle round the side of the building to where I presume the contessa kept her transport. There was a big turning circle where I was standing but otherwise no sign of cars. A moment later, Saul arrived on the back of his ride, visibly relieved to see me waiting. He descended and hurried over, taking my arm before anyone could separate us.

'What now?' I asked.

There was no obvious door to the castle. A deep arched passage led through the wall but neither of us fancied going that way—with the portcullis suspended overhead it looked too much like heading into a dragon's mouth.

Then a man appeared in the passage carrying a flashlight.

'I suppose that's our answer,' sighed Saul. Taking a firm grip of my hand, he led the way across.

'I recognize him—he's the butler from the contessa's house in Venice,' I whispered.

'If sir and madam would like to follow me,' the butler intoned.

'This is not a social call,' Saul said briskly. 'I think you know why we are here and you should consider your own risk of criminal charges if you prevent us from getting back our girls and my wife.'

'Very well, sir. This way.'

Oh he was good, this butler. He must have studied hours of classic film footage to get the subservient but sneering tone down to a T.

Our footsteps echoed in the passage. He led us out into a courtyard and across to where a door stood open. I could hear laughter and voices from inside.

'Looks like the contessa has company. What does that mean for us?' I asked.

'Possibly witnesses. If there's anyone not in her pay, it would work in our favour.' Saul stopped on the doorstep. 'OK, Crystal, I'm going to try telepathy. I know it makes you queasy, so I'm sorry.'

'That's fine.' I moved away and built up my shields still further. 'I'll run interference with the butler.' I crossed the threshold into a panelled foyer decorated with hunting trophies and swords—how unoriginal. 'Hey, Jeeves, where shall I hang my coat?' I called rudely. Out of interest, I tried dipping into the servant's mind to see if I could sense anything about his connections like I did when I was looking for something for my niece—and got a shock. His brain was whirling but not in a random pattern as most people's did; it was like getting on a roundabout, everything moving in an orderly circle: his duties, his loyalty to the countess, and his ties to his family. It was, well, almost robotic in its tidiness. I disconnected quickly, not wanting him to sense the invasion.

'Madam can leave her coat here,' the butler said, holding out his hand. I shrugged out of my jacket and passed it over. His expression did not change a jot—no smile, no glimmer of humanity.

Saul came in. I raised an eyebrow but he shook his head. OK, no normal telepathy. I pointed to my chest, asking if he wanted me to try. He shook his head again.

'Let's keep that in the locker,' he said in a low voice, 'for later if we need it.'

'Can I take sir's coat?' the butler enquired.

'You might as well.' Saul passed it over. While the butler's back was turned, I tapped my temple, pointed at him and grimaced.

'Hmm. Interesting. Eraser?' Saul asked quietly.

'I imagine so. Not natural. It seems she can reorder the mind to suit herself.'

'It would explain this set up.'

'This way.' Robot Jeeves headed towards a pair of fine wooden doors. He pushed them open to reveal a beautiful old sitting room, a huge fireplace with roaring fire, and a matching set of rose-coloured chairs and settees. None of that held our attention though for in the room were all the people we had come to find.

'Di! Oh my God, are you all right?' I exclaimed, hurrying over to my sister. She was sipping a glass of champagne, looking none the worse for her abduction. I didn't recognize the old-fashioned dress she was wearing—or the expression on her face for that matter.

'Sorry, do I know you?' Diamond put her glass down and stood up, holding out a hand to shake mine as if we were chance met acquaintances. 'Oh dear, your name has slipped my mind. I might have had too much to drink.' She grimaced ruefully at her glass, inviting me to join the joke.

'Diamond—it's me, Crystal. Your sister.'

'Don't be silly: I'm the youngest in my family. Mama and Dad were too old to have another. Not that Dad will ever admit Mama is too old for anything: he dotes on her. Sweet really, at their age.' She took another sip, her hand shaking as if her body knew something her brain did not.

'But Dad is . . . ' I let the last two words trail away because I knew they were useless. Her mental clock had been reset and she did not seem to know that our father was dead or that I existed. When I looked in her mind, I simply wasn't there. Everything and everyone that had touched her relationship with Trace had been deleted and, as I had been there from the beginning, I had been completely taken out of the picture. Memories of me had been sealed off like nuclear waste buried deep in concrete to stop it contaminating the other recollections. She was not the only one to be so blank. Phoenix and Sky were looking my way with polite interest; Karla was staring into the fire, not noticing that her husband had entered. He strode over to her and lifted her out of her chair.

'Karla, you will stop this now!' He put his face right in front of hers. 'Listen to me—find me in your head—your heart! It's me—Saul!'

'Good lord, what is he doing?' exclaimed Diamond, abandoning me and hurrying over to the pair by the hearth. 'Is he mad? Leave her alone!'

'Saul? Saul who?' asked Karla, her eyes dim. She looked as though she was drugged—I wished it was as simple as that but from the state of her mental landscape, she'd suffered the same erasing treatment as the butler—they all had; but with her, because so much of her adult life had been with her soulfinder, there was frighteningly little left.

The tiny dark clad figure in the winged chair on the other side of the fire now got to her feet. 'Do you like my revenge, Benedict?' she asked with bitter glee.

Saul released his grip on Karla's arms and gently put her back in her seat. He was struggling with such strong emotions that he was in no fit state to reply.

'As you can see, every soulfinder has been, how would you say? Lost,' continued the contessa.

'Nothing is more powerful than the bond between soulfinders,' he said in a low voice. 'Nothing.'

'Except me.' The contessa turned her attention to me. 'Ah, Crystal, you got back much quicker than I thought. I am amazed to see you here this evening. I wasn't expecting you to work out where I had taken everyone until, oh, tomorrow at the earliest. You have my congratulations. I underestimated you. Your lack of gifts made me think you lacked intelligence.'

'Why have you done this to my sister?' I swallowed against the lump in my throat. 'What has she, what have I, ever done to you?'

'Nothing—and it is unfortunate that you got involved in this. You see, my dear, to erase the soulfinder link you have to go so deep almost everything else goes with it. There's not much left in their pretty heads. They're not suffering; they are just . . . ' she searched for a word with a flutter of her gnarled fingers, 'vacant.'

I refused to accept that but the first thing was to get them away from her. 'In that case, surely your revenge is complete. Can we take them home with us?'

She perched her head to one side as if she had difficulty hearing. 'You are forgetting my son. I want him delivered to me—then you can have them back.'

'And if we do that, will you return their minds to how they used to be?' I asked.

'I would be lying to you if I said I could do that. No, I thought it only fair to take something permanently from the Benedicts as they have taken the honour from my house. Too much public damage has been done for that to be reversed.'

Saul held out his hand to Karla. 'In that case, we're going. Come on, Karla: the boys are waiting for you at the gate.'

'Boys?' Karla shivered and flinched back from the offered palm.

'Your sons. Our sons. Sky, Phoenix—you too. We're leaving. Yves and Zed need you.'

'What odd names.' Phoenix came forward and smiled up at him. 'You're funny. Why are you crying?' She wiped the tears from his cheeks.

Sky offered a tissue. 'Don't worry, Mr . . . um. Sorry, what was your name again? Anyway, we're having a lovely time. You mustn't cry.'

The contessa smiled at her guests. 'Do any of you wish to leave with Mr Benedict and this girl here?'

The four looked at us as if we were vaguely interesting specimens in a museum.

'Why would we want to do that?' asked Diamond.

The butler appeared at the door, flanked by a couple of bodyguards, almost as if he could hear Saul contemplating the odds of getting out with Karla thrown over his shoulder.

The contessa waved towards the exit. 'Thank you so much for calling. I'll expect you to be in touch, shall I, about my son?'

Saul did not reply. He turned on his heel and walked straight out, ploughing through the three men in the doorway. 'Come on, Crystal, we're not staying here. Rot in hell, contessa.'

For a mild man, the oath came with a horrid punch of ill will. I couldn't have put it any better myself.

Chapter 12

The drive down to our base in the lakeside resort of Malcesine
was passed in silence. Saul had delivered the devastating news
outside the gates in terse sentences, warning his sons not to
react as no doubt the contessa was watching and relishing. The
camera promptly exploded. I assumed that was the volatile
Zed's work but then saw Yves's grim smile. We had agreed to
depart and make plans out of sight and out of earshot.

I'd forgotten how beautiful Lake Garda was: deep slate-blue
waters, metallic grey mountain slopes rising from the shore,
little towns clinging to the edge, rimmed with cypress trees. I
had only visited in summer before; now the icy wind from the
Alps rippled across the surface of the lake, and the air had a
crystalline quality missing in the heat haze of August.

'What do we do first? Police?' I asked when we had parked
outside our villa, a pale lemon two-storey house with a roof
terrace. A vine wound round the gazebo, a handful of yellowed
leaves clinging on despite the brisk breeze.

Saul blew on his chilled fingers. 'Dealing with any sort of
bureaucracy always takes longer than you think possible. I'm
not *inclined* now to go that route.' He said the formal word

with heavy menace. No, he was *inclined* now to draw blood. We all were.

Victor gazed back up the mountain slopes to where we could just make out the black silhouette of the little castle on the crag. It looked so innocent from this distance. 'We'll need . . . I don't know . . . maybe a helicopter or something to break in there. I've never tried getting into a place like that before. We might be able to blow the gates and get the cars in but it would be easy to block our retreat. Trace?'

'Air is the best of our bad options,' agreed Trace.

'I'll have to put the girls out somehow—asleep I guess would be best—so we can carry them out. It sounds like they'll not come willingly.'

''Fraid not,' I confirmed.

'Then we'll have to get in ourselves—hire our own pilot as the red tape with the police takes too long. I'm not waiting for them to change their mind,' said Zed.

'Yes, but how do we get a helicopter pilot that can do a stunt like landing on that handkerchief sized bit of mountain at short notice?' asked Will.

Stunt? 'Actually, guys, I do know how.'

Xav swung round to me. 'If you have the answer, we will be your humble servants for the rest of our lives.'

'I'll hold you to that. The film crew. We saw that they're in the mountains setting up the action sequence of the Steve Hughes movie. The photographer on the set told me they had stunts with helicopters to work out. I know the director a little . . .'

'And Steve, according to the international media, is your "boyfriend",' growled Xav.

'A kind of friend at least. I can get you in to see them and then you'll have to take it from there.'

'No problem,' said Victor. 'I can be very persuasive if necessary.'

First port of call was Lily, whose mobile number I had. She was more than happy to hear from me. 'Oh, do come by, Crystal. I'm bored out of my mind here and so cold!'

'Would it be OK if I brought a friend or two?'

'Sure. Who are they?'

'You remember Xav?'

'Of course—the gorgeous American.'

Listening in, head resting on my shoulder, Xav raised a brow at that.

'Well, he's kind of my boyfriend now.'

Xav shook his head and pointed between our two hearts, then linked his fingers together.

I almost missed what Lily said next. 'Oh, shut up, I'm so jealous!'

'His brothers and dad are over from the States. They want to see what you're doing.'

'Not much down here. All the action's up on the ski slopes. Maybe I could arrange passes for tomorrow. How many of them are there?'

'Eight.'

'Eight!'

'Is it still OK?'

'Sure, after that fantastic shoot in Venice, James owes me a favour—or eight.'

'I'll be right over. There's something I need to tell you.'

Lily's hotel was only a couple of streets from our base, so it took no time to track her down. Work all done until the real shoot began, Lily was delighted to see me but a little surprised when I turned up with the entire Benedict clan in tow.

'Wow, girlfriend, where did you get these guys?' She nudged me. 'Are they all spoken for?'

'Nearly all. Not those three.' I pointed to Victor, Uriel, and Will. Trying to pretend this was mainly a social call so she didn't get spooked, I played along with the flirting.

She sighed. 'Shame I'm too old for them.' She may have said that but I noticed she lingered a little longer chatting with Uriel as she took drinks orders.

'Where is the set exactly, Lily?' Xav asked.

'There's a nature reserve up on Monte Baldo—great pristine slopes already snow covered. It's a bit of a drive. If you want to visit, you'll need to be in four by fours as the roads up are pretty treacherous.'

'Don't worry, Miss George, we rented some before we came,' said Saul. 'We live in the Rockies so are familiar with these conditions. We already had a drive up there earlier today and our cars managed fine.'

'Great. They're filming a shot where a stuntman, standing in for Steve, drops from a helicopter and skis down the run, shooting bad guys all the way.'

'How many helicopters are they using?' asked Victor.

'I think three—one for the stunt, two for cameras. We're lucky with the weather. They couldn't fly if it got too windy.'

There was a knock at the door.

'Come in!' called Lily.

Steve Hughes walked through. I could feel Xav stiffen beside me. 'Hey, Lily, do you want to go for a drink? Oh, you've got company. I hope I didn't interrupt.' He gave them his hundred-watt film star smile, not intimidated by standing among a group of men all taller than him. He spotted me at the back. 'Hi, it's Crystal, isn't it? How are you, sweetheart?' His voice dropped into what I thought of as his golden syrup register, saved for members of the opposite sex.

Nice of him to remember my name. 'Oh, fine, Steve. Just nursing a broken heart according to *Gossip Magazine*.'

Steve did not get my sense of humour. He actually became worried I was serious. 'You did understand, didn't you, that it was just a date?' He glanced at the door, contemplating leaving the messy emotional stuff to Lily to deal with.

'And there was little old me thinking an evening out with you was inevitably going to lead to a big Hollywood wedding and hundreds of babies.'

He frowned. The hundreds of babies bit had been a broad enough hint for him to understand. 'You aren't serious?'

Poor little humourless mega star. 'That's right, Steve. Meet my boyfriend—my *real* boyfriend I mean. This is Xav. The others are his brothers and father. They're from Colorado.'

Xav did not offer his hand for a shake. He put his arm possessively around my shoulders. 'Good to meet you.' His tone suggested the opposite—unless the meeting involved pistols at dawn.

Steve now looked really anxious. He had leapt to quite another conclusion as to why I should be here with my boyfriend's entire family in tow. 'I didn't touch her, you know. All that stuff in the press—just speculation.'

'But you did kiss her.' Xav fixed him with slash of a stare.

'Because the train on her dress was ripped—we didn't want that on the front page. I was doing her a favour.'

Xav really growled this time.

'I mean it was very nice for me too, of course.' Steve backtracked, realizing that had sounded vaguely insulting. 'But I won't kiss her again. Ever.'

'Let the poor man off the hook, Xav,' said Will. 'It's fine, Mr Hughes; we aren't here about that incident.'

'You're not?' Steve looked hugely relieved.

'No. We've got a serious problem.' Victor moved forward, smooth as skates over ice. 'Victor Benedict. I'm with the FBI.'

Steve shook his hand. 'Bit out of your jurisdiction, aren't you?'

I was impressed that Steve hadn't immediately been intimidated by Victor; I would have been shaking in my boots to be the focus of the attention of the iciest of the brothers.

'I'm here in a personal capacity. We all are. The story is wild even for the movies so brace yourselves.' Victor included Lily in that comment. 'I'm going to let you in on a secret because we need your help.' He then sketched out what had happened since Trace met Diamond in Denver. I noticed that he did not use his persuasive powers, but was trying to convince them with the unvarnished truth. I suppose it would be a violation of human rights to bend someone to your will without overwhelming cause. That's what put Victor on the side of the angels rather than devils like the contessa. She wouldn't have hesitated.

When Victor finished, Steve sat on the sofa with a heavy groan. 'Sorry, guys, but this is all too much to believe. Is this some kind of set up?' He glanced over his shoulder as if expecting a candid camera crew to jump out on him. 'Or a really weird pitch to get me interested in your next movie?'

Saul sat next to him, his wise face a reassurance after the dose of incredible news. 'We couldn't be more serious, Mr Hughes. Not everything in this life revolves about film making.'

'Try living in my world.' Steve gave a self-deprecating laugh.

Lily folded her arms. 'OK, you've just spun us an amazing tale but I take it being a Savant isn't like religion: we don't have to take it on faith. If you have these powers, why don't you prove it to us? Then we can decide if we will help you.'

Victor blinked once then smiled. 'I like this friend of yours, Crystal. She's nobody's fool. OK, who wants to go first?'

Yves stepped forward, hand raised.

'Good idea. Just don't do more damage than we can pay for.' Victor moved back.

'Oh, I wasn't thinking of anything like that.' Yves cupped his hands together and closed his eyes. When he opened them, he had a ball of fire spinning in the space between his palms.

'What the—!' exclaimed Steve, leaping over the back of the sofa.

'Crystal!' squeaked Lily.

I patted her arm. 'It's cool, Lily. Just watch.'

'It is not cool! It is a freaky great big fireball!'

True. Still, I loved watching Yves work. I'd never seen his power at play before. He smiled at Lily, his dark eyes glittering with mischief. The fireball shaped itself into a flower—tall and thin with a trumpet mouth that spat out tiny sparkles. A fire-lily.

'For you,' he said, presenting it to her, letting it hover above his palm.

'I'm convinced—I'm convinced!' Lily ducked behind me.

Yves laughed and let the fire go out. All that was left was the faint scent of smoke like the aftermath of a sparkler.

Steve shook his head. 'How did you do that? I've never seen a special effect like it.'

'Not special effects.' Zed stepped forward. 'It is the power of the mind over natural energy.' The fruit bowl lifted up from the table and began spinning like a flying saucer. Zed directed it towards Steve. The oranges and bananas floated out and began circling the bowl like planets around the sun.

Steve stared very hard at the display, trying to work out how it was done.

'It's real: not a trick,' confirmed Saul. 'Put the bowl down, Zed.'

I could tell by Zed's expression that he would love to hit Steve over the head with the fruit until he was convinced.

Everything in him was crying out to hurry up and save Sky, but this had to be done step by step. We needed a helicopter and our best hope was to get Steve on our side. He would pull more weight with the crew than anyone else. The bowl settled back on the table, the fruit dropping gently in, piece by piece.

Steve lifted up the bowl and then set it back down. 'No wires. Wow. OK. I believe you now. You have awesome powers.'

'But you can see why we don't advertise them to everyone. It would be like you publishing your phone number so any fan can ring you night or day,' said Victor.

'Yeah, I get that too. So this old witch has your women in a fortress, done some weird hypnotism thing on their minds and you need a helicopter?'

'Yes, that's it exactly.'

Steve looked to Lily. 'Am I crazy? I'm thinking of helping these lunatics.'

'I believe them, Steve.' Lily rubbed her hands together. 'It's new territory for me too but I agree that we should do what we can.'

'We would be really grateful.' Excited by this breakthrough, I squeezed Xav's hand. He returned the pressure. 'We can't waste any time with going through official channels—she's done so much damage already.'

Steve gave me an assessing look. 'So what do you do, Crystal, with your mind powers?'

'I . . . er . . . find things.'

He didn't look very impressed by that. I think he would have preferred to find he had been linked, albeit briefly, with someone who blew stuff up or made them fly in the air.

'And your boyfriend there?'

'I heal.'

'Useful. I'd like to know more about this Savant business. You sound like handy friends to have on your side.'

'But right now we need you on ours,' reminded Victor. 'Helicopter?'

Steve dug his phone out of his jacket pocket. 'Consider it sorted.'

'Can you persuade the pilot?'

'Won't be a problem.'

Victor got up. 'I could help—if you hit a snag.'

'I won't. You see, you are looking at your pilot. I have the licence and five years' experience.' He winked at me. 'Got tired of falling short of the action hero image so decided to go make it real.'

A banana bobbed up out of the bowl on a collision course with the back of Steve's head.

'Xav!' cautioned Will.

The banana flipped over and settled in Xav's hand like a gun.

'He really, really bugs me,' he muttered to me.

I snatched the piece of fruit, peeled it and stuffed the end in Xav's mouth. 'But just at the moment, he's our new best friend so play nicely.'

'So what's the plan?' Steve hunched over the map of the area Victor had produced.

'We are working on guesses here as our intelligence from inside the castle is just what Dad and Crystal saw today,' Victor admitted. 'She has our girls but not locked up as they don't know they are prisoners.'

'So the plan is to go in, fetch and get away fast,' said Steve, studying the terrain.

'Yes, but she has her fortress wrapped up pretty tight.'

'I can see that. How close do you want me to get with the helicopter? The noise is going to give us away.'

Will tapped the map. 'I think your pals making movie magic are doing us a favour in that department. Her guards will have got used to the overflight of helicopters setting up the stunt. We can count on them thinking it is just another test. They won't get worried until you put it down right by the front door.'

Steve nodded. 'It might be a good idea to do a couple of dummy runs so if they do look the first time, I can do the "hey I'm a movie star" thing, give them a wave and go on my way. It might annoy them but aside from a phone call to the director, they won't retaliate.'

Saul rubbed his chin. I could tell he was using his gift to sense in what degree of danger we were putting Steve. 'That's an excellent thought, Mr Hughes. Where's your helicopter?'

'On set. I'm not expected to be in it for the close ups until tomorrow. They've got a location camp established on a stretch of flat land near the top of the road. The scene involves me being at the controls, then handing them over to Jessie, my co-star, and jumping out of the door. I'm doing all but the jump.'

'Then what?' asked Xav, his interest snagged by something Steve had said.

'Then I ski down the slope fighting the villains. The stunt guys do that too. They're shooting that next week.'

'Dad . . . ' Xav began.

'No, Xav.' Saul shook his head. 'Too dangerous.'

All the Benedicts seemed to understand what Xav had in mind but I had no clue. 'What's going on?'

'Problem is that, even if we break into the castle grounds, we still have to get close enough to get inside the walls.' Xav pointed to the satellite image of the fortress. 'See that sweet little slope there: it goes all the way down the side of the crag?'

'What? The garden you mean?'

'In summer yes; just now you said it is a snow slope full of obstacles—statues, trees, ponds—ending in the . . . well, just ending.'

'Yes, in a sheer drop—not as severe as up by the fortress I grant you—but a suicidal jump.'

'It's OK: I'll have plenty of time to pull up before I reach that. I can go hide in that copse, then circle back to help you guys.'

'If you're still alive.' Zed batted his brother over the head.

'Why on earth would you want to do that?' I asked aghast.

'He is making himself bait. If he draws enough guards out after him, the rest of us can sneak inside by the back door.'

'If the place has a back door,' said Steve. I had to agree: it didn't look likely.

'It will have because we'll make one: rope over the wall in a dark corner.' Trace pointed to the north-eastern battlement.

No way did I want Xav to be quarry for a bunch of gun-toting guards. 'Can't we come up with another distraction? Blow something up?' I looked to Yves.

'I could but I wouldn't want to risk harming our girls. We don't know exactly where in the fortress they are or how they will react to a crisis in their dazed state. And it would tell the contessa that we had come back to get them.'

Xav nuzzled the top of my head. 'Don't worry, darlin', I move fast on skis. They don't have a hope of catching me.'

'Faster than a bullet? I think not.'

'I won't give them a chance to get off a shot. Besides, I was thinking to present myself to them more like an idiot wanting to get in their face—a drunken friend of our movie star here—skiing through the garden for a dare. I'm hoping they'll just want to thump me, not shoot me.'

'I'd say you've got that character down word perfect, seeing how you act that way all the time,' grumbled Victor.

'It could work,' agreed Steve, really getting into the spirit of the idea. 'If you hang out of the helicopter as I buzz their roof, you can shout and jeer—you know the kind of thing. I can fly drunk, no problem.' He must have seen my face. 'Pretend drunk, honey: I never drink and fly.'

'And while you crazy boys are doing all this, what are the rest of us doing?' asked Lily.

'Steve waits for the signal that we've got the girls, then lands on the turning circle. He then ferries the girls to the set,' said Trace, 'while we make our way back to our vehicles. A clean getaway is key. We'll need some drivers, maybe two vehicles with the engines running, up on set where he keeps the helicopter. We'll have to move fast and get clear of the area as I doubt the local authorities will look kindly on our invasion and I'd prefer not to spend the rest of the night explaining it to them.'

'I drive. I can do that.' Lily rubbed her upper arms, nervous already.

'Are you sure? I mean, you could stay back here and keep out of it.'

'I want to help. I think it would be worse waiting to hear the sirens and besides someone from the movie needs to be there in case your presence is questioned by the security guards.'

'Thanks. That would be great.'

'I will stay with Lily,' volunteered Saul, though with regret. 'I think my best wall climbing days are behind me and I know I can trust you to bring your mother out for me.'

I curled up against Xav as they tossed plans to and fro, feeling more than a bit useless.

'This is madness,' I whispered. 'You've all gone crazy. You sound like you are plotting one of Steve's movies, not a rescue in the real world. I don't want you to do this.'

He was silent for a moment, no doubt weighing up how best to answer me without causing one of our bust ups.

'You're worried about me?'

'Of course! About all of you.'

'You said it yourself: this is the real world, not an action movie. The guards won't start firing real bullets at a little provocation. They'll get pissed with me, chase me maybe, but I'm really good on skis: I'll be gone before they have a chance to strap theirs on. As for the team breaking in, again, if they get caught, they are far more likely to get arrested than harmed.'

'But the contessa has really strong powers. What's to stop her turning on them?'

'They're prepared. They'll keep up their mental shields, which is something you girls did not have a chance to do.'

'I did—I think that's why I was OK. She bowled me over but didn't get inside. I always have shields up—part of surviving in a family of Savants doing telepathy when you can't participate.'

'And I'm extremely thankful that you did.' He bent his head to the curve where my neck met my shoulder, just resting there, breathing in the scent of hair and skin.

'What shall I do while you lot are breaking in? I can't drive—can't ski.'

'I don't suppose there's any chance of persuading you to stay here?'

'Yeah, right.'

'OK. I thought not.'

'I want to stay near you.'

'You could keep Steve company in the helicopter, which would free one of us up to join the rescue. Trace, Zed, and Yves will fetch their girls; Uriel will carry Mom; we need Will and Victor to protect their backs. That way you could be our link—I can send you messages from the others through our bond and you'll know how we are getting on.'

I liked the sound of that: it meant I'd be close enough to help if they ran into trouble. 'OK. I can live with that plan.'

'Hey, guys, Crystal is going to be in the helicopter, keeping Steve in the loop.'

Mr Benedict looked as though he would much rather keep me away from the danger zone but the others all swiftly agreed to the plan.

'Is there anything we've forgotten?' Yves asked as Uriel and Will went ahead to gather their coats and gear from the villa.

'Probably,' said Zed, but he didn't seem too bothered. He was so desperate that fussing over little details just annoyed him. 'Let's stop talking and get going.'

Chapter 13

I elected to join Steve and Lily in their vehicle for the drive up the mountain, which naturally meant Xav came too. It was late. The temperature had plummeted to well below zero. I was grateful for the down-filled jacket Lily had dug out of wardrobe for me. She had kitted me out so that I could pass as Steve's glamorous sidekick if anyone had binoculars trained on the helicopter, hence the shades and designer ski wear.

'Do the crew stay up on set all night?' I asked, wondering how many people we were going to have to talk our way past.

'Some are billeted in a nearby chalet,' explained Steve, 'but most come down to Malcesine for the evening. Only the security guards will still be there. There's too much equipment to leave without someone to look after it.' He negotiated the icy roads with skill, bolstering my faith in his claim to be a decent pilot. In an odd way, I'd say he was enjoying doing something real rather than an act of screen heroism. The pinewoods either side of us were eerily empty—dense shadows under the branches choking off other life. A little higher and the snow began, counteracting nightfall with the glow from the white surface.

'So tell me about this Savant world you are part of—how many of you are there?' Steve asked.

'More than you'd think.' Xav took up the conversation. 'We keep ourselves to ourselves as much as possible as we have gifts that many people would want.'

'Yeah, like you and healing. You could make a fortune.'

Xav stiffened slightly next to me, acting like a cat with his fur rubbed the wrong way. 'I suppose, but it's not about money—or shouldn't be. The reason we keep quiet is that there's too much need and not enough of us to go round. I can't heal everyone so I have to make my own path, do the good that comes my way rather than exhaust myself on a futile attempt to cure the world.'

Steve met Xav's eyes in the driver's mirror. 'You know, the more I hear, the more it does sound like my life. My position gives me power and I have to be careful how I use it. I can only say "yes" to so many good causes or I'd never have time to live. Sounds harsh, but you have to strike a balance.'

Lily checked the map. 'Next left, Steve.'

'Yeah, I know. I've driven this a few times.'

'Still I wouldn't mind a gift like yours,' Lily told Xav. 'It must feel great to be able to make a difference—save lives, cure cancer.'

'Not sure I could go that far—it takes a lot of energy to do a healing and a disease like that is an energy-eater.' Xav was in a sombre mood, not replying with a joke as he normally would. None of us could stop being worried about what had happened to Karla, Diamond, Sky, and Phoenix and that was making him uncharacteristically reflective. 'But the thing is, Lily, though we divide the world up into those with Savant gifts and those without, that isn't really true. You have a gift too—to make things. It's just as worthwhile in its own way.'

Lily turned in her seat to grin at him. 'Aw, thanks. I knew I liked you.'

'It's the Savants who think their skills absolve them from normal rules, such as the difference between right and wrong, that you have to worry about.'

'Like your contessa?'

'Exactly like her—and her son and the other guys we had arrested in London. They have a loose confederation carving up the world into their spheres of influence like they had the right to do so. I'm proud we stopped them.'

'I just hope your ladies aren't paying the price for that,' commented Steve.

The rescue team peeled off at the fork in the road. They were going to stash the vehicle out of sight and go into the grounds through the fence, finding a spot, thanks to Will's gift, where security was least vigilant. Saul followed our car up to the location. The snow-glow lit up the helicopter pad even though evening had fallen in the valley of the Lake. The company had rented a large car park meant for weekend skiers and sectioned it off as hard standing for the production vehicles and aircraft. It was a good thing we had Steve and Lily with us, as the security guards were understandably reluctant to let a convoy of two vehicles invade their patch so late.

'Hey, guys, how's it going?' Steve said breezily.

'All quiet, Mr Hughes,' said the chief guard warily.

'I've just come up to take my friends for a spin in my helicopter. Just going to do some preflight checks—don't let us take you away from your other duties.'

'I wasn't told about this, sir.' The guard checked his schedule.

'It's not official. And it is my helicopter.' Steve let his smile fade, reminding the man subtly just who the mega star here was.

The guard backed down. 'OK, Mr Hughes. It was sprayed with de-icer before the techies left but go carefully now.'

'I intend to.'

Barrier removed to let us through, we drove past the location vehicles to the helipad and parked.

'You brought your own helicopter all the way from the States?' asked Xav.

Steve rubbed his hands together, feeling the nip in the air now the door was open. 'No. I rented it so I could get about without the hassle. Don't worry: it's the same as the one I fly back home.' He strode over to the smallest of the three helicopters, a black Gazelle according to the writing on the tail. Relishing the association with the top box office draw, the hire company had given it a paint job especially for their celebrity client: 'Steve' in large letters down the fuselage. Hmm, subtle.

'Is he for real?' Xav muttered. 'I can't compete with that.'

I burrowed closer to his warmth. 'I wouldn't try. He lives in a world of fictional heroes—that's who he's trying to keep up with; I like mine to be a bit more down to earth.'

'That's a relief. Come on, I think he's ready.'

We got out of the car and joined the others by the Gazelle. I could feel the telepathic messages passing so kept my distance from Mr Benedict.

'OK,' said Saul. 'The boys are through the fence and heading for the back wall. I'm not sure how far the dampening field stretches but they're still outside it.' He paused, listening to the voices winging to and fro. 'Steve, Victor's given me the go-ahead. Buzz the roof a few times then let Xav off in the grounds in full view of the front door. While he's doing that, the boys will go over the back wall as arranged. Xav, you keep in touch so you know when to call off your distraction. Yves will short the alarms and CCTV the moment the guards pursue so that'll add to the confusion. Steve, you circle and wait for Crystal to give you the signal to land. All being well, they'll be packing our girls out and with you before the contessa realizes what's going on.'

'Understood.' Steve rubbed his hands together. 'I'd prefer a few rehearsals but I suppose we'd better make the most of improvisation if things go wrong.'

'I'm afraid you're right. The telepathic link might fail if the contessa thinks to set up a dampener again. In that event, it's essential the girls be taken to safety even if that means letting my boys figure out their own escape route. Agreed?'

Steve nodded.

'Piece of cake,' said Xav.

'Xav, you're the one who is going to be on your own the most,' Saul said. 'Will says to make sure you haul your butt back to the vehicle rendezvous. He doesn't want to have to come looking for you.'

'Tell big brother that he doesn't have to worry about me.'

But I could tell Will and Saul were anxious about Xav's part in this and as they both had a gift for sensing danger, I found it far from reassuring.

'Xavier, you have given me more grey hairs than all my sons put together.' Saul frowned, then corrected himself. 'To be fair, you *and* Zed. Just try not to add to them tonight.'

Xav gave his dad a hug. 'I'll do my best.'

'Let's get this show on the road.' Steve climbed into the cockpit.

Saul helped me into the rear seat. 'Watch your backs, all of you. Karla will never forgive me if any of you get hurt trying to rescue her.'

Xav put his arm around me as we sat in the back to watch our pilot ready the helicopter for take-off. It was a small craft but could carry five passengers at a squeeze. The plan wouldn't have been possible without snow on the ground to guide us—almost as good as landing lights; as it was we were all acutely aware Steve was risking a lot to help.

He's not bad for a self-absorbed movie god, is he? I asked Xav. We had to use my kind of telepathy, about which I was still uncertain, like a kid wobbling on her first two-wheeler bike; but the whine of the engine was so loud, even in the soundproofed cockpit, that normal talk was impossible and Steve would hear us on the microphone in the ear defenders we were wearing.

Hearing you loud and clear, cupcake. Boy, is that one powerful bridge you build. You might need to rein it back a bit.

Sorry.

Don't be sorry. With any luck, it'll bust through any barrier the old witch throws up. As for your guy here, he's bearable as long as he keeps his hands to himself, Xav conceded.

He only kissed me once and it was nothing like yours.

Glad to hear it. He paused. *Mine were better, right?*

I couldn't help teasing to lighten the unbearable tension we were both feeling. *They were different, that's for sure.*

Better different or worse different? His arm tightened around my waist, a warning to go carefully.

I turned into his embrace. *His was kind.*

Kind? Xav turned the word over in his mind. *That doesn't sound very impressive.*

Oh, I was impressed that he cared to shelter me from the press pack.

And?

And what? Wasn't I a little Miss Innocent?

How did it compare to mine? he growled.

His gave me a little thrill I have to admit . . . but yours blew my socks off.

He kissed the space between my eyebrows above the bridge of my nose, urging the memory to stick. *Good. Just you remember that, Crystal Brook. And I can do much better, I promise.*

I bet you can. It's a shame now's not the time to find out.

Yeah, when everyone's safe, you and I have unfinished business to settle.

I suppose we do. I wasn't sure of my moves in this relationship. I know we were meant to be together but that didn't mean I could go straight to being uber-cool about the whole soulfinder thing like Diamond had done.

Sensing my need for reassurance, Xav glanced at Steve but he was too busy flying to pay us any attention. *I'll just take a little instalment now.* He bent down to kiss, warm lips soft against mine. I leant in, kissing him back, trying to use my mouth to say what I hadn't yet admitted: that I loved him and was scared rigid about what he was going to do. As he had on the movie set, he rubbed tiny circles on my spine, a magic touch that melted away the tension. He shifted to hold the back of my neck firmly, taking control of the angle our lips met and I was happy to let him take command. The boy kissed like a champion and I was more than ready to pick up a few tips. For a few seconds I was worried he would notice my clumsiness but then I forgot everything but enjoying the kiss. This wasn't a test I had to pass but a pledge, an exchange of what we felt for each other.

He broke off the kiss. *It's OK—we'll be OK. I'm coming back to you whatever happens tonight.*

I'll hold you to that. Just warning you: I'll kill you if you let any harm come to you.

Excellent. Sweet, moderate response from my understanding soulfinder. Aren't I lucky?

'Hey, lovebirds, you might want to know that we're approaching the castle now,' called Steve through the mikes in our earphones, not sounding that put out that he was playing gooseberry. Probably a nice break for him. 'I'm going in low. Time to cover up so they don't recognize you.'

I pulled on my ski hat and glasses. Xav was already suited up in his ski gear. He put on helmet and goggles, a little awkwardly, as he had to hold the earphones to one side to keep talking to Steve.

Xav scanned the castle grounds, matching it to what he had seen from the satellite image. 'That's a good place to start the run.' He pointed to a terrace outside the ground floor windows of the castle—the same sitting room where we had seen Diamond and the others. 'How low can you get me when you drop?'

'A couple of feet off the ground. No wind to speak of so I won't be battling the elements.'

'I'll throw out the skis first then follow. I'll need a few moments to put them on so if you can use the helicopter to shield me.'

'Will do.'

Be very, very careful, I begged.

With you to come back to? Sure, I'll take care.

'Second approach!' called Steve. 'And yes, Houston, we have their attention. Get ready for inane movie star mode.' We leant to his side and whooped and jeered at the security guard who had emerged from the tunnel to check out the disturbance overhead. 'Grab the champagne, honey. It's behind my seat.'

'Champagne?' I found the bottle in a box at my feet.

He grinned. 'I am Steve Hughes. Got my reputation to think of. Never fly without the Dom Perignon on ice. Crack open the rear window and fire the cork at him. That'll leave him in no doubt as to our intention to be idiots.'

It was an odd moment to realize I'd not opened a champagne bottle before but I'd have to learn quickly—Steve had his hands full and Xav was readying to jump.

'Distraction enough for you, Xav?' Steve asked.

'Perfect. I'll go out the other side.'

Steve circled and began to lower the helicopter as if coming into land on the terrace. The guard raced back into the building, gathered some reinforcements and emerged into the garden.

Steve waved at the reception committee, making the helicopter dip and swing as if the pilot was under the influence. 'Champagne cocktails, anyone?'

I levered off the metal top, surprised that that didn't do the trick of popping the cork.

Give it a twist, Xav said, amused at my incompetence.

I did as he suggested and the cork rocketed out of the window, followed by a spurt of foam. The guards reached for their weapons but then called out in disgust as they saw the champagne pumping over the snow-covered flowerbeds.

A blast of air from behind told me that Xav had made his exit. I bent over Steve's shoulder. 'He's gone.' I turned the gesture into what looked like a kiss on the cheek.

Steve nodded and began a steep bank away from the castle. As we circled I could see Xav straightening up from fixing on his skis.

'Oh no.' No one heard my groan in the noise of the helicopter but I could see Xav doing a little war dance on the terrace, a come-and-get-me-you-losers finger wave. He shouted something at the guards and then pushed himself off, taking the end of the first terrace in a flying jump.

Trace?

Crystal? That's some powerful link you've got there. I could feel Trace rubbing his temples.

Sorry, no time to sort it out. Xav's away. Tell Yves to do his thing.

Will do.

Steve did another circle of the castle. We both watched the little black figure of Xav winding his way through the steep gardens. Two of the guards had disappeared, only to emerge from the garages on the snowmobiles. They jetted off in pursuit, the others watching, the robot butler keeping in touch with a walkie-talkie.

'Your guy is hell on skis!' Steve exclaimed.

He sure was. It was like watching a razor blade slicing through white silk. Xav weaved in and out of an avenue of classical statues, jumped a flight of steps and tucked in low to build up speed for a dash down a narrow hedge-lined path.

'I hope he knows he's got company.' Steve pointed. Knowing the grounds, the snowmobilers were cutting to the end of the run, taking a track down the side of the gardens that avoided the obstacles with which Xav was having such fun.

Hell-on-skis, can you hear me? This is flying cupcake.

Go ahead.

You've two snow monsters meeting you by the summerhouse.

Copy that, FC. How are the others doing?

I switched mind channels and found my bridge to Trace. It was a little fuzzier this time but still working. It proved that my kind of telepathy could beat the contessa's dampening field. *Where are you guys?*

Sky's resisting Victor's attempt to put her to sleep. She may be small but she fights like a tiger. Zed's just trying to catch her. Mom, Diamond, and Phoenix already down. Wait—that's Sky out for the count. Coming to the front.

I tapped Steve's shoulder and gestured that he should land.

Trace suddenly burst back in. *Will's hit. He's hit. The contessa took a shot at us in the hall—some ancient revolver. Get that helicopter down.*

I could see the guards on the terrace turn to the house—they'd heard the gunfire too. Our rescue was slewing off course fast.

Xav, Will's injured. I could see Xav falter then carry on with his slalom. We didn't have enough seats on the aircraft if they were carrying out a casualty. I'd have to get out. 'Steve, we've a ganshot victim and possibly an armed mad woman firing on us from the castle.'

'How bad's the injury?'

'Don't know. Where's the nearest hospital?'

'Other side of the lake.'

That meant miles—and we had the complication of a cargo of brainwashed soulfinders and a pack of guards heading our way. 'We'll need Xav.' This couldn't be happening. *Xav, you'll need to get back to the helicopter. We're going to have to squeeze you in so you can treat your brother.*

Will do. I don't know how he was going to get from the bottom of the hill to the top but he sounded determined.

You'd better have that helicopter down 'cause we're coming out. That was Trace.

My head was reeling with all these different voices and demands. 'Now, Steve!'

Steve dropped the Gazelle in the perfect centre of the turning circle and cut the engines.

What about the contessa? I asked Trace.

Disarmed. Zed used his powers to snatch the gun out of her hand. Here we come.

I opened the helicopter door as I saw them emerge from the archway. Uriel was carrying his mother in a fireman's lift, Trace had Diamond, Yves Phoenix, and Zed followed up with Sky. Last out of the building was Victor who was helping Will.

'I can't take them all.' Steve had come to the same conclusion as me.

'Girls have the seats. Will and Xav on the floor. I'll go with the boys.' I wasn't used to being in command but someone needed to take decisions. I jumped out. 'Xav's heading back.'

Trace placed Diamond in my old seat, his mother next to

her. Once they were buckled in, Yves and Zed did the same for their soulfinders and Trace knelt to put a rudimentary bandage on Will's shoulder, keeping up the pressure to stop the bleeding.

'Lay him on the floor,' I suggested.

'Got company!' bit out Steve, pointing to the butler and his men. They were racing towards us from the archway.

Zed threw out his arm and the ancient portcullis started to creak and grind. Yves clapped a hand on Zed's shoulder, joining in the attempt. It was slowly descending but not in time to stop the man at the front. Uriel punched his fist at two nymph statues either side of the terrace steps. They toppled on top of the butler like a couple of Steve's swooning fans.

'Where's Xav when you want him?' muttered Victor, emerging from the helicopter having wadded up a blanket to put under Will's head.

'I'm going to have to get this baby airborne,' warned Steve. 'If they decide to use those guns of theirs on us, I don't want to take a bullet to the fuel tank.'

It was hardly as if Xav was dragging his feet. 'He's coming,' I snapped. *Xav where are you?*

I got the impression of fists flying. He had tackled one of the men off their snowmobile—the one built like a barn who had given me a lift earlier. *With you—in a—moment.* Using his ski to swipe the second man off his snowmobile, he jumped on the back and headed up our way, leaving the drivers rolling in a drift. *Got two following me—warn my brothers.*

'Xav's coming in but he's not alone. He's taken a snowmobile and the two men are chasing him on the other one.' We could hear the engines now roaring up the hill.

'Crystal, get under cover over there!' ordered Trace, pointing to the trees lining the drive.

Knowing better than to argue when an operation like this

was under way, I ran for the pines. The five Benedict brothers knelt around the helicopter, ready to defend it from any direction. The 'whomp!' of an explosion in one window of the castle told me Yves had just deterred a guard from taking aim from an upper storey. I felt the pressure of rapidly expanding air on my back so dived off the driveway, rolling to hide behind the nearest tree. I looked over to the castle and saw that fire was now licking the curtains at one window. Hopefully that would divert some of the castle servants from coming after us.

A snowmobile shot into the turning circle. Xav leapt from the back and bolted for the helicopter. Victor swapped with him, taking control of the snowmobile. Xav jumped inside and Steve took off the moment the door was closed. I breathed a sigh of relief. He was safe, so were Will and the other passengers. Now all that remained was to get the rest of us out of here.

Chapter 14

From the sick feeling in my stomach, I guessed the telepathic messages between the brothers were flying thick and fast. I crouched down, head on my knees. Now was not the time to get overcome by my weakness. Zed and Yves jumped down beside me.

'You hurt?' Zed asked, hand on my back.

'No.' I took a deep breath. 'Telepathy. I'll manage.'

'Do your sort to us and we'll keep the rest to a minimum,' Yves suggested. Their attention was pulled back to the turning circle. Victor was gunning his snowmobile directly at the guys coming up the hill. 'Oh, for the love of . . . what is he doing now?'

Zed gave a wicked smile. 'I think big brother is a bit angry.'

'Jeez—take cover, everyone.'

The air was humming with power.

'What's going on?' I asked. I could feel it—the hair on the back of my neck was prickling—but I knew I was not in its path, whatever 'it' was.

'Our Vick's pushing a mental snowplough in front of him,' said Zed. 'Those guys are going to run right into one hell of a primal scream.'

Yves's normally gentle face looked quite viciously pleased—payback for Phoenix. 'You really don't want to get on the wrong side of Victor.'

I could feel the impact when the snowmobile topped the rise and ran straight into Victor's mental barrier. The man on steering threw his hands up to cover his face and toppled back, taking the passenger behind with him. The snowmobile veered round in a circle and smashed into the plinth holding a sundial.

Yves pulled me up. 'That's our signal to move.' He led the way, Zed following up behind me, guarding our retreat.

Where are we going? I asked Yves, projecting myself into his head by the fainter trail of our newly developing friendship.

He checked a pace. *Wow, that's weird.*

OK, I do telepathy differently. Get over it.

Sorry. I sensed rather than saw him grin. *Over the fence and back to the car. We're expecting the police to arrive any second to help their poor little old contessa against these American house-breakers.*

She shot at you!

Self-defence.

She had our people hostage!

And they were perfectly happy there. There was a pause. *You can do something for them, can't you, Crystal? You're a soulseeker—you can find them if they've lost their bonds with us?*

I ducked under a branch, keeping in his footsteps. *The truth? I have no idea but I'm certainly going to try.*

Zed and I . . . Desperate to have Phoenix back, Yves wanted to beg, plead for me to do it but he knew he was asking the impossible so I felt him change his mind about what he was going to say. *We understand. You mustn't blame yourself if you can't. None of this is your fault.*

That made me only all the more determined to succeed. *There must be a way—and I won't stop until I find it.*

We reached the boundary fence: tall and forbidding, it looked as if the suffering serfs of the Count of Monte Baldo had laid the stones centuries ago.

Er, Yves.

What's the matter?

You've never seen me in the gym classes at school.

'Zed, cupcake here needs a boost.'

'Cupcake?' I was going to murder Xav.

'Sorry. Xav's been going on and on about you, it's kind of hard to shift his voice from my head.'

Right on cue, I heard Xav launch his message to me like a meteor falling into my personal atmosphere.

Where the hell are you, cupcake? You were supposed to be safe on the helicopter.

His voice was so loud with outrage I stumbled.

'You OK, Crystal?' asked Zed, taking my arm.

'Xav is not pleased with me.'

'Tell him to butt out. We're rescuing ourselves here.' Zed yanked the rope they'd thrown over the stone wall to check it was still secure.

Count the seats, Xav. It was me or Will and you. How is he?

Working on him now. We're using Steve's Winnebago dressing room as our ER. Bullet caught him high on the right shoulder.

Concentrate on that. I'll be out of here shortly.

Uriel, Victor, and Trace emerged from the trees, coming from a slightly different direction to the one we had taken. Now we were all gathered, Zed swarmed up the rope and dropped down out of sight. This was going to be so humiliating. I was slowing everyone down.

'You next, Crystal,' said Trace, doubtless wondering why I was staring at the rope as if it were a python dangling before my eyes.

I jumped, hauled myself a few metres up, felt my arms give

and I dropped back to the ground. I tried again and this time only succeeded in banging against the wall like an incompetent bell ringer lifted off the floor by her rope.

'I'm sorry: I can't do it. I've never aspired to be an action hero, never developed the upper body strength for more than lifting my coffee cup.'

Trace climbed the rope as nimbly as a monkey. 'Vick, tie the rope around her.'

Sweet of them not to tease as I was hauled up the side like a sack of potatoes. Tears of fury at my own incompetence stung my eyes but I was too annoyed to allow them to fall. I swiped them away instead.

'Sorry,' I muttered when I reached the top.

'It's OK, Crystal.' Trace untied the rope and threw it back down to the next brother. 'Can you manage now?'

I swallowed as I glanced at the hefty drop. Fortunately the snow had piled up against the wall so there was a soft landing. 'Sure. I'm a ninja. Just didn't want to embarrass you all.' Doing an ungainly bottom shuffle on the ledge, I took the rope leading over the other way and half-fell half-let myself down. I landed with a jolt on my butt in the snow. Zed plucked me out of my hole and gave me a hug.

'Ninja, hey?'

'You heard that?'

'We all heard that. Must tell Xav.'

'I'll kill you if you tell him how I let you down.'

'You haven't let us down, Crystal. You're doing fine.'

His brothers dropped lightly beside us—each elegant landing a reproach for all those PE lessons I'd avoided. All six of us were now gathered outside the castle grounds and I began to feel a little less anxious.

'Dad says Will's going to be OK,' Trace reported. 'Lily's taking him to hospital by road—Xav's with them—and Dad's taking the girls to the villa with Steve. Asks us to meet him there.'

The car was parked just down the track, hidden behind a tangle of brambles. We piled in. I had to practically sit on Trace's lap to fit. Uriel reversed and headed back to the main mountain road.

'Phee looked OK, didn't she?' Yves asked his brothers.

'Yes, they were all fine—on the surface at least,' confirmed Uriel.

'Sky can sure fight,' added Victor admiringly. 'She wasn't going to let me encourage her to fall sleep when she didn't want to.'

'Probably saw your colours—knew you were fibbing when you said you just wanted to check she didn't have a fever.' Zed tapped the window beside him restlessly, itching to get back to her.

Victor shrugged. 'That sleep message works best when I can touch someone's forehead.'

'Surprised Mom let you get away with it,' said Uriel. 'She hasn't fallen for that since you were ten.'

'Yeah, but she didn't remember, did she? Didn't know any of us.'

No one had anything to say to that.

The road wound to the right, coming in sight of the fork in the road. A police car was parked across, blocking our exit, blue lights flashing against the sentinel pine trees.

'Suggestions?' asked Uriel lightly. 'Vick?'

Victor shook his head. 'Can't manipulate their minds. Too many—and it wouldn't be right. They're just doing their job.'

'Then we stop and talk politely.' Uriel slowed. 'Things not to mention, guys: our girls, Steve and Lily, anything to do with the castle. We've just been for a moonlit drive.'

A policeman stood in the centre of the road and raised his hand. Uriel wound down his window as he drew alongside.

'Problem, officer?'

Yes, there certainly was a problem, as the man explained in rapid-fire Italian as his colleagues surrounded the car, me as his translator. They were all to get out and consider themselves under arrest. No, he wasn't impressed by Victor's and Trace's law enforcement credentials: this was Italy not America. No, we were not to talk to each other. The only phone call we would be allowed now would be to our lawyers.

So he didn't know about telepathy then.

The charges? Breaking and entering the contessa's castle. Assaulting her staff. Arson.

Lined up along the side of the vehicles we were patted down. No weapons or even a match were discovered. One by one the brothers were handcuffed and put in the back of a police van. I was left standing on the roadside. I could see that the Benedicts were far from happy to leave me alone with Italian police officers.

'What about me?' I asked the man in charge, a hard-faced public servant who looked sincerely tired of dealing with out-of-control tourists, the main source of crime in this holiday destination.

'You, signorina? You are not under arrest.' He signalled for the van doors to be closed. 'Those men we know about but the contessa said nothing about a young female being present at the time of the break-in.'

It would be foolish in the extreme to talk myself into being arrested. 'Where are you taking them?'

'My police station is not big enough for so many. I expect they'll be transferred to Verona in the morning. You can call the station at eight when the office staff go on duty. I would like you to come in and give us a statement. They will tell you then where your friends have been taken.' He headed for his vehicle, leaving me alone with our car. The keys were still in the ignition where Uriel had left them.

'But, signor, I can't drive!'

He looked sorely tempted to abandon me there. 'Officer Fari will drive you down to the station and park the vehicle there. You can send someone to collect it in the morning.'

I could feel Yves tapping on my mind, having worked out how to reverse the mental pathway I had built to him.

I'm OK. I assured him. *One of the policemen is driving me back to Malcesine. Worry about yourselves.*

I'll tell Dad what's happened. You tell Xav, OK?

OK. Not a conversation I was looking forward to.

Just tell him not to do anything stupid, like get arrested alongside us. He needs to stick with Will.

There was a spurt of radio noise from the officer's receiver. I deciphered the message amid the static. *I think it's too late. The contessa knew they'd be heading to a hospital. Xav's been picked up already. Lily and Will are continuing to the hospital under guard.*

Yves swore. *Any news of Dad?*

No one has mentioned him—or Steve. If they thought a Hollywood star was under suspicion, surely that'd be flying across the airwaves? I think the contessa is just not interested in him—like she disregards me.

I suppose we should be grateful for that. We'll see you soon as we raise bail. Do your best with the girls.

'Ready to go, signorina?' Officer Fari, a man in his early twenties and more disposed to be friendly than his boss, had noticed my 'out to lunch' expression.

I ran my fingers over my forehead. 'Sorry. I've had a bit of a shock.'

He nodded. 'Let's get you home then.'

I climbed in the passenger side and watched him familiarize

himself with the controls. We slowly set off after the police car. The van had long since departed.

'What were you doing out here, signorina?' the officer asked. The implication was why was a nice girl like me hanging out with five suspicious characters?

'Just taking in the sights. One of them is my future brother-in-law.' *Xav, are you all right?*

No. I felt rather than heard his cursing. *They wouldn't let me stay with Will. Apparently I'm under arrest for assaulting the contessa's guards. They are taking me to join my brothers. What about you?*

Not under arrest—not yet. A policeman is driving me down the mountain and then I'm going to meet up with your dad. Yves is confident you'll all make bail but I'm not so sure. The contessa is a powerful person round here.

Know any good lawyers?

I'll get on to it.

What would help most is getting our girls back. None of this makes sense unless they can testify that they were kidnapped.

I suddenly felt immeasurably drained. Would this horrible day never end?

Not so horrible. You found me, remember?

Yeah, and you're ending it in jail. Way to go, soulfinder.

Love you too.

How was that a declaration of love?

Wasn't it? I could feel that Xav was amused, despite everything. *You can't hide the fact that you care what happens to me.*

Of course I care!

See. Love you too.

OK fine, you're right. I love you, you infuriating menace who promised me that he would come back. I warned you that I'd kill you if you didn't.

I look forward to it.

I don't want to spend the best part of my life visiting you in jail.

Crystal, there ain't no jail that can hold the Benedicts when we put our minds to it.

Nor do I want to spend it on the run from the law.

Aw, you, me, obscure tropical island: what's not to like? He projected a picture of him in Hawaiian print shorts and me in a grass skirt and a strategically placed garland of flowers. I could feel my cheeks heat.

Xav!

What? he asked all too innocently.

You're embarrassing me, you muppet!

I can't help your imagination, darlin'.

I shot back a picture of me, fully clothed, placing a boot on his rear and propelling him into a rock pool.

Yeah, that could work for me too.

The boy was . . . what was that word my old teachers loved? Incorrigible.

Why, thank you, fair maiden. I take that as a compliment.

'Are you sure you are all right, signorina?' asked the officer, perplexed by my silence.

'Fine. Just upset.' *Got to go, Xav. My driver is getting suspicious. Speak soon. Over and out.*

'Don't worry: if they've done nothing wrong, they'll soon be free,' said Officer Fari cheerfully. 'I can't see my chief wanting to keep so many American visitors locked up. Not good for tourism and, in this financial climate, I can't see that being popular with the local authorities.'

He was a kind man, this officer. 'Thanks. I'll hope for the best then.'

'Then again, if they are guilty, you might want to keep your distance.' He turned into the police car park. 'You wouldn't want to find yourself dragged into a tussle with the contessa in the courts. Her cousin is the chief prosecutor around here.'

With that sobering assessment, I hurried back to the villa we had spent so little time in that afternoon. The lights were blazing, confirming that Saul and Steve had already arrived back, hopefully still with the girls. I rang the bell. Saul answered and at first said nothing, just pulled me into a wonderful, all-encompassing hug.

I realized then how much I missed my father, but an embrace from Saul was not a bad substitute.

Chapter 15

'Is everything OK here?' I asked, struggling with the sense of loss like a pedestrian controlling an umbrella on a windy day. I couldn't let my emotions go metaphorically inside out—not now.

'As well as can be expected. Come on in.' He stood back. I took off my jacket and boots and entered the living room. Karla, Diamond, Sky, and Phoenix sat in a little group up one end; Steve hovered by the door in case they made a break for freedom. I wondered what was going through his head. His life was doubtless strange, what with being a movie star, but I would bet he had never spent a night like this before.

'Crystal's back,' Saul said with forced cheerfulness.

Diamond's eyes turned to me, chillingly cold. 'We met this afternoon, I believe.'

I nodded. It hurt to feel her utter rejection of me but I knew she wasn't to blame.

Karla stood up, placing herself in front of the other three, mother bear protecting her cubs. 'I don't know what you think you are doing, Mr Bennett . . .'

A muscle in Saul's cheek ticked, the only sign he betrayed

of his pain. 'Karla, I'm Mr Benedict. You are Mrs Benedict. You're my wife.'

She waved that away. 'I don't know what planet you are living on, *Mr Benedict*, but I demand you let us go immediately. We were enjoying such a lovely weekend with our friend, the contessa. I can't imagine what possessed you to carry us out unconscious! I'll be reporting you to the police.'

I dipped into my power to see what had happened to her soulfinder bond. It was like the mind of the butler all over again; everything that made her unique was spinning around like a mad carousel, or perhaps in this state, a swarm of bees. I couldn't penetrate that cloud, couldn't get near to see if the essence remained within the cloud.

'Mr Benedict.' Diamond stepped forward past Karla. I could feel she was exerting her peace-making powers on us. 'I'm not sure what drove you to do what you did, but surely you can see this is wrong? We would appreciate it if you would just step away from the door and let us go.'

I slumped in a chair, fighting off despair. My power compared to the contessa's was like a fly going into battle against Godzilla. 'Go where, Di? The contessa is nothing to you. I'm your sister. We share a flat in Venice, remember? Do you mean to go there?'

Diamond looked at me as if I were a puzzle she couldn't solve. 'Sorry? A flat? In Venice? I know I have a flat inherited from my grandmother, but I don't remember you.'

'Yes, our nonna.' Something clung on to the wreck of her mind. 'So what about Mum? Silver, Steel, Topaz, Peter, and Opal? Your nieces are currently making themselves sick with excitement because they are expecting to be your bridesmaids at your wedding to Trace next weekend. If you don't believe me, phone Misty.'

'Misty?'

'Your niece. She's fifteen and she wouldn't lie to you as her gift means she has to tell the truth.'

'I remember Misty but she's only little. I can't be getting married. I have no idea what you are talking about. Stop it, stop it!' Diamond put her hands over her ears and sat down on the settee.

Steve put a comforting hand on my shoulder. 'It's no good, Crystal: they really can't recall anything about the people in their lives, not from the last few years at least. Saul's been talking to them since they woke up and got nothing but this.' He gestured to the defensive postures of the four women. Putting myself in their shoes, I guess I knew why they were like that: they'd woken up in a strange place with 'strangers' around them. At the moment they only knew each other.

But their powers were still functioning. That gave us a chink in their armour that we could use.

'OK, let's try this.' A little energy returned to me as I grasped my new strategy. 'Sky, you can sense a fib by watching my colours. Is that right?'

Sky nodded, her blue eyes suspicious. Good for you, girl, I thought. I don't want you to trust me; I want you to trust yourself.

'Watch everything I say. Phoenix, you can glimpse my thoughts?'

Phoenix glanced at Sky. 'I can. How do you know?'

'We've talked before but you don't have access to that memory. That's not important right now. Without doing your time-stopping thing, just see what I'm saying. Will you do that?'

Phoenix gave a curt nod.

'OK, here goes. Your minds have been tampered with by the contessa.' I held an image of the disastrous end to the hen party in my head. 'Is what I am saying true?'

Sky bit her lip. 'You believe it.'

That would do. 'Diamond is my sister.' I thought of all the years we had together, images of her playing with me as a little girl and her, the glamorous older sister; our recent history of flat sharing. 'Phee, am I right?'

'Yes, I can see she's been part of your past.' Phoenix folded her arms across her chest, brow wrinkled in thought.

Sky took Diamond's hand. 'She is your sister. She's not lying.'

OK. That was the easy part. 'Do you know what a soul-finder is?'

'Of course,' said Diamond. 'We are all Savants.' She was now looking at me with a kind of aching desire in her eyes to remember me, willing the barriers in her mind to fall.

'So am I. So is Saul.'

'And Mr Hughes here?' Karla pointed to Steve. 'I suppose he's one too?'

'No.' Just a superstar. 'He's . . . our friend.'

Steve held up his hand. 'Ma'am, I haven't known these guys long but I can say that they are good people. Please trust them. That old witch up the mountain has screwed with your minds.'

'Thanks, Steve. Now, please try to follow this very carefully. You were taken because you are the soulfinders of the Benedict men. The contessa wanted revenge for your part in the arrest and disgrace of her son in London earlier this year.'

Sky's face drained of all colour. 'She's telling the truth—every word.'

'Karla, your soulfinder is right in this room.' Saul went on his knees before his wife and took her hand. 'I'm here.' He pressed her palm against his chest. 'Every beat of my heart has been for you since the first day we met.'

Something in Karla snapped: she went from stiff spine to collapse in a second. Reaching out to touch his cheek, she asked plaintively:

'So why can't I remember you?'

Tears brimmed in Saul's eyes. 'Because your memories have been stolen.' He kissed the inside of her palm. 'We're going to try to reverse it but I swear to you, Karla, that even if we can't, we'll make new ones. We'll start again. I can't live without my soul.'

Sky curled up on the settee next to Diamond. 'Who's mine?' Her voice seemed to be coming from a very scared place deep inside.

'Zed. He carried you out of the castle.' I had to keep this simple for her. 'He's amazing—really devoted to you.'

'And me?' asked Phoenix. Her tone was angry. Good.

'Yves. You are going to love him all over again when you meet him, believe me. You're married.'

'I'm what? But I can't be more than eighteen!'

'My son was very persuasive,' said Saul proudly.

'And me?' Diamond held out a hand to me. 'Crystal, isn't it?'

I knew she hadn't remembered but was just checking she got my name right. 'Yes, Di. You're my big sister—you've been looking after me since Dad died.'

She closed her eyes. 'I remember him. The contessa didn't take that from me but I don't recall him dying.' A tear slid down her cheek. I could kill the contessa for making her go through her grief again!

'You remember the earlier stuff before he died probably because your memories are nothing to do with Trace, your soul-finder. I guess she took anything that has brushed up against the fact that you are getting married next Saturday, including me because I was there when you met.'

'How can I get married?' Her question was not one which asked for an answer. Yes, it did seem impossible right now. The girls might have accepted our version of the truth but none of them were fully themselves. The spark had been snuffed leaving a hollowed-out candle behind.

'What are we going to do?' Sky asked but I was relieved to see her question now included all of us in the room.

Saul stood up. 'One of our sons is in hospital, Karla; the others are in jail. We can't leave Will alone. He was stable when Lily drove him to hospital but I can't bear the thought of him lying there without a member of the family with him.'

'My son's in hospital?' Karla shuddered.

'Will. Your fourth son. The contessa shot him.'

Karla sprang up out of her chair. 'Saul Benedict, what are we doing here if he needs us?'

Saul smiled. 'Now you sound like Karla. Steve, Crystal, can you help with the others?'

'We'll look after them,' promised Steve. He checked his watch. Two in the morning. 'I guess we should get some sleep now and go to the station as soon as possible in the morning. I'm sure the movie company will know a good lawyer or two.'

'Movie company?' asked Diamond shrewdly.

'Steve's an actor in films,' I explained. 'Steve Hughes.'

'No!' Phoenix's eyes rounded in surprise. 'I know you—I've seen your films. You're amazing. God, it's so good to remember something normal.'

He gave her a salute. 'Glad I could be of help.'

'I just didn't expect you to be here. You're not as tall as I thought.'

'I think you'd better stop there, Phoenix,' I warned. 'Steve has been a total star tonight and we don't want to crush his ego now.'

Karla had momentarily been sidetracked by the news that

their rescue had been more bizarre than she had dreamed; now she returned to her priority. 'Mr Benedict—Saul. You have a car and directions?'

Saul patted his pocket. 'Yes, dear.'

'Then let's go. Diamond, look after the girls for me.'

My sister nodded. 'I will.'

Steve got out his phone. 'I'll just text Lily and let her know you're on the way. She says he's still in theatre but should be out soon. The doctors are surprised that the wound was beginning to heal so soon after the trauma.'

'Xav's doing,' explained Saul, helping his wife into her coat. 'Your fifth son is a healer. He's Crystal's soulfinder.'

'A healer? How lovely.'

The door closed on their conversation.

'I have to say this is the strangest night of my life.' Steve gave me a hug; somewhere during the adventure we had moved from being chance acquaintances to tried and tested best mates. 'would you like me to stay or go back to my hotel?'

'I think we'll be OK now. Can you be back at seven thirty?'

Steve grimaced. 'James isn't going to like that but, hey, what's the point of being me if you can't ask for a delay in a shoot from time to time. I'll get Lily to tell him.'

I had a sudden flash of insight. Steve might not be a Savant but his brain wasn't so different from ours and a lot of his attention was given to the little blonde costume designer.

'You know, you should ask her out.'

'Who?' He tried to look innocent.

'Lily. She's your best friend, isn't she?'

'I . . . I suppose.'

I tapped my temple. 'I do have a gift and it's telling me that she's the one for you.'

Steve looked as if I'd just taken a plank to the back of his head. 'How do you know about that?'

'As my friend would say, it's my special spidey sense.' *Xav, I wish you were here for this.*

What's that, Crystal? I got a glimpse of a concrete cell and a hard bed. The boys had been processed and locked up for the night.

I'm matchmaking. Steve and Lily.

Yeah . . . yeah, that'd work. Anything to get rid of my rival. How are the girls?

On our side but not yet recovered their memories.

Well done.

'Crystal.' Steve snapped his fingers in my face. 'I'm talking to you.'

'Sorry. Can't do this telepathy thing without checking out of the here and now. You and Lily—it's obvious. You've just not gone there because your publicist has been running your life and Lily's too real.' I remembered what he had said about liking meeting people who did something proper, made stuff with their hands; that comment took on a whole new meaning. 'She may not buff up your image but from where I stand, I doubt you need much buffing.'

He gave me a sheepish grin. 'Crystal, if you weren't already spoken for, you'd be in danger of being on my list too.'

'Yeah, but I'm way down there after Lily. She'll be good for you—keep your ego in check.'

He zipped up his jacket. 'I'll give it some thought.'

'You're just worried she'll turn you down.'

'No!' He sighed. 'Yeah. She knows me, you see.'

'A life of bimbos in awe of you or a real woman who sees through the razzmatazz? I rest my case, m'lud.'

'Jeez, you're sharp. I hope Xav's got some good defensive moves.'

'Believe me, he gives as good as he gets.'

With a nod to the others in the room, Steve left for his hotel, hopefully in the right frame of mind to download his weird experience on to Lily—forging another link between them.

The girls were looking at me with quizzical expressions.

'Have you always been like this?' Diamond asked.

'Like what?'

'Does my sister sass movie stars and order them about?'

I had been doing that, hadn't I? 'Not until today.'

I showed the three of them where they could sleep but I doubt if any of us got much rest that night. I could hear sobs from Sky's room and Phoenix's voice murmuring comfort. Diamond was trying to be strong for us all but I could feel she was suffering in the bed next to mine.

'I'll sort this out, Di. I promise,' I whispered.

'Crystal, I may not remember yet, but I want you to know that you are the best sister anyone could have. Thank you for coming to rescue me.'

I hugged the compliment close. 'Anytime you need me, I'll be there.'

Chapter 16

The next morning, Steve and I accompanied Diamond, Sky, and Phoenix to the police station so we could make our statements together. None of them had wanted to keep on the old lady clothes the contessa had given them. Wearing jeans, jumpers and T-shirts borrowed from Lily, the girls seemed subdued, still piecing together what they could from their memories.

'It's like trying to make a whole cloth from cobwebs,' confided Diamond as we followed the others along the sunny pavement edging the lakeside. A chill wind ruffled the grey-blue water; pastel-painted villas made a cheerful frill to those cold depths. 'Threads kept pulling away leaving great holes where there should be, I don't know,' she sighed, 'just much more stuff.'

'Trace sends his love.' Xav and I had had a long talk that morning. His brothers were keen to use me as their intermediary but he was being strict with them not to weigh me down with too many messages. Their priority was to get bail so they could see if something could be salvaged face-to-face now the girls understood who they were to them.

'That's sweet of him. But what if I never remember him?'

'Then you'll have to start again, like Saul told Karla.' One of us had to resist the sheer panic that threatened at that prospect.

'Yet how can I live with him if the soulfinder bond is only one way? It's like I've lost a limb and keep trying to walk on it.'

'People survive extraordinary things, Di. You'll get through this.'

The police station was in a bright yellow building that looked more like a primary school than the local centre of law and order. Only the discreet sign 'Carabinieri' on the black gate attested to its more serious function. Having a movie star with us certainly helped get us seen: no waiting around in reception; we were ushered straight into the interview room. Overnight, Trace's and Victor's contacts had been working behind the scenes and the report of missing persons in Venice tied together with the rescue. It certainly helped our case having Diamond giving a clear account of how her hen night had turned ugly, mainly gleaned from what I had told her as her own recollection was missing. She could give no information as to who had carried out the kidnapping, other than asserting that the contessa had been present in Venice and at the castle and that Diamond had had no desire to go there, having planned to spend all her time preparing for her wedding at home.

'You were held against your will?' asked the officer. It was the same man as the one who had arrested the brothers the night before: Inspector Carminati, according to the label on his door.

Diamond frowned. 'It is hard to say exactly what happened. I believe something was given to us to make us cooperate.'

'A drug?'

'Perhaps.' This was the closest she could get to explaining why she and the others had appeared before many witnesses to be contented guests of the old lady.

'We should arrange a blood test then.' The officer made a note. 'That's if there are any traces left in your system. Mr Hughes, what is your part in this?'

I translated the question for Steve.

'I was just helping my friends here rescue the ladies from the castle.' Steve folded his arms, betraying not a hint of regret for his part in the adventure.

'Why did you not stop to ask us to intervene?'

That was the million dollar question, wasn't it? So much of this didn't make sense unless we exposed the Savant dimension, which we were reluctant to do to any but the senior officers in international law enforcement who were already aware of our existence on a strictly confidential basis. Unfortunately, most of those were in Rome and had very little influence here in the north.

Steve shrugged. 'It was the fastest way to resolve the situation.'

'The contessa has not complained that you trespassed in your helicopter so I am not going to press any charges but, let me tell you, Mr Hughes: in Italy, we do not like vigilantes who take the law into their own hands. This is not one of your movies.'

Steve looked supremely unimpressed. 'No, what this is, is much weirder. You need to lock that old woman up—she's totally out of control.'

I chose not to translate that particular comment. 'He says thanks and that he understands.'

The officer had more English than he let on for he sniffed scornfully at my very free interpretation of Steve's words. 'If the local mayor wasn't so impressed by having a film made in his area, I would not hesitate to send your friend packing, celebrity or no celebrity.'

I gave him a helpless smile as if to say, what could I, a mere girl, do to rein in an A-lister?

'There is clearly more to this situation than I understand.' The officer tapped his papers straight. 'I can't, however, do anything further for you as your associates are already on the way to Verona where they are going to be interviewed and where they can apply for bail. If this is granted, they may be out by this evening.'

'What about Will Benedict?'

'The one in hospital?'

I nodded.

'He is also considered under arrest but matters are complicated by the excessive force used against him. We're looking into that. I suggest his name be included in the bail application.'

'What about the allegation of kidnap?'

'One step at a time, signorina. We need evidence to support that. So far we only have witnesses to testify that your sister and her friends were willing guests and appeared to arrive under their own volition. It was the forceful departure carried over the shoulders of their family members that was suspect.'

'But can't you see that it doesn't add up? They don't know the contessa—why would they want to stay with her and ignore their own family? She abandoned me on an island in the lagoon, for heaven's sake! I was lucky not to get hypothermia.'

His hard face softened for a moment. 'You have a witness to that?'

I remembered the banker from Milan. 'Yes! I've left his business card back in Venice. A very respectable witness. He said we were to contact him if we needed his statement.'

'Then I suggest you do that. But in Venice. The contessa has already returned to her home there as her castle is damaged by fire. If a crime was committed against you, it appears that was where it took place. There is little point pursuing it with me.'

I hadn't been expecting that suggestion, or his tone. 'So you believe me? I thought you'd side with her.'

Inspector Carminati stood up, signalling the end of the interview. 'I may be only a policeman in an obscure corner of this country, but I am not an idiot, Signorina Brook. I too read the papers. If these men were part of the operation that brought about the arrest of the Count of Monte Baldo as you claim, then I can imagine that his mother might be out for revenge. We all know the count around here—he has always been bad news. I'm not surprised justice finally caught up with him.'

'So you'll . . .'

He held up his hand, interrupting me. 'Whatever my personal thoughts may be on the subject, we must obey the law. So far the only offences that have been substantiated with anything approaching evidence are those committed by the Benedicts. I suggest you hurry up and prove that they had a sound reason for their actions.'

We left the office to find Lily and James Murphy waiting for us in reception.

'Lord Almighty, Steve, what have you got yourself mixed up in?' the director fumed. 'We have the press camped out there. One whiff of Steve Hughes visiting a police station and they're arriving in their droves. Not to mention what you've done to my shooting schedule.'

'Calm down, James,' said Lily, patting the Irishman on the chest to remind him to get a hold of himself before he had a coronary. 'Everything all right, Steve?'

The actor held out his arms. 'I need a hug.'

Blushing slightly, Lily obliged. At least something had been settled last night then.

'W . . . what?' James shook his head as the two exchanged a kiss. 'I won't ask.'

'Crystal and her family need to get back to Venice.' Steve dug out his sunglasses, preparing to avoid the cameras. 'Can we provide a driver?'

'Yes. But you are staying here, aren't you?' asked James suspiciously.

'For the moment. I don't think I can do anything but attract unwelcome publicity to them. Is that OK, Crystal?'

'More than OK. You've been amazing. A real hero.'

Steve gave a self-mocking grin. 'Nice to know I do have it in me.'

Lily squeezed his waist. 'I'm proud of you.'

'We'll go out the back way.' James made some rapid arrangements on his phone. 'I'll get my driver to help take Crystal and her friends home.' Poor James was hurrying to get me out of Steve's orbit as I was so clearly a disruptive element. 'You, my dear movie star, have got to get your butt up the mountain and do the stunt before the weather changes.'

Steve slipped his hand into Lily's back pocket; she put hers in his. 'Thanks, James. And sorry about this. Lily and I will explain on the way up—but I warn you, you aren't going to believe a word.'

The director groaned. 'Just tell me I'm not facing an expensive law suit.'

'I hope not.'

'Is there someone I can shoot for this?'

'That's already been done—and it's not a joking matter.'

James wagged his finger at me. 'Crystal, remind me why I ever let you near my film?' He wasn't really upset with me, just exasperated by the situation into which I had dragged him.

'Because I was tall, Mr Murphy.'

'From now on, Murphy,' he muttered, ushering us out of the rear door, 'do not work with children, animals, or tall girls.'

Rio d'Incurabili, Dorsoduro, Venice

The wedding dress had been delivered while we were away. Signora Carriera had taken it from the messenger for Diamond and hung it up in her room so that it was the first thing my sister saw when she got home.

'Oh my God.' She sat on the bed, staring at it. 'I can't wear that.'

'It's beautiful, Di. Give yourself a few days. The wedding isn't until Saturday and we might have sorted you out by then.' I brushed the lace overskirt reverently: it was fabulous. I wanted her to feel wonderful wearing it, not this desperate, empty person who couldn't recall any of the most important people in her life.

'Will you phone Mama and the others for me? I wouldn't know what to say.' She cleared her throat. 'I mean, I don't even know what they are really like, do I?'

'Yes, I'll do that.' I took the phone out to the garden to make the call. Telling Mama that her golden girl had lost so many memories was one of the most difficult conversations I'd ever had. Our mother leapt to the conclusion that it had to be my fault because I had organized the hen party. I don't think she really grasped the seriousness of what had happened to her daughter and was seeing it as an extension of the embarrassment I had caused ending up in the papers with Steve. I was so used to being the family screw-up that it took me a moment to remember that I was blameless for once.

'Hang on a minute, Mama, you can't say that.' I cut her off mid lecture about my part in spoiling my sister's life. 'Diamond doesn't blame me and I know I am not responsible for the choices made by the contessa.'

'But what about the wedding!'

My mother's mind could be amazingly narrow-focused; that was probably why she had never asked herself what the wider implications of my gift might be. 'The wedding isn't the important thing here. Diamond and the others are.'

'I'll come out immediately. I'll . . . I'll get Topaz to organize a ticket for me.'

I didn't think I could cope with another person in the flat at the moment. Mama was more likely to be a burden than a help, hovering and wringing her hands. I hadn't really realized how much in need of care she herself had become since Dad died, but my siblings had paid more attention; no wonder Diamond had stepped in to fill her shoes for me.

'Please, don't come just yet. We're sorting it out.'

'But Diamond needs me!'

I thought ruefully of the number of times I had needed a mother over the last year but that had never been on the agenda. 'Diamond needs most right now not to be upset. She doesn't remember us properly and it might be too painful to have you here.'

'You'll call every day, let me know how she is?'

'Of course. She might even ring you herself when she can.'

'I'm coming out on Tuesday whatever happens.'

'That's fine. We've a room booked for you. I'm hoping that this situation will have been sorted by then.'

'But who's sorting it, Crystal?'

'I am.'

Silence. 'I see.'

'You should have more faith in me: I'm a soulseeker, Mama.'

'A what?'

'Soulseeker.'

'No. You can't be. They're . . . they're like gold dust.'

A line from the Bible came to mind, the one about a prophet never being recognized in his home town. To my family, my default identity was always going to be the big disappointment. 'Why don't you ask my brothers and sisters why they never noticed? Why you never realized.' I took a breath, reminding myself that bitterness was ugly and pointless. 'Anyway, it's a good job I am one because apparently I stand the best chance of restoring the soulfinder links.'

'Oh, Crystal.'

'So, don't worry, Mama: I'm on the case. Got to go.'

'I hope you succeed.' She sniffed. 'I do love you, you know.'

'Yes, well.'

'I do.' Her tone was firm now. 'You were always your father's favourite, his baby girl, and I felt I had to make it up to the others by paying them more attention, but that did not mean I loved you any less than I did them.'

'Didn't it?' My question was genuine. I had always doubted that she cared.

'I've not been a good mother to you, have I? I'm sorry.'

This was not something that could be sorted out on a single phone call. 'Look, we'll talk when you get here. Oh, by the way, I've found my soulfinder too. Xav Benedict. Trace's younger brother.'

'What!'

I ended the call on that little bombshell. I'd give her time to get over the embarrassing gush of enthusiasm before I rang back. I switched off the phone. Mama would be busy for a while passing on the news but I would wager that my brothers and sisters would all be wanting an update directly from me and I couldn't face any more for a few hours.

The garden gate slapped shut. Peering out from behind my tree, I saw six very welcome people coming in from the street.

'Hey, Xav, over here!'

Xav peeled away and ran to me, vaulting Barozzi's table to shave a second off his dash.

'Am I pleased to see you!' He lifted my feet off the ground with his hug.

'I don't know: are you?'

'Of course I am.'

'Whoa, you'll crack a rib if you squeeze me any tighter, you muppet.'

He put me down. 'What's with this muppet thing, Miss Piggy?'

'English English for "you idiot"—but in a nice way.'

'Neat.'

'Is it OK to go in?' Trace called.

'Yes, fine.' Well, not fine, but we all knew what I meant. 'I think they're making sandwiches for lunch. Go slowly with them, won't you? They're not . . . ' I twirled my hand, unable quite to put my finger on it.

'Not yet on the right page,' suggested Yves, looking up at the upstairs window with unbearable longing.

'Something like that.'

Xav hadn't taken his eyes off my face. 'We'll be along in a moment.'

'OK. I'll make coffee.' Yves led the way inside.

As soon as we had the garden to ourselves, I tackled Xav, bringing him to the ground.

'You . . . ' poke, 'promised . . . ' another poke, 'you'd come back . . . ' light thump on the chest.

Xav let me sit on him as he threw his arms wide. 'And here I am.'

'Only after spending the night in jail. You got bail OK?'

'Yeah, thanks to Yves's millions. One time when none of us minded raiding his piggybank.'

'But what if you hadn't?' I couldn't bear to think about the 'what ifs?'.

'Then I would've expected you to bust us out with your ninja powers.'

'I'll kill your brothers. I asked them not to mention that.'

'Cupcake, they couldn't help themselves. There's not much to do inside but talk. They told me you did good.'

'I was crap, but we got out.'

'Dad said to tell you all that Will's getting on really well. Apparently the doctors are amazed by his recovery—almost as if someone with a healing touch got to him first.' Xav grinned so I pummelled him again for good measure. 'Ouch, I surrender! They are hoping that he can be transferred to a hospital over here. Dad is just sorting that out with the insurance company. Can I get up now?'

I sat on my haunches and thought about it. 'I don't know, Androcles. I have you right where I want you: under my paw.'

'That's my girl. Knock 'em when they're down. Come here and give me a kiss then.' He beckoned, pointing to his lips.

I leant forward, letting my hair brush his face and neck. Ever so gently I let a butterfly of a kiss play over his mouth. Sitting up swiftly, he caught me against him, taking the kiss further. If I had been a lioness I would have ended up purring.

'Sorry I scared you,' he whispered, my head resting against his shoulder.

'No more scary skiing and taking on bodyguards, two against one.'

'I'll try to avoid that in future.'

I sniffed. 'You smell of cheap cigarettes, soulfinder.'

'My accommodation last night was not that great, to be honest. Let's go in so I can change.'

The atmosphere in the apartment was awful in its quietness. Sky was sitting beside Zed, letting him hold her hand, but there was no enthusiasm in the gesture on her side. Yves was showing Phoenix something on his computer like polite strangers met in a public library. Trace and Diamond sat at the kitchen table looking through the list of everyone expecting to come to the wedding; it broke my heart to hear him remind her of her friends and family and her whispered answers. Uriel and Victor stood at the sink, shoulders touching, brothers seeking solidarity in face of the horrible odds stacked against the happiness of their family.

Uriel's face lit up when he saw me. It felt good to be someone's glad thought.

'Hey, Crystal, everything OK?'

'Yes, thanks. What do you reckon, Victor?' I gestured to the girls. 'You know more about the mind than I do but I don't understand what's happened to them.'

Victor rubbed the bristled edge of his jaw. All the brothers were looking like outlaws thanks to their rough night. 'Sky let me take a look in her mind as I'd been there before and I'm familiar with it. She once had gaps in her memory brought on by childhood trauma but this thing that's been done to her: it's completely different. I can't get near the real her.'

'Go on.'

'There's no false information planted that I can detect; it's more like she's a locked box. I don't know if when we lift the lid there'll be anything much inside.'

'I wish I knew what the contessa had done exactly, then I might be able to reverse it.'

'How much do you remember?'

'To me, when she attacked, it felt like being mown down by a lorry.'

'Same as my mind-plough? The one I used at the castle?'

'No, not quite. I could feel the power of your attack; it had a sound, a hum. Hers was more like a blow to the back of the head—unexpected, numbing.'

Uriel jumped up so he could sit on the counter. 'She's a spider.'

'What do you mean?' asked Xav.

'Spiders often paralyse their victims then put them in store . . .'

'Before sucking them dry,' finished Xav. He glanced over at the girls. 'Oh God, tell me they aren't really the . . . the empty husks they feel like. My brothers would never recover—and Dad. Not to mention the girls themselves—what they'd feel if they knew.'

'They do know,' I said quietly, remembering Sky's sobs last night.

Victor tapped his fingers on his forearms. 'That actually gives me hope, Crystal. I'd be more worried if they had no idea what they were missing. The brain has an amazing ability to recover. Look at stroke victims—all sorts of head trauma cases. Maybe there is something inside the locked box after all.'

Xav curled his arms around me. 'Let's not get too hung up on our metaphors. OK, the contessa is a spider but that doesn't mean she had the whole set of spider abilities. I mean, I didn't see her shoot webs, did you? Fricking pathetic spider woman—we can crush her like a bug.'

I tapped the back of his hand. 'I wish.'

'Yes, we can. We have you—our spider exterminator. We have our girls with us and on our side. C'mon, no madwoman is going to take the Benedicts down without one hell of a fight.'

Yves looked up suddenly. 'Hey, guys, you'll want to see this.' He had tuned into a rolling news channel. 'We've made the front page.'

We clustered around the screen. A sympathetic Italian reporter was interviewing the contessa as she sat ensconced in her antique armchair. She was dressed in black and looked convincingly frail, a poor little granny bewildered by the battering her home had taken at the hands of young louts. I had never hated anyone so much as I did her just then.

'What's she saying, Crystal?' Yves asked.

I listened for a bit. 'She's telling her side of the story, how her ancestral home was invaded by a bunch of redneck Americans who objected to her socializing with their partners. The implication is that you are all xenophobic, anti-old worlders. She's also—the cow—implying that Victor and Trace abused their law enforcement contacts to persecute her, just because her son had been caught up in a complicated financial transaction and was then arrested on false charges. She's making it sound as though the whole thing has been a set up to disgrace her noble family.'

'Our motive?' snapped Victor.

'Well, you do have access to a large bail fund. She's suggesting you've been making illegal gains from your police work and is calling for you to be suspended or sacked.'

'Any mention of Savant matters?' asked Trace.

I listened some more. The reporter was practically calling for Trace and Victor to be hanged, drawn, and quartered. 'No . . . no. I guess that would prompt questions as to her own abilities, changing her defenceless victim to someone more than capable of looking after themselves.'

Trace turned away. 'We've spent years flying under the radar and now, thanks to one night, we're big news. This is going to ruin everything.'

'As she no doubt intended,' cut in Victor.

'I think she is doing revenge in the old Italian way—complete and cruel. "You hit me once where it hurts, so I'll blast you out of the water." It's not enough to take our soulfinder links; she also wants us disgraced, as her son has been.'

'If they'd put her in charge of the criminal Savant network, they wouldn't have fallen so easily in London, that's for sure,' said Uriel.

'I don't care if I lose my job, but I'm not losing you, Diamond.' Trace reached for her.

My sister squeezed his hand in sympathy.

'I beg to differ as I do mind being fired.' Victor flipped his phone in his hand, debating who it would be best to call. 'I think it's time we started a serious counter attack. First thing is to get a statement taken from your Milanese banker, Crystal. I want every little detail on record so we can go after her with our version of events.'

Xav gave an unexpected whoop.

'Jeez, don't do that!' said Yves, clutching his chest.

'I've just had a really evil idea.'

'My favourite kind,' noted Zed. Sky gave him a glimmer of a smile.

'The old witch is expecting her notoriety in Italy to play in her favour—we are unknowns. She can project on to us any

kind of baloney as no one had any idea who or what we are—
we've done too good a job at keeping our heads down.'

'I'm not getting the evil part, bro.'

'She did not factor in that we have one of the biggest names
on the planet on our side. Steve Hughes, Crystal's boyfriend,
rushing in to save his girl's sister like the hero he is.'

'I thought I was your girl?' I muttered.

'You are, darlin', but we're talking about the make-believe
land of publicity—which is where the contessa has taken this
battle. How about you put a call in to your Hollywood hunk
and get him to give an exclusive interview to some international news corporation? Talk about blowing the contessa's
story out of the water; she won't even be a rubber duck afloat
on the ocean when his warship sails into view.'

'Do you think he'll do it?' asked Phoenix, rubbing her temples roughly. I could sense she was trying to cudgel her brain
into remembering. Yves took her hand and kissed the knuckles
before she hurt herself.

I nodded. 'Yes, he'll do it. He might even get something out
of it for himself as I imagine that right now he wants to distract
the press from his new relationship with Lily. This will give
them something to write about for a few weeks.'

'You might have to give an interview,' cautioned Trace. 'Are
you ready for that, Diamond? Crystal?'

'Anything it takes,' said Diamond firmly. 'Just help me say
the right things.'

'Always,' promised Trace.

If Diamond was brave enough to do it in the knowledge
that only a fraction of her mind was functioning properly then
how could I refuse?

'Sure. I'm up for that.'

'Great.' Xav rubbed his hands together. 'Let's make some
calls.'

By the time Saul and Karla arrived back from transferring Will to a Venetian hospital, the story was running on every major news channel. The arrest of the Count of Monte Baldo made a nice background piece. The BBC had found photos of the operation in Central London and shared them with the other media outlets. The contessa's version of his innocence was now heavily undercut by the wild-eyed, pasty-faced police mugshot taken while he was being processed. This was then matched with the six shots of the Benedict brothers taken in the Verona police station.

We watched the whole news package unfold.

'Hey, you look like a serial killer,' Zed mocked Victor. For guys who had shunned publicity, they were making the best of their newfound fame. I thought they all looked gorgeous, especially Xav. I wouldn't be surprised if they started receiving fan mail from TV viewers.

Then came the interview with Steve, conducted picturesquely on the top of the mountain, his helicopter as backdrop.

'Yeah, I rushed to my girlfriend's assistance. Of course I did. Her sister is very important to her.'

'What about the contessa's claim that Diamond Brook and her friends were just guests?' asked the reporter.

Steve snorted. 'That's one weird lady. I mean, when you have a house party do you knock your guests out, abandon one on an island to freeze, and then hold the rest hostage from their family? I prefer to send out invitations and make sure everyone has a good time.'

The reporter preened, doubtless hoping to be a recipient of an invitation for Steve's next private bash. 'I'm sure you do.'

'Seriously, maybe she's lonely; but to me what she did sounds like the actions of one severely disturbed woman. Her son's in jail, she sees the means of getting revenge, and then she takes it way too far.'

'Why did you not bring in the police, if it was a hostage situation?' So the reporter wasn't such a pushover after all.

Steve treated us all to his brilliant smile. 'Why wait when we had the helicopter and could do it ourselves? We weren't going to do any more than knock on the door and ask to take them home.'

Yeah right.

'It was the contessa who escalated the situation. She shot one of my friends. None of us was armed.'

The piece then cut to a report from outside Will's hospital where he was described as in recovery. That would generate a nice wave of sympathy for our side.

The final section was the interview Diamond and I had done that afternoon outside our apartment. Di looked pale but resolute; I looked as glamorous as I could manage, trying hard to live up to my reputation as Steve's model girlfriend. Diamond gave a brief explanation of what had happened, similar to the one she gave to the policeman. I backed it up with a fuller description of being stranded in the lagoon wearing nothing but an evening gown. The press liked that little detail and even got me to describe the cut and colour.

'Are these the actions of a sane woman?' I asked.

The reporter chose to end the piece on that question before spinning off into speculation about Steve's and my non-existent romance.

Celebrity power: don't you just love it?

Sitting next to me on the settee, Xav kissed my neck. 'You did really well. Take that, contessa.'

'I just hope it doesn't inspire her to do anything worse.'

Victor got up. 'I'll go visit with Will. Anyone coming?'

To my surprise, Diamond offered. 'If he's to be my brother-in-law, I'd better meet him properly.'

Trace smiled sadly and joined her by the door. So they had decided to travel in hope towards the wedding, had they? 'I'll come too.'

After they left, the rest of us decided to make an early night of it. Having survived on far less sleep than normal, I was expecting to go out like a light but instead I tossed and turned on my pillow, my grand prix car of a brain racing around the circuit of our predicament.

Our publicity battle with the contessa reminded me of the history of two Italian Renaissance cities, lobbing insults at each other from behind their fortifications. It was doing nothing to save the devastated valley between them—in our case, the ruins being the minds on which the contessa had exercised her malign gift. I had promised to sort it out but unless I had the map to show me what she had done, I had not the first idea where to start.

Maybe I could bargain for information? I thought of her son: would he tell us how his mother's power worked in exchange for some leniency in his treatment?

But Xav had told me that his case was still going through the courts. Until he was sentenced, he would not be interested in striking a bargain with us.

What about the contessa herself: what would she want in exchange for information?

A soulfinder? If not for her, maybe for the son she loved and any Savants among her grandchildren? It was the one thing I could offer that any Savant could not refuse. I was sitting on a deal clincher.

I threw off the covers, put on my trackies and jumper and crept out of the bedroom. Xav was really going to kill me if he knew what I planned. It was an enormous risk I was taking but I couldn't face myself if I kept failing the girls and their soulfinders, not when there was something I could do.

On my way to the front door, I almost tripped over Barozzi and stumbled into the settee.

'Going somewhere?' asked Phoenix. She was sitting by the window, watching the moonshadows play on the garden wall.

'You gave me a scare!' I patted my throat. 'Just letting the cat out. I won't be long. Don't wait up.'

It was a sign of how unlike her normal self she was that Phoenix was not more suspicious of my explanation.

'OK.'

I paused at the door. 'Phee, why are you here and not at the hotel with Yves?'

She gave a lopsided shrug. 'Just didn't feel right.'

That decided me. I could not bear to think of how much Yves must be hurting sitting alone in his hotel room without his wife. 'You're welcome to stay as long as you need, Phee.' I eased my feet into my wellingtons. 'See you in the morning.'

At the moorings by the Accademia Bridge, I found a gondolier about to go off-duty. A stout man with a chubby face like a worn-out cherub, he was packing up for the evening, accepting a hefty tip from his last cargo of lovers. He was transferring his gear from his shiny gondola to a scruffy little motorboat for his commute home.

'How much to take me to Contessa Nicoletta's island?' I asked.

'A hundred euros,' he said casually, standing at the back of his bucking boat like a bareback rider on a galloping horse.

I snorted. 'Yeah, and I was born yesterday. Look, I'm not a tourist and you're probably going home to the Guidecca so it's not far out of your way.'

He looked me up and down. I looked nothing like I had that afternoon in front of the cameras, as I was wearing my most comfortable and baggy clothes. 'Why are you going there so late?'

'Emergency staff meeting. You must have heard the rumours about the contessa's difficulties.'

He grinned. 'Yes. Funny old bird, never liked her. Sounds as if she's really gone off the deep end this time. What do you do for her?'

'I work for her chef.' Fingers crossed behind back.

'All right, signorina, in you get. I'll drop you at the watersteps for twenty euros. You'll make your own way home, OK?'

'Fine.' That's if I got to come home. Just now I couldn't worry about the details of after.

With a couple of pulls of the starter motor cord, my aging cherub propelled me across the choppy wide water of the Canale della Guidecca.

'You want me to sing?' he asked cheekily.

'Not paying for it.' I hunched my head against my knees. I was shaking with nerves and did not want to show it or he would suspect I was up to something.

'I give you one free.' He began his not so tuneful rendition of Italian opera arias. Gondoliers usually inherited their boat and mooring from their family; it was a shame the genes hadn't passed down musicality too.

I thought of the last time I had been taken somewhere by a man singing. It had been Xav driving me to the airport. *Hey, soul sister*—the song had proved to be correct. I prayed that I was not risking our connection by making this trip into the lion's den. But then, I told myself sternly, I was a lioness too; I was not going in without my own power to protect me. The old alpha female was about to find her dominance challenged by the new girl in the Savant pride.

Chapter 18

Left on the steps, I watched my gondolier head off home, probably to a house packed full of cherub-faced sons all practising arias to take over from Dad when they were old enough. I wished my life was so straightforward. I pressed the intercom.

No response.

It was late, at least midnight. Was my big adventure going to end with me sitting on the steps till morning? I eyed the wall. After my failed ninja moment of the previous day, I knew better than to attempt to scale it. I pressed the bell again, this time keeping my finger stuck on the button.

The intercom crackled. 'Yes?'

'Hello? Can you tell the contessa that Crystal Brook is here to see her?'

There was a brief silence then the gate hummed open.

'*Come into my parlour, said the spider to the fly,*' I muttered, that line of an old song drifting unhelpfully into my head. 'Stick with the lion image, Brook: it makes you feel more powerful.'

The garden was deserted. The dark outlines of box hedges stretched in a grid like a chess board; the pale grey shadows of statues looked like pieces left in the middle of a game played by giants. Without the warmth provided by the flaring torches at Diamond's party, the secret island was a haunting place. I felt a moment's pity for the imprisoned count growing up in this weird atmosphere; no wonder he had turned out so badly.

The butler opened the garden doors for me. If any other staff were in residence, I saw no sign. 'May I take your coat?'

'Thanks.' I stood with my hands in my pockets, feeling absurdly out of place in this elegant room.

'I will tell the contessa that you are here,' the butler intoned, shuttling off on his mission.

I drifted over to look at a gold-leaf clock on a marble side table. Black-faced cherubs held up the dial—cheerful relatives of my gondolier.

Crystal? Where are you?

I jumped as Xav's angry voice rocketed through my head like a missile from a catapult. *I'm just getting a bit of fresh air.*

Yeah, I got that. Phee told Yves and he woke me up. Where exactly are you?

Oh Xav, you aren't going to be pleased with me. My impulsive nature had run away with my good sense but I couldn't lie to my soulfinder. I let him glimpse my surroundings.

Silence.

Xav?

Yeah, I'm still here. Why have you done this, Crystal?

I've got to do something to save the girls. I've a plan.

Which you didn't want to share with me?

No, because he would have stopped me. *It wasn't like that.*

Don't fool yourself: it was exactly like that.

He was right. I would have gone ballistic if it had been me left behind while he waltzed off into danger. *Oh God, I'm sorry.*

Sorry don't cut no ice with me right now. I thought it was going so well between us—that we were a team.

We are . . . ! He was so right to be cross but I couldn't bear to think how I had hurt him.

That's just bull, Crystal. You decided that you had to play the hero, risking half my soul, without even asking me what I thought. That isn't team play.

The butler returned, showing no sign that he was surprised to find me with tears running down my face. 'The contessa will see you now.'

I nodded and swiped at my cheeks with my cuff. *Got to go, Xav. I need to concentrate on what I'm going to say to her.*

Xav was desperate now. *Please, don't do this. Turn round. Get out of there. I'll come get you.*

It's too late. I'm here now.

Anger rippled down our connection like an earth tremor. *Fine. Go ruin our life together with your idiotic plan! Don't expect me to be waiting around for you when you get back. Maybe I have plans myself that I don't want to share with you like, oh I don't know, throwing myself into a shark pool.*

I love you, Xav.

Don't you dare say that! You don't love me—not if you can do this to me. He slammed the door shut on our link, leaving me bruised and hurting so much I could barely breathe.

'Crystal, I must admit I am terribly surprised to see you back here.' The countess was sitting by the fire, her feet up on a footstool. I felt in no fit state for this confrontation but I had to do it.

'Will there be anything else, my lady?' asked the butler.

'Not for the moment, Alberto. Stay within call.'

He bowed and slid out of the room.

I bit the inside of my cheek, forcing myself to pay attention to the person in the library, not the angry soulfinder on the other side of the canal. 'Contessa. Thank you for seeing me.'

She waved me to a seat opposite her. I sat down. She studied my face for a few moments. 'An interesting tactic, coming here. Whatever do you mean by it?'

'I want to make a bargain with you.'

She folded her hands in her lap. 'What have you to bargain with? I would have thought it was clear we were going to fight this one to the death, so to speak. Intriguing choice: going public with that actor fellow. I had not expected that. But neither did I expect you to come here with what I think you regard as an olive branch, am I right?'

'Yes.'

'Hmm. Do you want something to drink?' She raised her hand to a little bell on the side table.

'No, thank you.'

She let her hand fall. 'Well then, tell me your bargain.'

I took a breath. 'I'm a soulseeker. I am offering to find the partners of your son and grandchildren—your own if you care to look for him—if you tell me what you did to my sister and the other girls.'

Apart from a slight flare of surprise behind her dark eyes, she showed little reaction to my announcement. Instead, she arched her fingers together and said nothing.

What else could I say? 'I understand that you are playing this game to make the damage even on both sides: disgrace for disgrace, loss for loss. What if I offer a prize that makes up for not depriving the Benedicts of their soulfinders—your family gaining theirs?'

I waited.

'You really are much more interesting than I first thought,' mused the contessa. 'In a few years, when experience has mellowed you, you might even be a worthy opponent.'

Not the response I had anticipated. 'I don't think I understand you.'

'No, you would not. There is so much you do not understand, standing on the brink of your gift like a child with its toes in the water, gazing at an ocean.'

'But surely you want your children and grandchildren to be happy? This whole thing has been about your son—I'm sure you care for them.' Even though you are an evil old bat, was the subtext.

She stroked one gnarled hand over the back of the other. 'And you think that finding them their counterparts would make them happy?'

'Yes?' I wish that word had come out more as an assertion than a question.

She resettled herself in her seat, turning her body towards a portrait of a handsome man that hung beside the fireplace. He had the slicked-back hair and chiselled looks of a 1950s matinee idol. 'I had a soulfinder once. My husband. He died.'

'Oh. I'm sorry.'

'No, you are not.' For the first time she showed real depth of emotion, squeezing the head of her walking stick and tapping it on the floor. 'You don't understand what that is like—losing the best part of yourself. Far better never to have known that happiness than to live with its loss for the rest of your life.'

'If you know how painful it is, why are doing this to my family then?' I couldn't comprehend why anyone would want to torture others with the same pain.

'Oh the women aren't suffering,' she waved a disdainful hand in the air, 'I've curtailed their connection to their partners, tidied it away so it won't harm them again. Only the men are in pain—that is my revenge.'

'But can't you see that it is only a half life—if that—that the girls are living?'

'You have no idea,' she spat the words at me, 'what a life

lived in the presence of full, raw longing for something you can no longer have, what that does to you.'

I could guess: it would produce a bitter soul like the one sitting opposite me.

'But isn't it their choice to make, not yours?'

'Rubbish. When one is a soulseeker, one makes that choice for others all the time. Why do you believe that you will be doing good for them?'

The recognition echoed through me like the siren for *acqua alta*. 'What? Are you telling me that you're a soulseeker too?' It would explain so much.

'Of course. We soulseekers are the only ones who have any power to manipulate soulfinder bonds. I thought you would have known that?'

She made me feel horribly ignorant. 'I've only been one for a day. I don't know much yet.'

'You are fortunate. You have not had time to do any damage with your gift; it is not too late for you to turn back.'

'But I want to make people happy—whole.' I recalled the feeling I experienced when I was with Xav. Even arguing with him was being so much more, well, *technicolour* than the black-and-white emotions I had felt towards other boys. I couldn't—wouldn't give that up.

'So what will you do when the Savant who comes to you for help has no soulfinder, thanks to death in accident, disease, or war? This is not an academic question—it will happen.'

'I don't know.'

'Or when the soulfinder has been so damaged by their up-bringing, or perhaps suffers from some kind of mental illness that means they are impossible, even dangerous, to live with? Would you shackle a pair like that for life?'

'I . . . I'm not sure. Is it my part to decide what a Savant does with the discovery?'

'If you open the door, you are responsible for what comes through it. Do you have the courage to face that? You think you will be fulfilling dreams; maybe you are only ushering in a nightmare?'

She was chipping away at my certainty that my gift was a blessing; I had never been very confident and she had found my weakness and was exploiting it. Her points were worth considering, but not now, not when there was real suffering already happening, not this hypothetical sort. I realized she was distracting me from the main reason I had come here; I had to find a way of turning the tables.

'I don't know what I will do, contessa, but you can't deny I had the courage to come here and face you. I don't think I lack bravery.'

She inclined her head in acknowledgement. 'That's what gives me hope for you.'

I thought about my mother and father; since his death, I had never once heard my mama lament knowing him. 'But, please, answer me honestly: do you not remember anything good about your time with your soulfinder? Was it not worth knowing him even for the short period you had together?'

Her eyes hardened. 'You dare to talk to me of Giuseppe so lightly? You cannot know—cannot understand.' She clenched her fist against her chest. 'You have no conception of what I suffered when he was murdered.'

A wave of pity swept through me. She had faced the worst. Death to illness was one thing; but someone else choosing to take a loved one from you another. Little wonder she was so bitter.

'I think,' I said carefully, 'I think you were probably more like me then than you realize. I have listened to you and I am hearing the words of someone who had hopes—illusions as you now think them. You loved him, I'm sure of that. And knowing your nature, I imagine you took your revenge for him.'

She smiled, a sour expression. 'You've seen Alberto and my staff?'

I nodded.

'They are the sons and relatives of the man who killed my husband. I disposed of Minotti himself first, naturally. He was supposed to have been our friend, but he betrayed us in the foulest way. You don't know, Crystal, what it is like when there's an argument between Savants, how it can run out of control.'

Actually, I did: that was what Diamond had dedicated her life to preventing.

'My foolish husband and Minotti were vying for supremacy in northern Italy, business, as if that mattered! I warned them, but they carried on with the stupid battle. Minotti was losing his influence so he tampered with the brakes on Guiseppe's car—he didn't even have the gumption to challenge him to his face.'

'That's terrible.' I needed no special power to know that the rest of the story was going to be ugly.

'It was. My soulfinder went over a cliff on the road to Garda—his body broken and mangled—leaving me with a fatherless child and a righteous desire for vengeance. I swore my son would never know the same pain as I felt then. I found a new use for my soulseeker power; I found I could erase, reorder so that emotional links were broken. No one knew because they never remembered afterwards what I had done. Until you came along, that is.'

I had to say it, even if it angered her: the parallel was screamingly obvious to me. 'So you tampered with your son's brain as Alberto's father did the brakes. You've done the same to your butler and staff. How is that just?'

'No!' she shrieked, thumping the floor again. 'It is not the same. I have kept them from true harm.'

'You haven't let them live.'

'Don't you come in here, you ignorant child, and tell me you know better!'

My alarm grew as I felt her gathering herself for an attack. 'I'm not. I'm telling you I think *you* know better. You've become like this Minotti, the person you hated for taking your soulfinder from you.'

'How dare you!'

'Your son committed crimes and when the Benedicts helped catch him, you have forced the car of their relationships off the cliff.'

'No, this is not the same at all.'

'And as for keeping Alberto and the others as your . . . your slaves, how can that be justified? It was the father, not the son, that harmed you. You are keeping life from them because your own died that day. Your motivation is like that of the dog in the manger—if I can't have it, neither can anyone else!'

Her mental attack slammed into my head. I had my shields raised and they held. I kept telling myself that this was what I had come for: if she didn't take my deal—and clearly she wouldn't—I had to know how she turned her powers against her enemies, but it was excruciating. I felt as if I was standing by a jet engine running full blast with no covering for my ears to dull the roar. I tried to breathe through it. She surely couldn't keep this up for ever?

Sweat trickled down my spine. I closed my eyes. I could feel her groping for my connection to Xav, seeking to yank it into her control, but her mental hook skittered off the walls I had built, grappling irons failing to catch on my battlements. That was how she worked: she reversed the soulseeker power;

instead of following the connection she reeled it in, a spinner hoarding the thread so it could not be woven.

Enough. I had my answer.

Xav, I need you.

Crystal, what the hell is going on? He could feel the attack I was under but I had no space to show him the source as any relaxation of control might let her in.

Thank God you're still there.

Always, you infuriating . . . he rejected a lot of unflattering words and settled on my own favourite insult . . . *muppet.*

I had known in my heart of hearts that he wouldn't really leave me as he threatened; that had been temper talking and I now owed him big time. *I need you to help me. The contessa is trying to get our link.*

Dammit, Crystal!

I'm going to drop my shield and reverse the attack but I want you to hit back with me so she can't reel in our connection.

I don't understand.

No time to explain—it's a soulseeker thing. You've got to shock her so she lets go. Do something unexpected.

You mean use force. I caught a glimpse of him thinking of the final combat in the movies, Harry versus Voldemort, Spider-Man versus the Green Goblin.

No. She's far too powerful. I can't win a duel of strength.

So, what?

I could feel my shields beginning to shudder. My head was splitting. *Can I leave that for you to decide, Xav?*

Crystal, you're in pain.

I'll let you sort that out too later. Let's do this. On the count of three.

Don't give me much time, do you?

One . . .

Crystal!

Two . . . three!

I dropped my shield, trusting that Xav would do his part and yank our connection out of her claws. I went straight to her mind. She had no shields to speak of; so concentrated was she on attack, she forgot about defence. With part of my consciousness, I saw Xav doing a slalom down our connection wearing a Kermit costume, me as Miss Piggy. Unexpected but effective if the contessa's astounded expression was anything to go by. I got inside her barriers and found that her mind was a confused mess, like a circuit board where the wiring had been bodged by amateurs. Grief had ruined her. But this was no time for pity; I had to protect me and mine.

Sleep, I ordered her, recalling how Victor had exerted this power. She resisted but she was slipping. He'd also said touch reinforced the mental command. I crossed the gap between us and put my hand on her forehead. *Sleep*.

Her eyes closed and her chin fell on her chest. Her mental presence vanished from the room, leaving just Xav and me.

Hey, Kermit, come in.

You really OK? Cupcake, you scared me to death—I think I could hate you for that.

No, you don't. I felt exhausted but relieved. *You can tell me off when I see you. And yes, I'm fine. I'm getting out of here but I'll need a lift.*

Not another rescue? I charge a lot for rescues.

I smiled, remembering our first flirting conversation. *I'll pay up, I promise. Can you get me a ride from the contessa's island?*

I'll see what I can do.

Meet you at the water-steps. There's something I've got to check out first before I leave.

I hope it's not dangerous?

No, I don't think so. See you in quarter of an hour?

I'll be there.

I stood up. The contessa was asleep, her breathing shallow. She looked so small and frail; I couldn't find it in myself to hate her any more. What would I have been like if I had lived through what she had done? I could only hope I wouldn't be so unbalanced in my thirst for revenge but I could see her now as human rather than as a monster. I'd probably even forgive her if I could undo some of the damage she had inflicted, for after all, it was her ill-intentioned actions that had forced me to find Xav.

I rang the bell. Alberto arrived swiftly.

'Signorina?' He glanced at his mistress in consternation. 'Is something the matter?'

'No, your mistress is just sleeping.' I studied him. He had the same almost-but-not-quite-there expression as I had seen on Diamond's face. I had thought it his natural butler school manner, but now I knew it was foisted on him. The poor man had been a victim for so long, would trying to reverse that be worse than leaving him as he was? The contessa had warned that these were the kind of decisions I would have to face if I used my powers but I refused to chicken out just because I was scared of making a mistake. I asked myself, instead, if I were in his shoes, what would I want someone to do?

I'd want someone to free me.

'Excuse me for a moment, Alberto.' I closed my eyes and reached out to his mind. I was faced with that carousel of tidy emotions, raw ends snipped off and woven in an enclosed circuit that went nowhere. I could now see what she had done: she had created a pattern that was like life but not life. But in doing that she had got it wrong: pain and suffering, longing and sadness could not be avoided as they were the flip side to all the best things. I couldn't help him just yet—I could possibly do more damage by attempting a fix without more understanding of my own abilities—but I could at least offer him some help.

'Signorina?' Alberto was unnerved by my silent study of him.

'Alberto, are you a Savant?'

'Signorina?'

'And there are other Savants on the staff—your relatives perhaps?'

He arched a brow. I took that as an affirmative.

'I would be very grateful if you could arrange for me to meet them the day after tomorrow.'

'Whatever for?'

'I have something for . . . for the emptiness you know is inside you.'

'Emptiness?' The butler was rightly bemused by my abrupt drive off the track of normal conversation into the personal.

'You've been, um, manipulated. By the contessa. If you really think about it, you might realize that you know this somewhere inside you.' He frowned, like a child facing a maths problem beyond his level of understanding. 'I am not asking you to believe me, just give me a chance to help. You see, I'm a soulseeker. Oh, and don't tell your mistress that I'm coming back.'

'I don't know what you mean.'

Poor man. 'I know. Can you at least let me in when I return? I won't do anything you don't want and I'll only come if I think I know how to . . . to unravel this problem.'

He gave a cautious nod.

'OK. Can I have my coat then?'

This time his face brightened. Back on the normal script of butler duties, he felt much happier. He handed over my jacket. 'Goodnight, signorina.'

'Goodnight, Alberto. See you again soon—I hope.'

Chapter 19

Xav must have paid the driver of the water taxi handsomely to come and fetch me at this late hour. My soulfinder said very little as I emerged from the garden gate, just scooped me off the steps and dumped me next to him on the padded bench.

'To the Zattere,' he ordered the driver.

Catching his urgency, the pilot revved the engine and pulled away, prow of the boat slapping against the little waves on the lagoon.

'Are you still mad at me?' I huddled against him.

'Yes.'

'I'm a bit impulsive.'

'I'm getting that picture.'

'So are you.'

'Er . . . excuse me, but I didn't go shooting off alone to face down our enemy.'

'Jumping out of a helicopter and skiing through a garden, anyone?'

'Humph!' He put his arm around my shoulders. 'At least you knew what I had in mind.'

I bumped my head against his chest. 'Yes, I know. And that's what I'm sorry for—that I didn't tell you. I had this pressure building inside me and when I saw everyone suffering I just had to do something about it.' I wrinkled my brow. 'I don't think I was being totally rational, more like following an instinct.'

He sighed. 'And was the instinct right?'

A huge white cruise ship came into view, having cast off from the moorings at the far end of the Dorsoduro. It sliced through the waters of the canal, strings of lights like Christmas decorations, tiny faces at the windows staring back at the city they had so briefly visited. The vessel felt far too big for the medieval landscape it sailed past.

'I think my instinct was right. I now know what I'm up against and why.' I filled him in on the background to the contessa's particular gift.

'Another soulseeker?' Xav asked as our boat bucked in the wake of the cruise liner. The contessa had been like that, throwing our world at sixes and sevens.

'I don't think she's been doing any seeking, more like hiding.'

'And she's done this to others, not just our girls—to her family and the staff?'

'Yes. She's one mixed-up lady. She's been out of control for years, spreading her poison secretly to the Savants she knows, even her own blood. She says that, on the one hand, she's doing it to keep her son safe, avoid the pain of loss, and yet, on the other, she clearly uses her powers as a kind of punishment. It's not some well thought through master plan, more the erratic reactions of someone who is hurting.'

'You're being very generous.'

'Yeah, well, I took a peek inside. Her mind is all scrambled, love connecting to hate, kindness to cruelty.'

Xav smiled down at me, a lock of his hair falling forward to brush my cheek. 'You are a very sweet girl—when you're not being totally infuriating and impossible.'

'And you are one infuriating boy—when you're not being totally sweet to me.'

'Then I'd say we were well matched.'

The water taxi drew up at the landing place. The pilot lassoed a line around a post to pull us alongside. 'Here we are, ladies and gentlemen: the Zattere.'

I hopped ashore. 'Do the others know I was gone?'

'Of course.' Xav got out his wallet and counted out the fare. 'You can't expect me to shoot off after our soulseeker without Will and Dad knowing something was up and Zed foreseeing scary snatches of you sitting with the contessa.'

'Oops.'

'You're part of the Benedict family now, like it or not. Get ready for a lifetime of all my brothers, my dad, and my mom when she's back to her old self, telling you off when they think you've put yourself in danger.' He passed the driver his tip and rejoined me on the jetty.

'Aw, but I've got this big brave soulfinder to protect me now.'

'Darlin', you can't hide behind me—you're too tall.'

'Leave this girl some illusions.'

'C'mon. Let's face the music.'

When we reported our safe return at the hotel, Xav did actually protect me from the worst of the roasting Victor and Saul had planned, arguing it was too late to scold me properly. He promised to tell them what had happened if they would let me get some sleep.

'Tomorrow's going to be another big day. She's gone through enough tonight.'

'You will promise not to leave the house alone again?' asked Saul, hands on my shoulders to make his point.

It felt so great to be told off by a father again; I really wanted to hug him but instead I tried to look repentant. 'I give my word.'

'Then get some rest.'

I couldn't quite meet his eyes, feeling a bit shy. 'I'm going to try to reverse what was done. I think I might know how.'

'You do?' He couldn't hide his flash of hope.

'Well, maybe. I can't promise that I'll succeed.'

'Of course you can't, sweetheart. Until the morning then.'

Xav walked me the few yards home from the hotel foyer and gave me a goodnight kiss by the gate. Funny, it was the first time our relationship had fallen into anything like a traditional dating pattern, what with having started with the passionate kissing *before* we got to go out.

'I really, really hope I can do it,' I whispered.

'I've faith in you, Crystal. Try to have some in yourself.'

'The contessa said I'd have to take tough decisions—that I could do more damage than good.'

'I suppose she's right, but taking no action is a kind of decision.'

'Yes, that's what I think too. She tried to stop people living and that's worse.'

Xav ruffled my hair. 'Go and get some sleep. We'll sort this out in the morning.'

'Can I say "I love you" now without you biting my head off?'

'I don't know—that seems like a good idea.' He opened his mouth wide and did the mock-Vampire thing on my neck.

I pushed him away. 'Are you never serious?'

'Um,' he pretended to think, 'no. You?'

I laughed. 'Not often.'

'I love you, Crystal.'

'Back at you, Xav.' I let the gate clang shut behind me, hugging that thought all the way up to my bedroom.

* * *

There was a mood of expectation the next morning when I surfaced from a dreamless sleep. Everyone was gathered in the living room and kitchen of the flat trying to pretend they weren't waiting for me. I got a bit of a shock as I padded from my bedroom to the bathroom to find Steve and Lily had also showed up.

Memo to self: get rid of Disney PJs before meeting world megastar and trendy costume designer.

'Hey, guys, give me a moment,' I croaked. I locked the door and checked the mirror. Yep, it was as bad as I had thought: my hair was standing up on one side and a bird's nest on the other. I did a quick repair job and scuttled back to my room to put on my most comfortable clothes. I'd snagged a jumper borrowed from Xav so that was almost as good as a morning hug.

'OK, I can do this.' I looked out of the window. Life went on as normal out there: Rocco chasing the birds, Barozzi watching him with indolent amusement, one eye cracked open as he lay on his table command post. The sight reminded me how Signora Carriera had been torn in her loyalties after we went public with our side of the story but had come down on ours when she talked to Diamond. She knew my sister too well not to realize that something was seriously wrong. She had given me the rest of the week off until after the wedding to deal with the family crisis. She was turning out to be a good friend; I'd not thought to have a real buddy from another generation. Then again, neither had I expected to be on best mate terms with Steve Hughes.

'C'mon, Crystal, quit stalling.' I forced myself to leave my bedroom. So many expectations were piled on my shoulders this morning I felt like a dairymaid carrying a too-heavy yoke. I was bound to spill.

'Hi, everyone.'

Xav pressed a coffee mug in my hand and kissed my cheek. 'Hi yourself.'

'Will, you're here!' I rushed to the middle brother's side where he lay spread out on the settee.

'Miraculous recovery apparently.' Will touched the bandage over his chest. 'I couldn't occupy a hospital bed when all I really need now is rest and my brother's TLC.'

Xav bowed. 'My specialty.'

'I'm so glad to see you're going to be fine.' I patted his uninjured arm.

'Hey, with you on my case, I know I'm going to be more than fine. Supremely happy was what I had in mind.'

Uriel appeared at the back of the settee. 'He's just worried you're going to do me first and push him to the end of the line.'

'No, you're too nice.' Will grinned. 'It was Vick I was really concerned about, that he'd intimidate you into doing his soul-finder first. You know, one of his "I'm too scary for my shirt" looks.'

'He does have those down to a fine art,' I agreed.

Uriel bent closer. 'That's because they are real. I hope his partner is one unflappable lady.'

'I'm guessing destiny will make her a complete marshmallow and he'll have to get in touch with his softer side and save his steely looks for anyone who dares offend her.' Xav rubbed his hands. 'I'm gonna love it.'

I crossed the room to greet Steve and Lily.

'Taking a break from filming?' I asked Steve.

'I did my shots yesterday. The stunt guys are doing the rest. Lily persuaded me we should be here in case you needed any more support.'

Lily tweaked his ear. 'Liar. You ordered me to pack as soon as the camera stopped rolling.' She smiled at me. 'He is very loyal to his friends.'

I was so happy for her. 'I can see that.'

Was cool-man Steve actually blushing at our praise? He cleared his throat. 'I'm . . . er . . . sorry to report I've brought the press pack with me. They are presently paddling outside your gate. Do you know you're under water out there?'

'It happens.' I shared a grin with Xav and then I hugged Lily, drawing her aside. 'Everything, you know, *all right?*'

She smiled. 'Funnily enough, yes. I understand it's thanks to you that he plucked up the courage to ask me out.'

'You've been circling it for years, admit it; I just brought the plane down to land.'

Steve rolled his eyes. 'Thank you, Crystal. She really needed to know what a coward I've been.'

'Enough socializing.' Xav took me by the shoulders and sat me down in front of a plate of fresh pastries. 'Eat.'

'What's this? Have you gone all masterful on me?' I teased.

'No, just fattening you up for the kill.' He stole a bite of my croissant, the sure-fire way of getting me to snatch it from him and stuff it in my own mouth.

I lowered my voice. 'It does feel a bit like that.'

'You will be fine. You're our soulseeker. Look what you did for Steve and Lily.'

'Strange to think that my first success was with people outside the Savant world.'

'I'm coming to realize we make way too much fuss about the difference.'

'You told Lily that everyone has a gift.'

'That's right. Being an awesome craftswoman must be up there with Savant gifts—or starring in a box office hit. Maybe we should think about lowering some of our barriers?'

'So I've hooked up with a true democrat, have I?'

'I guess. But I do know that we are all special—and that's not just hot air. Look at Lily: she's Steve's happiness, isn't she?'

They were so sweet together; Steve had none of his brittle star aura when she was in his orbit. 'Yes, she is.'

'Just like you are mine.'

'Aw, shucks.' I made it into a joke but we knew it was true for both of us.

We were both aware of the sideways looks we were getting. I'd drunk my coffee, eaten my breakfast, debated philosophy, flirted, now I really had no more excuses.

'OK, let's do this.' I brushed off the crumbs. 'If you wouldn't mind sitting in a circle. I'm going to start if that's OK with everyone.'

'What are you going to do, Crystal?' Victor asked.

'Last night I let the contessa attack me so that I could find out how her gift works.' From Saul's and Will's grim expressions I could tell neither were fans of my go-it-alone daring. 'Her power is the same as mine, except she reverses it, cutting off the links rather than following them. She then "tidies them away"—her words—which explains the unnatural neatness in her victims' minds. It's like she gets them muffled up from the real world.'

'Go on.' Victor chose a seat opposite me. The soulfinders were sitting together on the floor or sharing armchairs.

'I'm guessing here but I think I have to unravel the ends. It will be the job of the soulfinder to reconnect with his partner so you'll all have to be there with me. Trace, I'm going to attempt this with Diamond first. You have to be ready.'

My brother-in-law-to-be nodded.

'And Xav, I'll need you too because it might be a bit chaotic. I'm not sure, but I might do more damage.' Bearing in mind the contessa's warnings about the adverse outcomes my gift could bring, I was worried I wasn't able to get fully informed consent with the girls this way. 'Di, do you understand? Do you still want me to go ahead?'

My sister met my eyes. 'Yes, I do. I'm not going to stay this way. I can't bear it.'

That would have to do.

'Zed, can you bring us together like you did before?'

'Sure.' It was going to be an immense strain, supporting his entire family, but I was hoping for a domino effect, once one started to unravel, that I could quickly follow with the others.

'Xav, you're going to have to let me fly solo once we're in. I can't be protected.'

He took my hand. 'It'll hurt you.'

Yeah, that was the part I hadn't quite admitted to myself. I shrugged. 'Life hurts. That's what the contessa doesn't get.'

'What do you guys want us to do?' asked Lily.

'Stand by just in case. Intercept any disturbances.' I curved my lips in what I hoped looked like a smile. We'd already un-plugged the phone and disconnected the door bell thanks to media city outside. 'Make tea.'

'I'm great at tea,' volunteered Steve. 'Lily, let's go to the kitchen and leave the floor clear for our friends.'

'Over to you, Zed.'

I sat back in Xav's arms, my favourite place in the whole world. He dropped a kiss on the top of my head.

'It's going to be OK,' he whispered, more an order to me to make it so than a conviction.

'Piece of cake,' I muttered, borrowing his words from two days ago.

Going into the family bond was easier this time as I knew what to expect. Xav's protection allowed me to see and hear what was going on without being knocked about by their tele-pathic communication. It struck me that, potentially, with Xav's help, I would be able to take part in normal Savant te-lepathy if he was there to shield me. But that wasn't something to experiment with now.

OK, I'm going to step outside when I'm close enough to Diamond.

Xav rubbed my upper arm to show he'd understood.

Here goes.

The familiar sickening sensation of being assailed by mind-junk struck me as soon as I let go of Xav's shelter. I tried to jump on the carousel whirling in her mind but was pushed back, sent spinning away. Dizzy—sick—this wasn't working. Xav had to catch me and put me back within his walls.

OK. That went well.

Uriel touched my mind. *Remember, your mind is as powerful, more powerful, than what you are imagining. You have created an illusion of a carousel to understand what's happening but it doesn't really exist.*

Trace was at my side. *You have to believe you are big enough to stop that merry-go-round.*

That went to the heart of it, didn't it? I had always struggled to think of myself as having any worth. The last few days that had set my world up in its end couldn't change that so quickly. The idea that I could undo damage done by a much older, much more experienced Savant was laughable. Yet I couldn't cling on to the second-hand belief others had in me for this; I had to have faith in myself.

Xav sensed my determination. *Ready?*

I nodded and let go. The carousel was my image and I was free to change it. OK, so I'd shift it to something familiar. Space junk—that was how I had thought of it for years—and this time I was like a rocket sent up to intercept. I entered Diamond's slipstream, feeling the barrage of her concerns striking against me.

It hurt. Like flying through razor-edged debris. The pain didn't stay outside; it zinged through my body, nerves on fire.

You'll have to stop. That was Xav.

No, I can do this.

I felt as if I was burning up on re-entry to her atmosphere. He put his hand on my neck, trying to cool me down with his powers. It helped a little, just enough for me to clear a space in my mind to get on with my task.

Crystal, are you sure you know what you're doing? asked Saul. He had been trying to keep out of the way but I sensed he was having as hard a time as Xav in letting me put myself in danger.

I have a hunch. Time to act on it. The contessa had been all about tidying raw ends away; I was going to be the one to mess it up again. I took hold of Diamond's streams of consciousness and pulled, heading in the direction of Trace. It was like trying to hold on to a meteor shower.

That's it! urged Trace.

Your temperature's way too high! warned Xav.

I kicked the connection as hard as I could out of the fake, tight orbit woven by the contessa, trusting Trace to catch it, and headed straight for Karla. No hesitation this time; I dived right in, grabbed a handful of the stuff that was her and hurled it to Saul.

Your nose is bleeding. Xav's tone was urgent. *You've got to stop.*

Not now.

Phoenix next. She was trying to help me. I could sense her seeking memories of Yves for me to latch on to, the recent moments when he had calmed and comforted her after the trauma. She used her power to time-freeze them so they bobbed out of the whirl of stuff in her mind.

Yes, that helps! I encouraged. It was easier this time to catch a thread and pull it with me. Yves was shadowing me every step of the way, waiting to grab.

Crystal, you've got to stop! Come back and finish later. Xav was really really shaken. I could feel him put a tissue to my nose, then dab the corners of my eyes.

Please. Zed's plea cut across Xav's appeal. He had been so patient, helping the others, holding the bond together. I couldn't back out now.

Sky next.

She had picked up the hint from Phoenix to use her gift and was putting the brakes on her orbiting material as much as she could manage. I saw the faint connection to Zed fluttering, end already loose for me to catch, the colour flaring out to attract my attention. I skimmed away, feeling the strength of my imagined rocket boosters flagging. I wasn't sure I'd done enough. If the link fell and got tangled up again, I worried that I'd do more harm to her.

I'm here. I've got it. Zed somehow managed to fly alongside and take it from my grasp. I sensed rather than saw the pulse of power that travelled down the connection. The circuit had been repaired; the electricity of their relationship now flowed at high voltage once more.

I'm coming in, I told Xav. But I wasn't. I couldn't stop my drift outwards, away from the consciousnesses I had visited. Without power, I was in space freefall, momentum carrying me into blackness.

Xav!

Got you. Not letting you go.

I realized I wasn't alone in mental deep space; he had always been there and could pilot me home.

Chapter 20

What was that phrase they use on TV? Don't try this at home. That was playing in my head as I came back to my senses. I was lying in my bed. From the long low shafts of light outside, it appeared that I'd missed quite a few hours.

'Xav?'

'He's . . . er . . . gone out.' Diamond sat at my side; she brushed the hair off my face. 'Here.'

She passed me a damp flannel.

'What? Why?'

'You overdid it. Had a bit of a bleed from your nose and your eyes.'

'Gross.' I cleaned off the last signs.

'Xav says you're fine otherwise. Ordered you to rest.'

'But didn't stay?' I found it hard to believe he was doing the sights while I lay unconscious.

'He said he needed to unwind. He was furious we all let you go so far. That boy would stop you so much as breaking a nail if he could.'

'My choice—totally my choice.'

Diamond bent over me and whispered. 'Between you and

me, I'd let him take his mad out on his brothers.'

I smiled. 'You might be on to something.' I suddenly realized the thing that I should have gathered immediately on waking. 'Hey, you're you again!'

'Yes, I'm back.'

'Really back? The link—your memories?'

Diamond sighed happily. 'Yes, really. So are the others. I had a crushing headache for a time but Xav and some tablets sorted that out. Fortunately, the contessa hadn't taken anything away, just buried it so deep that I thought I'd never get it back.' She squeezed my hand. 'But thanks to you, we did. I don't know how we can . . . '

'Stop right there,' I said firmly. 'I don't want thanks. I want you to be happy. Have a great wedding.'

'We will. I know it's kind of late notice—not to say unconventional—but I was wondering: would you be our best woman?'

'Really, me? Do I get to lose the rings?'

She laughed. 'Absolutely, because I know you of all people will be able to find them again.'

There was a knock at the door. Diamond looked up. 'Yes?'

'Is she awake?' Karla poked her head around the frame.

'Yes, I am.'

Xav's mother bustled in, Saul on her heels as if he daren't let her out of his sight for a second. Gone was that terrible vacancy; back was the little ball of fire that was the Benedict boys' mother.

'You wonderful, fabulous girl!' Karla kissed my forehead. 'We are so, so grateful—words cannot begin to describe. But . . . ' she frowned and put her hands on her hips ' . . . if you ever risk yourself like that again, Crystal, I will be very angry indeed. Xav is not the only one to be annoyed with the boys for letting you do that for us.'

I smiled, quite enjoying my ticking off. She was trying very hard not to be too pleased with me. 'Yes, Karla.'

'Humph! This silly man here should have known better.' She looked up at Saul, the decades of love for him shining in her eyes.

Saul took her hand. 'We're sorry, my dear. None of us wanted to put Crystal in danger.'

'So, are you really back to normal?' I asked.

'Not quite.'

'Oh?' I began to worry that I'd got something wrong.

Saul flashed me a devilish smile. 'We are better than normal. After nearly losing our bond, we realize how incredibly lucky we are to have each other. So I've decided it is time to take our second honeymoon. When the wedding is done, we're staying on. I'm not saying which hotel we are checking in to either—total privacy,' he kissed his wife's knuckles, 'us old sweethearts, alone at last.'

Karla wrinkled her nose. 'I am not going on a gondola, Saul Benedict.' This was obviously an already running discussion. 'The prices are outrageous.'

Saul tapped his wife's obstinate chin. 'Mrs Benedict, you certainly are. You promised to obey.'

'That was thirty years ago! Before the wedding ceremony caught up with the modern age.'

'Well, I for one am holding you to that. Gondola for two, in the moonlight, with champagne and roses.'

As the vow to obey went, that didn't sound too bad.

'Oh well. If you are going to make such a fuss about it. I suppose I could. Just this once.'

My sleep had restored me to something like my ordinary self, so when Saul and Karla left, I got up. The flat was emptier than the morning: Steve and Lily had gone back to their hotel, taking most of the press pack with them. Yves, Phoenix, Saul, and Karla had returned to the Calcina. Zed and Sky had stayed behind and were chatting with Will, Sky sitting on Zed's knee as if nothing was going to get them apart again in a hurry. Victor and Uriel were playing cards at the kitchen table. Trace looked cute in an apron, chopping vegetables with a surgeon's precision.

'You know, the restaurant across the way does great take-out lasagne,' I mentioned as I came out of the bedroom.

'Now she tells me!' sighed Trace.

Diamond pushed past. 'Ignore her. We are doing Nonna's recipe. Nothing tastes better than real home cooking.'

I popped up behind her, mouthing 'liar!'

Trace swallowed his laugh. 'You bet, darling.'

Diamond kissed him on the cheek.

As I turned to the others, I could feel that they were about to embark on a round of thankyous so I cut them off at the pass. 'Anyone know where Xav's gone?'

Uriel picked up the trick he had just won. 'He wanted some quiet time, he said. Shall I ask him?'

I pulled on my jacket and boots. 'No need.' I tapped my forehead. 'Homing pigeon in here.'

'You OK to go out?' asked Will. 'You looked really rough when you passed out.'

I guess I had looked like something out of a horror movie. 'I'm fine.'

'You pushed it too far. You shouldn't take the same risk again.'

'Says the guy who got shot.'

Will laughed. 'I now know why fate linked you with Xav. You are going to tease each other unmercifully.'

Victor threw down a card. 'Might make the world a little safer for the rest of us then.'

'Unless they turn their powers jointly on us,' suggested Sky, her old sparkle back in her eyes.

The Benedict brothers groaned in unison.

'OK, I'm outta here.'

'Dinner at seven. Mama arrives tomorrow, don't forget,' called Diamond.

It looked as if this was the last free time I would have for many days to sort things out with Xav. 'I'll be back, but in the non-Terminator sense, of course.'

I shut the door on Will's chuckles.

I found Xav sitting on the steps in the Piazza San Marco—the exact same spot where we had shot our scene for the movie. My heart did its little flip in my chest on seeing him with the backdrop of the bell tower and the water-filled square. The buildings were mirrored in the flood brought by the high tide, but I guessed that it wasn't his own reflection that he was studying. His thoughts were turned inward; his hands were held loosely over his knees, head down. I sat beside him.

'Hey,' I said softly.

'Hey.' He looked up, eyes warm but no greeting smile.

'Something the matter?'

'Just . . . getting my head around what happened. You wouldn't stop.'

'I know.'

'I thought you were going to have an aneurysm on the brain or something.'

'I'm OK.'

'Just. I had to patch up a few blood vessels, you know?'

Ouch. I touched my forehead. 'I didn't. Thank you.'

A tour party walked behind us, the guide waving a scrap of red material on his stick like the kind of toy you use to tease a cat. His pussycat followers gambolled after him, cameras rather than bells round their necks.

'I've been sitting here and deciding that you put me in the position of someone linked up to a soldier in a war zone. I hate sending you into combat but I know you had to go.'

I was relieved he wasn't outright blaming me. 'Thank you. This gift—it won't always be like this.'

He gave a huff that sounded full of scepticism.

'I'm learning my moves right now. I'll try really hard not to put so much of myself out there on the line next time.'

'So there will be a next time?'

I tapped my feet on the step. 'Yes, well, I did promise Alberto the butler that I'd go back and try to do something for him and his people.'

'When?'

'Tomorrow.'

'Jeez, Crystal, I'm not sure my heart can take much more of this.'

'Do you want me to break my promise to them?'

'No. That's the really, really annoying thing: I'm behind you one hundred per cent. I just don't like it.'

That was OK then. I leant against him. 'My advice? Don't walk behind.'

'Good rule. Not to say the view isn't mighty fine from there.'

I grinned. 'Walk with me. It looks like I need you to patch me up.'

'I can see I'm going to have my hands full, particularly when you have this tendency to bolt ahead and get into all kinds of trouble.'

I picked one up from his knee and draped it on mine. 'Consider yourself fully employed.'

We sat for a while just enjoying the sunset painting the ancient stones a blushing pink. It was a magical city, polished like the intricate mechanism of an old ornamental clock, out of date but still ticking away. Until time ran out for it, that is.

'How many lovers have sat here, would you say?' he asked, gesturing to the square with the sunken entrance to the basilica, the Doge's palace and ranks of waiting gondolas bobbing on the lagoon.

'Too many. We are in danger of becoming a cliché.'

'I don't mind; do you?'

'Not a bit.'

He held my hand, warm palm to my cold one.

'Your brothers are worrying we are going to forge a united front and turn our teasing upon them.'

'Sounds a plan.'

'But I've rumbled you, Xav Benedict.'

He arched a brow. 'Am I so simple to see through?'

'For your soulfinder. You've carved out a role for yourself in the family as the joker but, oddly enough you . . . '

He smiled. 'You're saying I'm odd?'

'If the cap fits, mate . . . Anyway, as I was saying: *oddly enough*, you might be one of the deepest thinkers, certainly the most compassionate. You use your humour, like Diamond does her peace-making, to defuse, to heal if you can.'

The humour faded from his expression to be replaced with something more like an aching vulnerability. 'I guess I might do that. I hadn't really thought about it much. It's just what I do.'

'But you can get it wrong, push the joking too far.'

'You mean I'm not perfect?' He sounded relieved rather than offended.

'Exactly. Sometimes the comedy stops people realizing you can be hurt as much as someone of a more serious character. It's not going to be easy for you being my soulfinder, is it?'

245

He squeezed my hand. 'In one way, it's the easiest thing ever, as natural as breathing, but I can't say I find you suffering a pleasant experience to watch, no.'

'I know. But it kind of feels right, doesn't it? That I'm linked to a healer? I need you to be the person I should be, use my skill to the full.'

'Happy to be of service.'

'But I don't want you to feel you have to be part of some sort of entourage around me, like Steve with his social secretary and minders. I felt like that when I was travelling with Diamond. We have to make sure it is the Xav and Crystal show, not mine alone.'

His shoulder bumped me. 'Sweet of you to worry about that, but do you really think I have an ego so easily crushed?'

Now I came to think about it . . . 'Er, no.'

'Cupcake, I'll turn the spotlight on for you with great pleasure, but once it's on, don't be surprised if I break out for a little tap dance of my own.'

'Happy Feet.'

'You said it. Come on, I've done my brooding, sorted it in my head for the moment: time to go back.'

'Trace is cooking Nonna's lasagna.'

'Wow. I must see this.'

'He was wearing her little apron and everything.'

Xav picked up his pace. 'Got a camera?'

The next day my family descended in force. I had not seen them together in one place since Dad's funeral and I had forgotten how quite overwhelming they could be when not staggering under the weight of grief. Peter, my favourite brother, a heart-stealer with his crop of auburn hair and big green eyes, gave me a crushing hug and swirled me in a circle as soon as he was through customs at the airport. He eyed Xav guardedly then decided he had to be a good thing as I looked so happy and offered his hand for a shake. I knew then that they were going to get along famously. My other brothers and sisters were too busy fielding infants to give Xav a hard time. Topaz in particular was ready to sing his praises when he charmed her reluctant toddler to get in the water taxi by making funny faces at her.

'You've got yourself a good one there,' she said, 'we're so pleased for you.'

Misty, the long-suffering eldest niece, was babysitting the middle two. She met my eyes and rolled them at her twin sisters who were already hanging off Xav as if he was their favourite climbing frame and they two little monkeys. Topaz's husband, Mark, corralled the final two of their six to sit on the bench behind us. He smiled at me but I could feel there was a new strain in their relationship. Topaz and Mark weren't soul-finders and now my sister could ask me to uncover who she should have been with. I wasn't sure what I would do if she did request the information.

'Is everything going to be all right?' I asked.

'We've talked about it,' said Topaz, immediately knowing what I had in mind, 'and we have decided we don't want to know. I do love Mark and he loves me. It might not be the kind of love that sets the world on fire, but we are good to-gether and the children need us.' She patted my knee. 'We are happy.'

'Xav says that we all have gifts. Mark may not be a Savant but he has his own power, doesn't he?'

'Yes, he's the kindest man I know and very witty. He makes me laugh.'

'Then maybe holding out for your soulfinder would have been completely the wrong decision.'

She nodded. 'That's what we think. What can be compared to sharing six wonderful children? There is more than one way of being complete, no matter what the romantics tell you.'

'I'm glad.' And I was. I had been dreading that she would ask me to tell her who her counterpart was and then I'd be responsible for wrecking a perfectly good marriage.

My family had come determined to make up for lost time and to put me centre stage, what with the discovery of both my power and my soulfinder, but I was adamant that this was Diamond and Trace's moment. Not to mention that with lots of under-tens bouncing off the walls, it was hardly the occasion for a heart-to-heart about how many mistakes we had made as a family, getting my gift so wrong.

Karla and Saul took on the responsibility for entertaining—good of them as I had the little matter of the contessa's staff to sort out. Diamond had insisted she accompany me as her gift could help the tensions in the household. Trace and Xav refused to be kept away so it was quite a party that arrived at the gate.

Alberto came to the steps to let us in. 'If you would follow me. We weren't sure if you'd come back.'

'I promised, so here I am.'

This was the first time I'd seen inside the walls in daylight. The house looked more dilapidated than I expected; the frames on the windows were sorely in need of paint; cracks snaked up the wall—a fitting image of the person inside.

'How is the contessa?'

'Not well, signorina. She has taken to her bed. We will not be disturbed.'

I relayed this information to Xav. 'Do you think I hurt her when we had our mind tussle?'

Xav refrained from pointing out that she had been the one to attack me and brought it on herself. 'I'll check on her if she'll let me.'

The staff had gathered in the spacious kitchen of the mansion, six men ranging from Alberto to the pilot. They were either brothers or cousins, all related to the original enemy, Minotti. It took a while for me to explain the background and why I was here. Fortunately, in their mind-numbed states, their reactions were muted: no one flew off in a rage or marched up to the contessa's bedroom to take their revenge. The prevailing mood was that of baffled sadness as to why anyone should do this to them for so long.

Now I knew how to go about unravelling her mind-muffler, I asked the staff to use their skills to help me break out their true personalities from the tidying away the contessa had done. It was new territory for me as there was no soulfinder to complete the process.

Alberto stood in front of the men, their nominated spokesman. 'Do you know what we will experience?'

I shook my head. 'I guess it will feel scary. You are used to being confined in a certain way of thinking. I won't do anything if you'd prefer to remain as you are.'

'None of us want that. We've discussed it and accept the risks.'

'OK, let's give this a go.'

It was simpler than I imagined. The contessa had had to be brutal to eradicate the soulfinder bond in Diamond, Karla, Phoenix, and Sky; with these men, she had merely kept dosing them with mild touches of her power, folding any emerging links back into the tidy pattern she sought, clipped close like the box hedges of her garden. Xav did not even have to relieve me of a headache when I finished with the last one.

'How do you feel?' I asked. The process was not so abrupt as the restoration of the soulfinder link, more like a gradual waking up.

Alberto sat in an upright chair by the old cooking range. 'I feel confused.' He frowned, like someone just catching a whiff of a bad smell. 'And angry.'

Diamond stepped forward and exerted her gift in the room. 'You've all served one very sad old lady faithfully for many years. You can reflect with pride on that excellent record, even if one that was unfairly foisted on you. You can now choose new lives.'

'Should we not make her pay for what she did to us?' asked the pilot.

'I think, signor,' argued Diamond, 'she has been paying a heavy price ever since the day your father took her soulfinder from her. What good would vengeance be but to carry on a family feud that should never have started?'

The man looked thoughtfully at Diamond and then nodded. 'Yes, you're right.' He rubbed his wrists as if just freed from shackles. 'But I don't owe her anything now. I'm leaving. Anyone else?'

From the chorus of voices I gathered that the contessa would soon require a completely new team of servants. Only Alberto looked torn. In my opinion, it wasn't right that he should feel responsible for someone who had cramped his life for so long.

'Go on,' I urged him. 'I'll make sure someone comes to look after her. She still has friends in this city—the priest at her church will sort it out when I tell him.'

'Tell him what, signorina? He won't believe what she is.' I welcomed the flash of humour I saw in Alberto's eyes; the real man was slowly finding his feet.

'You had a dispute about wages, of course, and all walked out in solidarity. No one will think that odd.'

'Thank you. For everything.' He paused. 'And if I asked you to locate our soulfinders, would you do so? Even after what we did to your family?'

I guessed this would be the first of many such requests. 'Of course—and you did not do anything you need apologize for: we understand you weren't responsible for your actions. You know where to find me.' It was the least I could do for people who had arguably been the worst victims of the contessa's form of madness.

Xav took my hand. 'Let's go see the contessa. I'll need you to translate.'

We found her sitting up in bed staring blankly at the window. Her bed was an ornate four-poster with dusty hangings. The drapes at the casement were faded crimson silk. Her eyes flicked to the door when we came in, then went back to the view across to the bell tower in Piazza San Marco.

'Oh, it's you. Come to beg for my help?'

I followed the direction of her gaze. The lace-covered table by the window was decorated with photos of her and her husband in happier days. She held a locket in her hand, gold chain spilling onto the quilt. I could guess that it contained another memory of him.

'Yes, it's me. This is Xav Benedict—you haven't met him properly yet.' I checked the water in the jug beside the bed. 'Do you need anything?'

'I'm not going to help you. I won't undo what I've done. I can't so . . . so I won't regret it.'

'I wouldn't expect you to. I managed to undo it myself.'

'You did?' She turned to look at me.

'It wasn't easy.'

'I thought it impossible. I always thought it too late to turn back once I had begun.'

'No, it wasn't. I have freed the minds of your staff too.'

She sank back on the pillows, her face grey against the white. 'Perhaps it was time. Should I expect to be murdered in my bed?'

'More than time. And no, they are not after revenge.' I poured her a glass of water. 'You should never have done what you did.'

Xav stepped to the bedside. She flinched as if expecting a blow.

He held out his hand. 'May I?'

'Xav's a healer. He's not going to hurt you.'

She inched her wrist closer which he took as permission. Closing his eyes, he examined her with his gift.

'There's nothing really wrong with you, bearing in mind your age. I think you are just tired, contessa,' he announced.

'Yes, I'm tired.' She pulled her hand away. 'Of everything. Of life.'

Tired and lonely, I guessed. 'Shall I send someone to you?'

'There's no one to send. My son's in jail.'

'His family?'

'They don't care about me. They just care about inheriting my money.'

'I'll ask the priest to come and sit with you.'

She nodded. 'Yes, ask Father Niccolo to come.'

There was nothing more we could do. Her tone was hopeless, but she had brought this on herself, which made it all the sadder.

Xav followed me out. 'Funny that our confrontation ends with me feeling sorry for her.'

'Me too. Perhaps I could arrange to see her son? Have a talk with him and sort him out?'

Xav tapped the banister. 'Meddling again?'

'Yes. I can't seem to help it.'

'I get that but I think it would be better if she did the unravelling. It would be more, well, *healing* that way.'

'You're right.' Xav had great instincts. 'I'll suggest it to her when she's recovered a little and tell her how to go about it.'

We joined up with the others in our waiting water taxi, closing the gate on the old house. I was acutely aware that I was heading back to a family-filled apartment in the city, leaving one very sad old lady alone with nothing but her bitterness. I was not so ignorant of the uglier parts of human nature as to think that I could not have been her had I gone through what she had. I vowed every day from now on to appreciate the happiness I had, not take Xav for granted.

And there was one person to whom I had to say sorry that I had taken her for granted. She was waiting in the apartment when I got home, youngest grandchild on her knee. She didn't see me at first so I stood for a moment, savouring the fact that she was there, still with us, putting aside her deep grief to be part of the family. Her choices were so much better than the contessa's.

'Hey, Mama. How are you?' I asked, giving her a gentle kiss on the cheek. Her short dark hair was tucked behind one ear; a pair of diamond studs given to her by our dad on their last anniversary glittering in her lobes.

'Oh, I'm having a wonderful time, thank you. All your friends here are so kind—and Trace's family are simply delightful!' She bounced baby Robin, cutting off some infant grizzles before they took root.

Tears pricked my eyes. 'Dad would have been so proud to see you now.'

'Oh, darling, what a lovely thing to say!' My mama beamed up at me. She knew what I was trying to convey.

'Having Xav means I understand. Sorry I was so . . . so angry before.'

She cuddled Robin against her shoulder, patting his back rhythmically. 'My bad years did not come at a good time for you—I realize that. I wish it had been different—that Charles could be here to see all of you wonderful children doing so well. I would feel more guilty than I do, but as Karla said to me this morning, you've come through with flying colours so maybe I should settle for just saying "I love you".'

'Yes, that'll do fine. I'm pleased not to be the family screw-up any more.'

She laughed. 'Oh, darling, give yourself time. You'll make more mistakes. No matter how old we get, we go on doing that. I should know.'

'Love you, Mama.' I hugged her, baby and all.

She cuddled me back. 'Love you, my little girl.'

The day of the wedding arrived and all men had been banished from our flat while the bride prepared. Lily was helping her dress, my mother and Karla in attendance, which was why I found I had a quiet moment in the kitchen with Sky and Phoenix. I leafed through the morning post, putting aside the congratulations cards for Diamond and Trace. We'd already had one wedding present: hearing that the contessa had dropped her charges against the Benedicts.

I opened one addressed to me—thick creamy stationery with a New York postmark. My jaw dropped.

'What's the matter?' asked Phoenix.

I passed her the letter. Sky joined her to read over her shoulder.

'Oh my gosh: Elite Models wants you!' Sky giggled nervously. 'Wow. Three weeks in the Caribbean for a summer fashion shoot.'

'They took the gossip about me and Steve seriously. They don't seem to realize I have no experience.'

Phoenix passed the letter back. 'What are you going to do?'

I brushed my fingers over the paper. It represented a dream I had so briefly indulged in but the answer was obvious.

'I get spots. Hate diets. I can't walk in high heels.' I chucked the letter on the side for a polite refusal to be penned later.

'So?' Phoenix grinned, pleased with my decision.

'The world can do without another model, but not a soul-seeker. And I was thinking that I'd set myself up near to where Xav does medical school, maybe take a few design courses while I'm at it. I like making clothes more than wearing them.'

'I hope he chooses Colorado then!' said Sky.

'Hey, no, California.' Phoenix waved away the idea of studying in the Rockies. 'San Francisco is much the best place to live.'

I tidied away the post. 'To be honest, I don't care if he chooses Nowheresville, Idaho.'

'Aw, that's so sweet.'

I thought again. 'Actually, maybe I do care—about the Nowheresville.'

Sky laughed. 'Crystal, looking at Xav's wardrobe choices, do you really think he'll be choosing that?'

'No. I'm thinking more Manhattan or London.' Phoenix was also amused. 'Funny thing is that Yves told me Xav has put his plans on hold to hear what you want to do.'

Sky hugged herself. 'You guys are so cute! I'm so pleased it's you. It's no big secret in the Benedict family, but everyone has a soft spot for Xav because he's, well, he's Xav.'

I grinned. Yes, Xav was Xav, unique and just what the doctor ordered.

Chapter 21

The bride was radiant in white lace over a satin slip; the groom dashing in morning dress; the Best Man (Victor) in grey was dangerously impressive; the bridesmaids and page boys looked deceptively angelic in yellow and white.

Xav, who had been listening to my internal commentary as we watched the newly married couple walk down the aisle, leant over.

'You forgot to add that the Best Woman isn't looking too bad either, not in that cream dress. Your own design?'

I nodded. 'And you don't look a complete disgrace in your suit.'

'Tell it how it is, cupcake. Shall we go?'

I took his arm and fell in behind the parents. I couldn't resist satisfying my curiosity so I reached out briefly to Uriel—not a proper examination, just enough to catch a hint.

'Interesting: South Africa,' I muttered.

Xav smiled at his brother's startled expression as Uriel felt my gift brush by. 'Is that right?'

I turned my attention to Will. 'I'm getting . . . tulip fields. Windmills with mice in.'

'*That's hardly surprising,*' Xav whispered back.

'Aw, you know that children's song too? Let's get him a ticket to Amsterdam.'

'What about Vick?'

'Hmm.' The third brother had many defences around his mind but I sneaked in for a little peek. 'Now that is unexpected.'

Victor's steel-tipped gaze swung round to us.

'What?' urged Xav.

I bit my lip. 'Shouldn't I tell him first?'

'Hey, soul sister, we're in this together.'

'OK. Prison. Afghanistan.'

Xav tripped over his own feet. 'I volunteer you tell him.'

'What happened to the "we're in this together"?'

'But it's Vick!'

'Coward.'

'OK, I'll tell him—eventually.'

'But don't forget to mention that she's innocent and needs his help.'

'You can tell that much?' Xav pulled me out of the line of people being arranged by the photographer. Those things always took hours. Steve's fans were out in force beyond the barricades put up by the movie people. Steve and Lily didn't notice—this was their normal after all—and were chatting happily away with Yves and Phoenix as they waited for their photo call. Xav and I found a little spot on our own in the church porch, a flight of angels cavorting on the wall beside us, scrambling haphazardly up a ladder to heaven.

I shrugged. 'Just an instinct about Vick's partner. Her energy is really . . . kind—and brave.'

'I like your instincts.'

'Well, here's another of them. Phee told me you'd said you'd put your medical training on hold for me?'

He nodded. 'I'll do what's needed.'

'I need you to follow your original plan. Where you go, I go.'

'You're sure?'

'One hundred per cent.'

He recognized the echo. 'Is this all part of the Crystal and Xav show?'

'Xav and Crystal show, you mean.'

'That too.'

He squeezed my shoulders gently. 'So what do you think about New York?'

I laughed silently. Phoenix had called that one correctly. 'I'd think it perfect—as long as you are there.'

'Thank you.' He kissed me so tenderly I felt as if my soul was unfolding, like petals on a rose.

'Hey, guys, stop fooling about!' called Zed. 'The photographer is waiting!'

Reluctantly we parted to find our families smiling indulgently at us. Confetti fluttered in the air, whisking over our heads and away to the lonely islands of the lagoon.

'We'll be right with you!' Xav called. He lowered his voice. 'After just one more kiss.'

About the author

Joss Stirling lives in Oxford and has always been
fascinated by the idea that life is more than what
we see on the surface. She loves travelling and thinks Venice
has to be an all-time favourite city in which to fall in love.

You can visit her website on www.jossstirling.com

Have you read the other books in the spine-tingling soulfinder series?

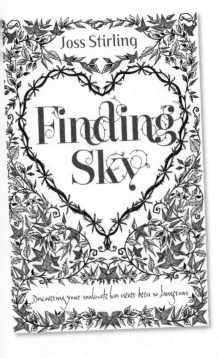

OUT NOW!

Who is *your* favourite brother?

All the Benedict boys are gorgeous, but who is your favourite? Is it brooding Zed, intellectual Yves, or charming Xav?

Let Joss know by visiting her website and joining the debate!

For competitions, news of the next book by Joss, and a chance to chat to her directly go to

www.jossstirling.com